Bones of an Inland Sea

Also by MARY AKERS

Fiction
Women Up On Blocks
Medusa's Song and Other Stories

Non-fiction
One Life to Give

BONES *of an* INLAND SEA

Stories by

MARY AKERS

Press 53
Winston-Salem

Press 53, LLC
PO Box 30314
Winston-Salem, NC 27130

First Edition

Cover design by Kevin Morgan Watson

Cover art, "Shipwreck" Copyright © 2013
by Tim Knifton, used by permission of the artist.

Author photo by Deb Sammarco

Epigraph from "In the Ladies Bathhouse," Copyright © 2010
by Anne Colwell, from the book *Mother's Maiden Name* (Word Press),
used by permission of the artist.

Printed on acid-free paper
ISBN 978-1-935708-89-6

For Wendy,
without whom this book would not exist.

And for Jack,
always a lover, never a fighter.

where we have hauled our bodies,
      not quite wholly water,
            to the sea, the body
of water we cannot wholly bear,
            we cannot wholly leave.

—Anne Colwell

Acknowledgments

Grateful acknowledgment is made to the following publications in which these stories first appeared, often in different forms:

"Beyond the Strandline," *Among Animals* (anthology)

"Bones of an Inland Sea," *Storyglossia*

"Christmas in Phuket," *Literary Mama*

"Collateral Damage," *Juked*

"Comfortably Numb," *Bellevue Literary Review* and the anthology *Home of the Brave: Stories in Uniform*

"Like Snow, Only Grayer," *Bellevue Literary Review* (2012 Pushcart Special Mention)

"Treasures Few Have Ever Seen," *Prime Number Magazine*

"¡Vieques!" *Guernica*

"Viewing Medusa," *The Good Men Project*

"Waste Island," *Magnolia Journal*

"What Lies Beneath," *Bellevue Literary Review*

"Who Owns the Moon?" *Freight Stories*

Bones of an Inland Sea

HOUSE OF REFUGE

Keeper Bunker maintained a careful record of misfortune. In his logbook, our tragedy read thusly: *April 19, 1886, the brigantine JH Lane, Alonzo Shute master, bound from Matanzas, Cuba, to Philadelphia, wrecked fourteen and a half miles north of Jupiter Lighthouse, on a reef three-quarters of a mile from Florida's shore. One-thirty in the morning, stormy, with a gale blowing ENE, a low tide, and high seas. Six crewmembers were rescued, among them the captain's wife.*

The words in his logbook represent only the barest of facts.

For instance, a captain's wife does not always set sail with gladness. Alonzo knew I feared the perpetually rolling sea—he has known me all my life—and did his best to allay my fears, but the creaking of the hull at night, the slapping of the waves that lulled him sweetly off to sleep, drove me to near insanity.

I admit to a certain nervousness of constitution. My mother would tell you I have always been this way: "A nervous child, Madeleine."

After our rescue, the keeper's wife took great pains to make me welcome, delighted as she was to have a female refugee. I was grateful for her kindness, but did not wish to be coddled, for coddling meant I had a loss to bear, and *that* I refused to accept.

She fed us immediately—a noon meal that she called *dinner*—and despite the anxious night, most of us, the men especially, proved glad of food. Over bacon, beans, and a heavy, pudding-like gruel, Sarah told us of our rescue, already making a story of the peril we had faced.

"That storm blew you in late." She dished a second helping of the steaming pudding onto each plate. "Come up out of nowhere. Samuel thought sure there'd be a wreck come morning. Climbing into bed, he said as much."

She poised the serving spoon over my plate; I put out a refusing palm that went unseen or unheeded, and she heaped a fresh mound upon my half-eaten pile. I took a small bite and moved the remainder around with my fork.

The German, August Fuhrman, held his laden spoon aloft. "*Vas ist* this?"

The question appeared to please her. "Spoonbread. My mother's recipe. You like it?"

"Is *gut.*" August opened wide his mouth and shoveled in the soggy porridge. Although uncharitable, I detested him at that moment, seeing in him a gluttonous sponge (who had throughout the journey taken more than his share at every mealtime) while my own husband was still out there, cold, wet, and certainly hungry. I pushed my plate away.

"It's best made with fresh milk, but I only get the tins here. Supply boat comes first of the month. Sam rows out in the skiff and brings back provisions, takes out my letters." She pointed to a desk on which a stack of envelopes sat, bound with twine. "Writing keeps away the loneliness," she said, smiling while her eyes drooped. "I do love this house. What we do is important…" Her voice trailed off.

"*Ja, ist* important," bellowed the German. He was entirely too hearty for a crewman without a ship.

Sarah smiled, encouraged. "Samuel went out looking, first light. Nine o'clock, he came back and said he'd spotted your ship—what was left of it—and took off again, rowing down-coast for help." She looked around the table. "Were there two boats when he got there?"

"Tree," said John Ahiskog, the tall, austere Finn. "The boats were tree." He wiped a hand down his face, trapping a few grains of gruel deep in his beard. I resisted the urge to remove them. Such melancholy tidiness seemed out of place, given that only hours before we had been clinging desperately to the bottom of a capsized lifeboat.

Just as I could not have told you all the things about the ship that my husband's log would tell (371 tons, out of Matanzas, Cuba, bearing

$13,640 worth of molasses in its hold) so I had little sense of our position on the ocean that night. I only know that the storm carried us too close to shore. Our ship grounded in shallow water and the crew dropped anchor and converged upon the deck. The wind whipped our ghostly blowing nightclothes.

Johann Jacobsson, first mate, offered an apologetic nod, perhaps ashamed at being seen thus; I offered a grim smile of reassurance. Three fortnights at sea, and we were not so modest as at the start of our journey.

The ship jerked and strained. The groans of the hull and the dread in the faces of the men made my knees quail. I sought Alonzo on the quarterdeck, while sliding and nearly tumbling overboard in my slippers. A foamy spindrift flew through the air; wet strands of hair blew about my head, whipping my face with all the fury of the wind.

Even as the tide was low (the very cause of our grounding, insisted Keeper Bunker, hoping to mitigate—for my sake—my dear husband's culpability, I know), the seas flew high against us. When Alonzo looked up from the helm to see me struggling toward him, I caught, for a moment, a look that contained all the fears of bringing me on board that I knew he felt but had not expressed. Just as quickly, the uncertainty in his eyes vanished, but fear continued to prickle around my hairline.

As I reached the lifeboat, a great rending groan vibrated through the soles of my slippers and there came a smell so pungent—so *distressing* and pungent—I knew at once that the sweet molasses—the thirteen thousand dollars of molasses—was mingling with the waves. Had it not been the blackest of nights, I am certain we would have seen the broken barrels rolling out to sea. Alonzo's answering groan told me that he, too, had smelled defeat.

With no time to contemplate the loss, Alonzo hoisted me into the lifeboat. The Lane's crew (a German, a Brit, a Swede, a Finn, and a fellow Mainer) climbed in. Alonzo manned the ropes and lowered us into the sea. He called down a promise to join me soon then left to attend his floundering ship.

My husband has always been a man of his word.

The lifeboat descended toward the raging sea. I clung to its sides. As if to answer my fears, a wave caught our craft broadside and flipped it over. In a blur of motion and wetness, I found myself underneath the very boat that had been intended to save us. The arms and legs of the crew thrashed in the water around me. A heavy foot tangled in my nightgown.

When a pair of strong hands gripped my shoulders I was certain I would be saved. But the hands pushed at me until I sank. I surfaced once and saw or sensed August Fuhrman, mouth twisted up in fear, mustache hanging soggy and bedraggled at the corners of his gasping mouth, sour breath assaulting my face. In trying to save himself, he was drowning me. Down again I went beneath his heavy paws.

Fighting a rising panic, I held my breath and went under as he made to climb atop me. Avoiding August's desperate, grasping hands, I surfaced outside the overturned boat and called into the darkness, "Alonzo?"

Thomas Jones, the Englishman, answered. "Mrs. Shute?" His reedy voice cracked—all of seventeen, he was.

"Yes." I sounded shaky, even to myself. A chill crept up from my churning legs. "Alonzo?"

"He is not here, Mrs. Shute."

"He will find us," rasped the smoky voice of Henry Whitlock, the other gentleman from Maine, a Downeaster. Even in the darkness and the turmoil, their voices were distinct.

The Finn, John Ahiskog, spoke with authority, and near-perfect English, from a point across the keel. "Hold the gunnel," he said. I located the Y of an oarlock and grasped it tightly.

Our pitiful capsized boat lifted and fell. We bobbed with it. Each time a wave rose around my neck, my lungs tightened in fear. I shivered violently and continuously.

When a large swell slapped against us, I gasped, swallowing a mouthful of seawater. My stomach churned in response. I clenched my teeth but the contents of my stomach climbed my anxious gullet and launched into the waves. I felt my face flush with mortification, glad of the darkness, but certain that the men had heard me retch.

Some time into our ordeal I thought to tie the sash of my nightgown onto the oarlock, thus giving my frozen fingers some relief. I fought to keep my nightgown close around my shivering legs and held my knees curled up and close together to preserve any small bit of warmth.

A few hours later (or had it been only minutes?), the Swede, Johann Jacobsson, informed us very calmly that he was letting go. Those of us still lucid tried to talk him into hanging on but some time later, when the storm eased and the seas became flat and calm, I realized Johann was no longer there.

I dozed for a short time. Inconceivable, but I must have, for I remember Alonzo floating beside me, admonishing me to hold on, that help was coming. I came to with a start, expecting to see my husband, but there was only the sky, lightening all around us.

The sun tipped above the horizon, revealing my fellow shipmates snugged around the boat. We were a desperate lot. Sometime in the night August had come out from under the boat and was now one of the five who remained.

I stared at the empty shoreline that spoke no hope of rescue, at the splintered ship that had been my husband's pride and joy, at the endless ocean that sought with every wave to consume us, but was careful not to look into the surrounding faces of four men clinging desperately to life.

I fixed my gaze on the spine of the overturned lifeboat. I memorized the knots and seams of her hull. I fought a heaviness in limb and spirit.

At noon, so Keeper Bunker has said, we were rescued. I could not even climb into the boat; three strong men dragged me ingloriously aboard.

As the lone shipwrecked female, I was given a room to myself at the House of Refuge. My berth was at the terminus of a narrow stairwell, up a set of steep steps, just under the exposed eaves of the gable. It had rough pine floors—an attic, converted—and a large clock that ticked steadily away in the corner. I was very grateful.

From the room's sole window, I had a view that faced the sea; I could watch for my husband's return. Mrs. Bunker had shown me the room, remarking, "We don't get many ladies here," and handed me a dress of her own that was too large in both bosom and waist but was warm and dry and welcome. My soggy nightclothes she took modestly, through a crack in the mostly-closed door; my slippers had long before been swept from my feet. I hadn't even noticed when they drifted away.

Once in my room alone, I took out Alonzo's log—Mr. Bunker had salvaged it from the Lane, wedged between the heavy sextant and the ship's sideboard. I stared at the tidy scrawl, the pinched letters, high and cramped. I touched the page then brought it to my lips, closed the book and held it close.

A deep sleep overtook me. The ticking clock pushed into my dream and then became Alonzo knocking at the door. "Come in," I cried, elated. Sarah softstepped in and was gone again as quickly as I roused. By morning light I saw a nightgown at the foot of my bed; I had slept, fully clothed, atop the spread.

I arose, rumpled as I have ever been, and looked out the window. The day was dawning blue and lovely. I smoothed my hair and dress, then paused at the closed door, listening for my husband's familiar timbre. I did not hear it.

What I *did* hear was the German's loud voice declaring that a woman onboard was a wish for trouble. After I had composed myself, I opened the door and stepped out. And my stockinged feet landed in . . .wetness? Feeling cross—for what else does a wet step engender?—I told myself that our proprietress was very busy and so to be forgiven for sloshing her bucket. She had been so quiet I had not even heard her mopping.

At breakfast very little was said to encourage or discourage me, and yet the mild remarks on the weather and the food felt cruel, dismissive.

"Mrs. Bunker, might I borrow the spyglass this morning?" I asked, as casually as I was able.

"Sure you can, honey, but Samuel has it. And please—call me Sarah."

"He is out looking?"

"He is. Don't you worry, we'll find your husband." She petted my hand.

"Yah," agreed the others, using the universal affirmative of a multilingual crew. August nodded vigorously. His yellow-white hair shook into his eyes.

"Perhaps I will just walk a bit, then. If you will excuse me." I rose and took my leave. "Thank you for breakfast, Mrs. Bunker."

The House of Refuge sat on a small rise. I had not even known such a place existed—a government dwelling built solely to house the shipwrecked and the stranded. It seemed a miraculous thing. The beach below alternated between flat sandy stretches and rocky piles. To the north I could see the remains of what had once been my husband's fine, sturdy ship. She was far away. There was nothing to be done but watch her slowly break apart. The carcass of the Lane held nothing for me now.

I removed the shoes that Mrs. Bunker had given me (like the dress, a size too large) and walked southward down the beach, scanning as far as my eye could see.

The ocean to the left and ahead was empty. The woods to my right were short and viney—nothing like the forests of Maine and nothing like the lush rainforests we had seen in Cuba. These trees were scrubby, twisted by perpetually blowing salt winds. The undergrowth was thick and tangled, the plants spiky and threatening.

An uneven ridge of driftwood, shells, and seaweed paralleled my walk. The ocean had given up her treasures during the heavy seas of the storm and I followed the strandline to a small glass float, unbroken. I picked it up and slipped it into the pocket of the dress.

Then, tangled in a bit of coarse fishnet, I saw a familiar shape. As I reached for the jumbled mass, a crab scuttled off and a small scream escaped me. It was my husband's polished wooden comb tangled there; I kneeled onto the sand and delicately pulled away the strands of twine and seaweed. Several tines were broken, but it was Alonzo's. I brought it to my nose. No trace of him remained. It was salty and waterlogged, but it was his. I pressed it to my cheek and felt the memory of combing his fine, thick hair with my hands on our wedding night when time was slowed and everything was sensation. In that instant I could smell his skin and felt powerfully that he was near.

"*Vas ist das?*" asked a voice too loudly and too close. A shudder passed over me.

"A bit of driftwood," I lied and tucked it quickly into my skirt beside the glass ball.

"You are finding *seeoberteile?*" August leaned down and lifted a small shell of spiraling chambers from the sand.

"Seashells, yes," I said, and continued walking, hoping he would leave me to my thoughts.

But August did not leave. He stuffed his hands into his pockets and kept pace beside me, scuffing at the sand with his heavy black shoes. Had those been the shoes he wore on-ship? I could not remember. In any case, they seemed to fit him well enough. I felt exposed in my bare feet and wished I could replace my shoes, but did not want to stop for fear of inviting conversation.

But conversation came anyway. "Kapitän Shute vill be find," August offered, and I was suddenly sick to death of this man.

"Spare me your predictions, Herr Fuhrman." My tone was icy but I had no time to regret my outburst because he simply laughed as if I had told a fine joke. I quickened my pace, wishing nothing more than to be rid of this ungentlemanly man who would drown a woman to save himself.

"You are frightened," he said, touching my elbow.

I jerked my arm away and turned back toward the House of Refuge. "I do not wish to be touched, Mr. Fuhrman." Then I walked away so quickly that he would have had to run to catch up with me. Fortunately, he did not.

At the end of that day, hope was still high. I sat on the porch with Henry and Thomas after dinner, waiting and rocking as the sun dimmed and the distant edge of sea and sky receded.

The tide was low; the rhythmic slap of Keeper Bunker's oars grew louder as he approached. When I saw he was alone, the disappointment almost swamped me. He pulled the skiff onto the sand and called, "Thomas, I will need help." When I stood, too, he said grimly, "Leave the Missus."

But I could not stay on the porch and idly wait. I rose to follow Thomas. Henry stayed me gently with his hand. "Not yet," he said in a voice that made my own throat hurt.

Through the fading dusk I made out a dark shape in the back of the rescue boat. It was wrapped in a heavy brown cloth and it was in the shape of a body.

"It isn't him," I told Henry. "That is not Alonzo." I shook my head to reconfirm my statement.

Thomas made his way to the water. Was it my tortured mind, or was he walking with deliberate slowness? Perhaps he did not care to face what was in the rear of the boat, either.

I moved Henry's arm aside and he did not restrain me further.

Thomas bent over the wrapped form, clenching his jaw so that the tendons stood out on his neck. Keeper Bunker looked up as I approached. "Not a good, idea, Ma'am," he said. "Thomas and I can handle this."

"I want to see."

"It ain't a pretty sight, Ma'am." He stood between me and the rear of the skiff. "Found the body tangled in the weeds about a mile south of the wreck; a day and a half in the ocean haven't been kind."

"It's fine," I said, not knowing if it was or not.

Thomas peeled back the upper portion of the shroud and I saw at once a shock of dark hair—curly and black. When he pulled it farther down, the skin was white as ivory, the face bloated beyond recognition, seaweed tangled around the ears and twined in the hair. Sand filled the lower lip to overflowing, like a too-large dip of snuff. The eyeballs were horribly gone. Crusted sockets stared back at me, swollen around the brow and cheeks, but the bloated chin was hairless; my Alonzo was bearded. This was not him.

I cried out, relieved, then just as quickly understood that the clean-shaven face belonged to Johann. Johann who had not been able to hold on a minute more and had announced it so casually. Should we have tried harder to keep him with us? Why had we not? Was this proof, then, that when we face our final destination we care only for ourselves?

Keeper Bunker tried to console me, reaching out his arm to encompass my shoulders, but I ducked away and laughed a choking sob. "No," I said. "This is Johann. Alonzo is still out there."

Thomas nodded his agreement and covered the face. He and Johann had been close. I had forgotten that, and when I remembered, leaned toward him and said, inanely, "It will be all right."

"He had a wife and two daughters." Thomas carefully tucked the ends of the shroud beneath his friend's head. "I suppose I will be writing them a letter." His face paled, and he touched his abdomen. In the exceedingly reserved tone that is the province of disappointed Englishmen, he said, "I do not relish it."

On the second day, a wretched rain descended, along with my spirits. It has always been thus: as the barometer drops, so does the tenor of my blood. The drumming of the rain upon the tin roof did nothing to drown out the noise of my clamoring thoughts. To make matters worse, this morning there was water *inside* the door of my room. How Mrs. Bunker had managed to slosh water not only outside but also *under* the door was beyond me. It served merely to further dampen my already soggy mood.

Breakfast was a thick gruel of oats, sweetened with molasses. When

I lifted the spoon to my mouth and smelled the molasses I burst into tears. The spoon fell back into the bowl with a splatter. I ran from the room.

As I climbed the stairs, I thought back to when Alonzo and I had been children. We had run with a mob that played our days away. Kick the can, and king of the mountain for any pile of any thing climbable. Alonzo and I had not been passionately attracted, but rather the best of friends, intimately inclined. Even as children our families often joked that we would one day marry. I, for one, believed it every time.

If anything, Alonzo and I knew one another too well. It was the classic case of finishing the other's sentences, of knowing when he was out of sorts, sometimes before he knew. Alonzo was my balm, my salve, my comfort. My twin, separated at birth, as we used to jest. The only thing we had not shared was a love of water.

The next morning, the doorstep was dry, thankfully, but nearer to my bed I found a small wet area. I knew Mrs. Bunker had not entered my room—I slept far too lightly to have missed that. Before bed, I had washed out my one surviving undergarment (Mrs. Bunker had proffered hers, but I could not bring myself to accept that final, utter indignity). Had I sloshed water then? Had I not wrung it out adequately, and in hanging it over the bed rails created a puddle in the night? That could be the only explanation.

A nagging dyspepsia drove me daily from the confines of the House of Refuge. At home in Maine, I would have the tasks of cooking, cleaning, keeping all in order, but here, in another woman's home, I was not afforded that comfort. Perhaps Mrs. Bunker did not understand that the busyness of work would be a balm, but in any case she refused my offers of assistance, saying that I had been through enough.

And so I took my restlessness to the beach, never knowing quite when August would appear. He often sneaked up on me, appearing like an apparition, and scaring me no less than one.

The third day, I walked along the coastline, toward the remains of the ship. As I approached her shattered hull—over a distance made deceptive by a stretch of treeless sand—a feeling of sadness overcame me. It had been Alonzo's pride and preoccupation. Our only child. For as long as I had known him he had wanted to captain a ship, and the JH

Lane had been the culmination of his dreams. So even I—who had no love-loss for the Lane—felt bereavement when I looked upon her.

As I walked, I cupped the backbone of Alonzo's comb in my pocket; I had slept with it under my pillow. In the other pocket, the round smoothness and surprising weightiness of the glass float comforted my otherwise restless palm.

And yet still I jumped when August spoke behind me. "*Guten Tag*, Madeleine."

That this man should use my first name as an address alarmed me even more than the suddenness of his appearance.

"You must learn not to startle a woman so," I admonished him. "And I prefer to be called Mrs. Shute."

"Voman alone is not safe." He smiled, but I felt a measure of menace to his words.

"I am not alone," I said, stroking the comb in my pocket. "I have my thoughts," I added, attempting to lighten the mood.

In the distance, the bulk of the ship was mostly gone, washed who-knows-where. Half a dozen outer hull planks remained like ribs, obscenely thrust into the air, perhaps jammed between rocks and so resistant to the waves that passed endlessly around and through them. It was undeniably sad to see such a grand ship so reduced, so denuded.

August turned his gaze to match mine. "She vas good ship," he said.

The fourth night, I felt fatigue upon lying down, finally. I had washed at the basin and donned Mrs. Bunker's nightgown and lifted the window for one last look toward the sea. In the darkness, I could find only the whitecaps, but their soft, rolling light comforted me in a way I had not been comforted by the sea before. For the first time I listened for the sound of the waves as I drifted off to sleep, finding peace in the perpetual slapping of the shore.

I slept through the night, mercifully, and in the morning, lingered as the sun's first light appeared, then intensified. I swung my feet over the bed and moved to dress, only to find myself standing in yet another puddle. This one, surely the result of my late night ablutions, but no less annoying when it was of my own making than when I had not known its source.

On that day's walk, a warm breeze off the ocean made me think of our last night in Cuba. It was a magical place, the harbor filled with the bustling noise of human activity, the nearby forests echoing with the most unique animal sounds—birds or monkeys, I could not discern. The air was warm and moist and a daily rainshower cleansed the afternoon streets and added sparkle to the wares of the women at market. There were peppers and fruits of every shape and color, and Alonzo let me assist in choosing what provisions we would bring onto the ship to resupply the larder. We purchased many limes at absurdly low cost.

In the strangest stall of all, we found a mix of fine jewelry and personal wares, most certainly the goods of a pawnbroker's trade, made more interesting, no doubt, by it's location in a large port city. Among a row of chains and lockets we found a gold pocket watch. Alonzo studied the face then turned it over to read the inscription: "*Tú eres mi corazón, no dejes nunca de latir.*"

"You are my heart," the shop owner translated, "never stop beating." And after that, of course we had to have it.

Even before the gold watch and the bazaar, the stevedores had offloaded our delivery of ice. Great chunks of Lake Quinnabacock had been cut the previous winter and stored in sawdust for the trip. They had only diminished slightly in size, and the Cubans were thrilled by the ice. It was a magical thing—to think that someone in the world had no knowledge of ice or winter or even snow. I had never considered that someone might not know what *cold* felt like.

After the ice was removed, our ship, lightened, rose considerably in the water. It would be a day at harbor before the molasses merchants brought their cargo and loaded it into our hold. We spent that night in the town of Matanzas. There was a holiday or a celebration underway; it was not clear what the people were celebrating, but they were a happy lot, singing and dancing, the women in colorful dresses and turbaned heads, the music vibrant with a syncopated beat that made me tap my toes. A toothless old woman approached and held out an arm draped with woven necklaces. I selected a finely knotted one, tan in color, with a small shell that fell just above my bosom. I did not know when I should ever wear such a thing in Maine, but there on the island it felt both natural and exotic. As did I.

Alonzo came alive on Cuba's shore. His exuberance made me open to the island's charms. At a cantina beside the marketplace, we ate a plate of small black beans mixed with rice and a wonderfully aromatic spice. There was an unknown meat, marinated and roasted on a spit, and bananas that were savory like a potato. I tried the proprietress's rum and burned a trail of fire down my throat. Alonzo laughed and had another sip himself—my ordinarily temperate husband—then asked the owner if she had something a woman could drink. The bent old woman emerged with a cup of cloudy liquid that tasted of citrus and coconut. It was delicious, but my head became quite dizzy.

We laughed and strolled the warm city streets, a breeze blew us arm-in-arm to the beach, where I sat with my bare feet against the sand. It was heady and romantic, even for a couple of old friends like us.

I smiled, toes in the sand again, to remember us so.

Then—as if he waited nearby until some memory softened my features—August appeared. His face was that of a handsome man's, but he lacked charm or grace and so did not appear handsome. I have never found looks to be a good indicator of character. A lovely outside has been known to belie an ugly interior.

Such was the case with August.

"You must be careful, Madeleine," he said, bending down to remove a tangled bit of driftwood from my skirts. I shivered at the implied intimacy of him lifting the edge of my dress and jerked it from his grasp. "You vill soon be pulling the whole beach along vith you."

"My skirts are not your concern," I said and turned away from him. I took a step to leave but he moved in front of me and held my arm. I pulled against him, slid through his grasp down to my wrist. He held it fast.

"Madeleine," he moaned. His eyes rolled back. He clutched my wrist so tightly that I felt the bones grinding against one another. Tears sprang to my eyes. He drew me to him.

"You're hurting me," I cried, hoping it would pull him out of the strange trance he was in, call him to his senses.

"I vould not hurt you, Madeleine. You know that I vould not."

His grip was as an octopus, sliding and tightening around me. I cursed my foolishness for having wandered so far from the House of Refuge. I could barely breathe. I cried out, but the wind blew my words down the beach; there was no one to hear me.

He advanced, pressing me backward. Waves lapped against my ankles and water spilled into my too large shoes. The panic rose in me until I couldn't breathe.

August's eyes were smiling as if he had told a clever joke; my struggle seemed to excite him. When he pressed closer, I lifted my heavy shoe and stomped upon his instep. He stumbled and loosened his grip. I shook my wrists free and ran down the beach, heading for the House of Refuge.

"Your husband is not coming back!" August yelled at my retreating back. "Your husband is dead."

I hate you, I thought. I hate you, I hate you, I hate you. Hot tears ran down my cheeks, cooling in the wind as I ran. My shoes flopped around until I mustered the nerve to turn my head to see if I was being followed. I was alone. August walked in the opposite direction. I could only see the hard curve of his hateful back; I despised that back with all my powers of loathing. Then I bent down and removed my shoes, poured the saltwater from them.

The tears would not stop. Whatever would I tell the others? I hoped that no one would notice my disheveled appearance. Even more, I hoped that I would pass no one on the way to my room and could grab a few hours of peace to still my raging heart. Even though I hated every inch of August, I knew that what he said could be true. It made me hate him all the more.

Mrs. Bunker met me at the door. "My goodness, Madeleine. What has happened to you?"

"Nothing," I said, patting my hair and smoothing my skirts. "I have been to see the ship." I don't know why I didn't tell the truth. Perhaps I worried I had somehow encouraged August, or that she would think I had. So I said nothing. And at dinner I politely passed the boiled potatoes, flinching only when his hand touched mine.

Once we were all eating, Keeper Bunker tapped his glass and informed us that we would be leaving the following morning. We would take a borrowed boat to Stuart, a buggy to Fort Lauderdale, then board a sidewheel mail steamer, the Isabel, on her twice-monthly trip to Charleston. From Charleston, we would board another steamer bound for New York City and then a railway train for the final leg of our return to Maine. It would take more than a week.

Keeper Bunker spoke until I could contain myself no longer. "What of Alonzo? Am I to leave without him?"

I expected the others to join in my protest, but there was an uncomfortable silence. I looked around the table at these men I had considered my friends. "Have we given up, then? Has the search been called off?"

"Mrs. Shute——" began our host.

"What is the matter with all of you? Do you not understand that he is still out there? We cannot leave."

Thomas cleared his throat. "Keeper Bunker has scoured the coastline. He has searched for days."

"So I am to just leave? With no sign of my husband? I am to go home...and what? Live my life? Waiting for Alonzo to walk through the door? Hoping for a telegram to arrive and tell me he is on his way?"

"Vat if he ist gone?" asked August, his features barely holding back the glee.

"You!" I shrieked. I felt the shrillness rising up within me, powerless to stop it. "You, who would force your affections on me, even when my husband is lost?" I looked around the table, unable to contain myself. "Do you know what this man did?"

Henry took his napkin from his lap and set it upon the table. He moved toward me but I pushed at the air as he approached. "Do not try to placate me. Do not *remove me for my own good*." Thomas rose as well, and I felt the walls closing in. "Does no one believe me?" I looked around desperately and called to Mrs. Bunker. She entered drying her hands on a towel.

"My heavens, what is going on in here? Madeleine?" Doubt raised her words at the end.

"Sarah," I said, desperation leading me to her first name, "you saw me today. When I came in from my walk."

"You were flustered," she said, addressing the men around the table. "All torn up by something or other. I figured you were mourning."

"I cannot mourn what I do not..." I let the sentence trail off, then recaptured my thought. "You saw me, Sarah. I ran all the way from— nearly as far as the wreck—and the reason I ran was because Mr. Furhman . . . attacked me."

Sarah's sharp intake of breath was followed by the group turning to hear August's response. Without waiting for him to speak, I continued. "He forced his affections on me. He was not gentle."

"Mrs. Shute," said August, "does not know vat she ist saying." He nodded kindly in my direction and I could sense the men believing him and pitying me. My fury and indignation deepened.

"I am clear-headed. I know what happened."

"She was very upset," agreed Sarah. "Are you sure you did not threaten her?"

"I vould remember, had I threatened a grieving vidow," said August.

At the word *widow*, all sense left me; I lifted a handful of food from my plate and flung it in his direction. Mashed potatoes landed against the side of his face and stuck in his drooping mustache. He wiped them away calmly and said, "She ist hysterich."

Sarah came quickly to my side and led me away. "He's lying," I screamed. "He's a liar. He tried to drown me, too. He is not the man he seems." Sarah took me to the divan and sat beside me while I heaved and cried. I tried to shake her off and rise but her bulk was greater than mine. I slumped back down and sobbed against her breast. I kept crying, "He attacked me."

When the shaking had subsided, Mr. Bunker entered with a steaming drink. It smelled strongly of spirits and gently warmed on the way down. I quaffed it in three long drafts and sat there with the residuals of my extended cry shuddering through my body. I was suddenly very tired.

Mrs. Bunker helped me to my room. I pulled the covers over my head, curled into a ball and sobbed. I must have slept, also, for I dreamt of Alonzo—that he climbed into bed with me. It was a salve to have him there, snuggled tight against me. After a time, he murmured that he could not stay, that he must go. I begged him not to leave, but in the dream he told me I would be all right. I said I was worried, where *was* he, couldn't he come back? He said not to be afraid, that he was fine and warm and dry. "I will always be here," he said. I believed him and I slept.

The dream had been so real that I awoke with wet cheeks, then turned over and found a wet spot in the bed. Had I cried that much? Had I lost my faculties in the night? Had there been a storm as I slept and the attic roof leaked?

At breakfast, amid discussions of the impending trip, the men politely ignored me. The prior evening's unhappy incident was not mentioned.

I wished that someone would bring it up, so that I would know I was not crazy, but the crew bristled with impending departure.

"The boat will arrive at noon," began Keeper Bunker. "We will—"

"My roof leaked during the night," I said.

"Pardon?"

"The rainstorm," I said. "It caused the roof to leak."

"I didn't hear any storm." Mrs. Bunker entered the dining area, dishtowel in hand.

"But—" I looked around the room, "—my bed. It's wet."

"You were very upset." Thomas' voice was gentle.

"The barometer was normal," Keeper Bunker said softly. "I checked before extinguishing the lamp."

"I heard nothing," added August.

"There was a storm," I insisted. "And the roof sprung a leak." I looked around at them, feeling a sudden chill.

"Wetness in your room?" Sarah tossed the dishtowel over her shoulder.

"It's been happening all week," I said. "The first time, it was outside the door, from your mopping."

"I haven't," said Sarah, concern softening her features. "I mopped before you came."

"And the day after that, it leaked *under* my door." I looked from face to face. On each, I saw a flat pity that angered me. "It must have been your mopping."

"I haven't mopped."

"Then you carried water, and it sloshed outside my door."

"Madeleine, you are tired. It has been a trying week. It is all right." She moved closer and touched my arm.

I shrugged her off. "It is *not* all right. All week long, the mornings have delivered some form of wetness to my room."

"Is your mind," said August. "Like before."

"I did *not* imagine it." Tears pushed at the backs of my eyes. I blinked hard against them and stared into the corner of the room. A fine crack ran down the plaster where the two walls met. It forked at the juncture of the floor.

I thought about the whole week of water, how each morning the puddle had been nearer to my bedside. And I began to understand that the water was not from Mrs. Bunker's mopping. It was not from my carelessness with the basin. It was not from the rain. It had appeared every morning after a night of worry over my husband. It had moved closer and closer to me. Last night, when I dreamt of Alonzo in the bed, I woke to water on the sheet beside me.

He had been here after all. He had kept his promise.

"I cannot leave," I said, under my breath. Desperation flooded over me. I had wanted a sign, hoped every day for a message from my husband. And I'd had not *one* sign, but five, each night that I had slept in the House of Refuge. I had slept and dreamed and Alonzo had been there, too.

I looked around the table. The same people were no longer sitting there. Instead I saw the faces of those who had survived, who would go on, who had not lost what I had lost.

"Excuse me," I said. I placed my napkin on the table, stood and left, without explanation. I climbed the small attic stairs slowly and thought of our days in Cuba, of the grand boat my husband had been so proud to captain, of the preciousness of our enduring childhood friendship, of the children we would never have ourselves. I pulled the covers back and crawled beneath them. Until it was time to leave, I would lie in bed, the clock ticking steady as a heartbeat, my arm across the wet spot, and say good-bye.

BONES

OF AN

INLAND SEA

Alicia's main goal—back in the mid-Carter, Cenozoic Era, before Silicon Valley spawned a population overgrowth of *Geekus millionairus*, before the *Me Generation* erupted on the scene, creating a fissure through which Reaganomics trickled down into American bedrock—was getting her paleontology professor into bed.

The Goal (as she came to refer to it) gave her something to reach for outside of academics; it gave her *purpose*. The Goal began as intellectual adoration; she adored her professor for what he could give her mind. Later, when he returned her attentions, she adored him—such a smart man!—for wanting *her*. His erudite desire made her more deserving; it made her valuable.

And even when Professor Baxter—Quinn—had mentioned the wife, Alicia hadn't been deterred, not so long as she remained nameless and insubstantial, a will-o'-the-wisp wife, if you will.

His ten-year-old daughter, though, was more tangible, as evidenced by Quinn's many relics: little Leslie Baxter's plaster-cast handprint propped on his office bookshelf (flanking a prized Silurian Eurypterid), a trio of lost teeth taped to a picture frame that held a photo of her with a tiny fish dangling at the end of a stringer.

It was the teeth that made the biggest impression on Alicia, something solid and real, little pieces of castoff bone, the archaeological remains of a child, treasured before they'd had the chance to be buried and retrieved.

Anyway, with a little distance—she has her own classroom now, her own fawning students to contend with—she understands how decent it was of Quinn to mention The Wife's existence. Andrea, she was— the A, Quinn said, pronounced like an O—*On*-drea. A priggish name. Alicia prided herself on *not* being priggish. Not an On-drea at all. A quarter of a century later and Alicia still remembers The Wife's name. She must have *become* real, then, solidified over time like a fossil's calcified remains.

In the years since, Alicia has refashioned the Quinn and His Will-o-the-Wisp Wife saga into something useful: a story to regale girlfriends with, over drinks, in the salsa-and-margarita joints that attract unattached women-of-a-certain-age.

Most often, it's the breakup story she tells. "We broke up in a pile of bones," she'll start. Except it wasn't really *bones* they'd been digging for, since an arthropod's shell takes the place of bones, but "bones" sounds better than "exoskeleton." Bones fit the theme of a dying relationship. So she lets her listeners think "bones" as she speaks about Quinn, old himself then—at forty-six he was exactly twice as old as Alicia, or *Lixia*, as he called her, some shortened version of delicious, which he liked to tell her that she was.

Sex with Quinn had been a revelation; a sudden under-standing that *this* was what all the fuss was about. She'd had other lovers before him, of course, and one even in the midst of their affair, just to prove (he went home every night to *On-drea*, after all) that he wasn't the only one with options. Before Quinn—B.Q. in their lovers' shorthand—her sexual trysts had mostly been one-offs with overeager frat boys, plus that one fumbling attempt in high school in the Methodist Church cemetery, but none of those boys wanted to do it in a real bed, take their time, bring *her* pleasure.

She tells her listeners that the end of the relationship came in a hotel near Niagara Falls, New York, honeymoon capital of the world. The siren-call of eurypterids had lured Quinn there. Eurypterids were small, smaller than a hand, related to scorpions. Western New York's limestone harbored a subterranean treasure trove of them, and it was Quinn's professional ambition to discover a new species and name it eponymously.

Already there was *Euripterus pittsfordensis* named for the town of

Pittsford, New York, discovered in the early 1900s when blasting the Erie Canal out of its surrounding shale. And also *Hughmilleria socialis*, named for Hugh Miller, an old-timey Scottish geologist who'd shot himself in the chest because he couldn't reconcile his search for fossils with a strict religious upbringing that said the world was made in six days.

Alicia considered the taxonomy of a Quinn-discovered Eurypterid. *Quinnbaxteria adulteralis?* Its outstanding features being a pair of elongated pincers, designed for mating with more than one female at a time…

Okay, so it's only with hindsight that Alicia thinks this way. At the time, she was smitten, smote by love. And aside from the Latin names—which she adored for their musical rhythms and exotic appeal (taxonomy had always been her favorite part of biology)—she doesn't remember a lot about the eurypterids. But Quinn has long been classified as The Man Who Taught Her To Appreciate Her Own Body. In the midst of Alicia's Great Sensual Awakening, small wonder that The Wife seemed inconsequential, unrelated to the things that she and Quinn did, an utterly unimportant aspect of their secret lives.

Besides, The Wife had been nearly the age of Alicia's own mother. Women that age didn't have lives; they didn't *need* a man, not the way Alicia needed Quinn. To women like The Wife, The Husband was something laughable, something to pityingly mock when he attempted to shop for groceries, wash a load of clothes, change a diaper.

Alicia had passed that long ago drive from Penn State to Niagara Falls trying to imagine the ancient inland sea that had harbored Quinn's eurypterids. She closed her eyes and dreamed big wavy expanses adrift with giant seaweeds, sheltering strange-shelled creatures zipping in and out and through, eating smaller creatures, eaten by larger ones, emerging from their briny home to crawl up into the intertidal zone for seconds and then minutes and then hours.

When she awoke, she sketched out a rough image of the prehistoric creatures from her dream. She would spend her free time, she decided, on a drawing for Quinn and present it to him at the end of the trip as a token of her love and admiration.

At the hotel check-in, he arranged adjoining rooms that overlooked The Falls; Alicia watched the water hurl itself ceaselessly over the steep precipice, trillions of droplets at a time. A fine mist hung over The Falls, refracting in the sunlight.

Quinn's decidedly unromantic destination was not The Falls itself, but the *escarpment,* which is what The Falls falls over. The long ridge of the escarpment ran east from the city of Buffalo toward central New York. It's what the Erie Canal's famous locks of Lockport had to climb and the only thing in the area that even slightly resembled the side of a mountain.

Alicia loved mountains—they gave a body purpose, something to strive for, to conquer—and Quinn—Professor Baxter—became her Matterhorn. By the time she finally scaled Mount Quinn, though, he was easy enough. Too easy, really. She would've liked a little more struggle, a little more sweat. But he was ripe and ready, and fell right off that old monogamy tree, smack into the palm of her hand.

And so, during that dig, they had the whole Thanksgiving holiday to spend together—nights!—all night long, in a real room, in a real bed, like a real couple.

In the years since that dig, Alicia has progressed to the age that Quinn was back then (it had been so *ancient!*) and she moderates the discussion as her own zoology students dissect a virtual fetal pig in her anatomy lab. The virtual pig allows for a no-muss, no-fuss dissection, electronically blipping between pages that show digestive, excretory, reproductive, and nervous systems. No more real pig dissections for *her* students. PETA would be proud, but Alicia isn't convinced. Dissection-by-proxy might be fairer to the animals spared, better for the environment, and cheaper for the schools, but there was definitely something missing. Her students wouldn't get their hands mucked up, wouldn't smell the acrid stench of formaldehyde in their nostrils, wouldn't attend their next class with preserved fetal pig beneath their fingernails. Life was messy and occasionally unkind—even to unborn pigs. Today's sheltered kids deserved the chance to learn that. And yet her students, with their *helicopter parents*—who had been known to actually call Alicia at home to argue on behalf of precious Brittany's or Josh's grades—would never understand the logic of unsheltering, of deliberate exposure. The parents were fossilizing their children before their time.

The fetal pig lies curled on the screen before her, larger than life. It looks distinctly humanoid, lying there with its tongue stuck out and its eyes tightly closed, lashes knitted together, ears folded back against its head, smooth skinned, with an umbilical cord tied off and a baby-like butt—smooth mini ham hocks.

She's seen this image a hundred times. Why the sudden likeness to a human fetus? It's the thoughts of Quinn she's been having; it has to be.

Last week, in a back issue of *Paleontology Today*, she'd encountered an obituary for Quinn; sixteen months old by the time she read it—and it seemed ludicrous to grieve, but she did. Sat right down and wept. The obituary mentioned his military service during the atomic testing in the 1950s, his forty-plus years of teaching, and his lifelong study of the eurypterids, which would have pleased Quinn. There was a brief mention of The Wife and his adopted daughter Leslie, also two young granddaughters, Tabitha and Reese.

She searched the obituary for mention of her, not honestly thinking she'd be there, but somehow looking still. They had been so important to each other. How could she not be mentioned? (*Also surviving, the adulteress who drove Dr. Baxter back to his wife and family in the late seventies…*) She was as invisible in his death as she'd been in his life.

That article had excavated too many long-buried memories of Quinn—and now he kept popping back up during the quiet moments of her day. She had to keep reminding herself that everything took place twenty-five years ago, not yesterday.

Alicia had lost loved ones before. Shortly after she'd started dating Quinn, her beloved grandmother died, and he'd held her through the worst of her sobbing fit, three days post-funeral. But the knowledge of *his* death has affected her in a different way. It's as if Quinn's dying has somehow shortened what's left of *her* life.

She isn't sure how to reconcile the remembered pleasure of shared flesh with the death of said flesh. Flesh is what she remembers most about Quinn, and now it's *all* he is. Flesh. Not a *virtual* carcass, like the splayed pig on the monitor at the front of the classroom, but really and truly dead. A man she had loved, had allowed into her body, a man she had craved was now a man no more.

It also makes the new life they created finally and completely dead. Yes, Alicia had been awake during the procedure, she knew the moment the fetus was gone—no need for the doctor to announce, "All done" as he had—but somehow, she realizes now, as long as she felt that Quinn was still alive, out there somewhere, a child of theirs was, too. Or the possibility of a child. The shared memory of their creation a living thing on its own. A virtual life being lived alongside hers. But now it isn't, because Quinn is gone. He can't carry his half of the memory any more and she feels the sudden truth of that more completely than she ever has before.

Had Quinn told The Wife about Alicia? Had she become an accepted anecdote between them? An explanation for occasional long stony silences? Or a hard suspicious knot that was never mentioned? Had he cherished their time together and kept it to himself for the last twenty-one years of his life? Had he taken Alicia with him to his grave?

She imagines her body locked away in a tiny room in his now decaying mind. She could be entrenched in the whorls of his brain, worn forever, invisible yet visible, a tiny, pearled, brain-scar of memory.

"Professor Sparks?" It's a student, interrupting her reverie, and she looks up, the eye contact enough to keep him talking. "Is there a slide for the lachrymal ducts?"

Lachrymal ducts? Do pigs cry?

If Quinn is dead, what does that make Alicia? Old enough to have found bliss with a man who is now old enough to be dead? Old enough to be a virtual grandmother? Alicia could be consoling her own child right now, consoling him over the loss of his father. Or *her* father. Doctors didn't tell you the sex of the child you'd aborted, if they could even tell. She knows because she'd asked, and realized as soon as she had that it was a dreadful faux pas.

So Alicia *is* old, then. Old by association. A near-miss grandmother. *Virtually* dead.

When pigs cry.

Back while Quinn was off busily unearthing evidence of ancient life, Alicia kept busy in the hotel room. She stayed away from the dig because he had other scientists working with him and when she did show up she got we-know-why-you're-really-here-Miss-Helpful-Assistant-who-isn't looks.

So Alicia's sketchpad was a blessing. She'd thrown it in at the last minute when Quinn asked her if she'd packed a book, if she had anything to read. That was the first indication that her role wasn't the one she'd imagined: Alicia and Quinn standing shoulder to shoulder in a dusty pit, sighing as they brushed fine layers of dirt from finds-of-the-century with soft-bristled brushes. She grabbed her sketchbook while the college van idled outside her dorm and Quinn paced guiltily around the quad.

Alicia didn't draw from life. No horses or landscapes, no still lifes or portraits. She drew fantastical images, ancient creatures, fossils on the page. Things with odd, long, stalked eyes and wings, with too many or too few legs and an excessive number of joints to the appendages. The Year of Quinn had been the year of the colorful dangling heart swarming with hundreds of leggy, crab-like creatures. Except for the one tiny, detailed study she drew specifically for him: a eurypterid looming large in the foreground, seaweed twining gracefully beneath it with a smaller eurypterid zooming through the background. She spent hours on the drawing, laboring to get it just right, lightly shading color into the water, the seaweed. She could hardly wait to present it to him.

On the final day of the dig, she lay under the covers in Quinn's room, waiting for him to emerge from his post-dig shower. The eurypterid sketch sat propped on the bedside table (on his side) in a small black frame with a beveled, green mat she had walked into downtown Niagara Falls to procure. He loved the drawing, said he would cherish it forever, said he loved her for spending so much time on something meant only to make him happy. No one had ever given him art before. He was *honored.*

He opened the bathroom door and stood in the steam looking slicked back and doughy. A paunch hung over his underwear like the crown on rising bread. But she loved him, didn't she? She wanted to spend the rest of her life with him.

The Wife loomed, though. What did she have that Alicia didn't have? She asked Quinn this as he made his way toward the bed, drying his ear with his pinky on approach.

He took it as a joke, she could tell by the way he smiled and kept walking toward her. The beginning of an erection strained his Fruit of the Looms.

"Why did you marry her?"

"You were in diapers," he said, holding valiantly to his happy hard-on. "Now let me into bed."

She lifted the covers and scooted over but continued the barrage. "I'm serious. What about me?" She hated the way her voice rose up at the end, hated the grating sound of it in her own ears, but she couldn't stop the momentum of her words.

He bit her shoulder. She sighed and dropped her head back. Yes, there was that. How could she do without *that*?

But when he pressed what was left of his erection against her thigh, tears inextricably stung her eyes. "I want more."

He gave a long sigh and turned away, pulling the sheet up to his shoulder. "We can just go to sleep. Whatever you want."

"Whatever I want?" She felt the desperation rising. "Maybe I want to be The Wife for a change." There, she'd said it. Quinn turned back and his face told her she'd crossed a line, so she pressed it home. "Maybe I want the white picket fence. Maybe I want to be the one you come home to every day."

A film like frosted glass descended over his eyes. "You know my situation."

"You'll screw me but you won't marry me."

"I've been straight with you."

"You could divorce *her*. You could love *me* forever. Would that be so hard?"

"I will love you forever."

"Oh, sure, but there's *On*-drea," she said, derisively. "On-drea with her hook in your nose, leading you wherever she wants you to go."

She rose from the bed and walked into the bathroom. She ran water so he wouldn't hear her crying. How had they come to this? When she turned the water off and opened the door, Quinn sat hunched at the edge of the bed, cupping the mouthpiece of the phone, talking low but trying to sound like he wasn't.

She turned back to the mirror but spoke loudly and deliberately from the bathroom. "Will you have to go back to the dig in the morning, honey?"

"Hang on," he said into the phone, then too loudly, "No, no turn-down, thank you." He returned to his call saying, "Sorry. Housekeeping."

Alicia-the-turndown-maid opened the door of the adjoining room and stepped inside, locking it behind her. She hadn't even set her luggage in here. The beds were made, the towels sat folded neatly on the rack, the soaps were wrapped, the toilet paper triangled. She picked up a bar of soap and bit into it. She screamed an animal sound and threw the shower curtain to one side, then turned the water on and stood under it in her nightshirt, letting the water blast her face. She shook her hair. Water strafed the walls. Quinn would always put his fucking wife first. Alicia would always be invisible. The Invisible Fucking Woman.

She turned and looked in the mirror. "Where are you?" she asked.

Quinn banged on the door. "Lixia, let me in." He banged some more. "I know you're there, Lixi."

She stepped out of the shower, dripped across the floor and sat in front of the TV stand, staring at the tucked, boxy corner of the bedspread with its geometric southwest-style patterns.

"I have my own key," he said, banging again.

When it got quiet she stood and walked to the door, pressing her ear against it. She thought she could hear him standing there, breathing on the other side, but she wasn't sure.

"I'm pregnant," she told the door, then listened again. She leaned against it, shivering, then went back to the bathroom and ran a bath. She stripped off the wet shirt and climbed in.

The phone rang ten times. She counted. When it stopped, she told the shower curtain, "You don't love me."

While the water was still hot and steam clouded the mirror, she heard the door open and close. Quinn appeared and stood there, staring at her.

When she said nothing, he moved closer to the tub and kneeled. "Are you sure?" He reached forward and rested his fingertips lightly on her abdomen.

She nodded.

"There's been no one else?"

She gave a brief thought to that one other time, that guy whose name she couldn't even remember now, but she stared defiantly and didn't answer. It had to be Quinn's child. Any baby growing inside her had to be made from love.

"It's just—" he said, "I didn't think I could." He stared into the water, his shoulders slumped. "There was some exposure, from atomic testing. And I'd always thought...even the doctor said...but, now you're...you've proven everyone wrong." He pressed wet fingertips against his closed eyes and the silence settled between them. The faucet dripped steadily. Then he raised his head and looked at her. "I'll leave her. I mean it, Lixi. I'm ready. We can be a family."

"God," she said, and stood. Water coursed down her legs. His expression changed to serious and he rested his hands at her waist and pulled her toward him. Then he put his arms around her and sobbed against her shoulder. They moved in tandem to the bed. Beads of water coalesced and cooled, puckering her skin. Quinn's face was red and blotchy. She had never seen him cry. He cried like a small boy, breathing in big sobs and rubbing his eyes. She knew it should have made her sympathetic. He continued to whimper so she stroked his hair. "Poor baby," she said.

He cupped her breast, then bent down and nuzzled it. He pulled it into his mouth and sucked greedily like an infant, still whimpering. This was a new element of her take-charge lover. Did he do this with his wife? She cringed in pain and distaste as he continued sucking and whimpering. Alicia wanted her passionate lover back, the man who controlled *her* passion, who led her on the path to pleasure. She didn't want a little boy.

"Quinn," she said. She thought she would tell him that she appreciated all the time they'd spent together, but that they both deserved better. Or that it was about her, not him. Or that she really needed some space, just a little while. Or that she'd really been feeling lately that it wasn't fair to his family. Instead she said, "Make love to me."

And the melancholy romantic notion of *one last time* fed her desire and her recklessness, and they rolled around and she bit his shoulder knowing it would leave a mark that his wife might find. He was the only man who could touch her to the core, she thought, the only man who ever would. The only one.

Other men *had* touched her as deeply, of course. There had been many lovers since Quinn, but he held that special place—the place that the body-memory of first passion takes.

The thing that Alicia never tells when she tells her tale of leaving Quinn is the pain that followed. The nights of lying in her bunk worrying and crying. Of sitting in class those last two weeks of the semester and watching Quinn teach and seeing the sadness and the droop of his shoulders and her hurrying to be the first one out the door so there would be no chance of him holding her back after class. Of crying when she got her grades because he had given her a perfect score. Of asking her roommate to say she wasn't there when he called. Of the time she saw his wife in the grocery store, horse-faced Andrea, and she followed her at a distance thinking, "Hey, Miss. Why the long face?" making a joke even as this woman's world was falling apart. She cringes at the thought of her own twenty-something callous disregard.

Over the years, Alicia-the-arthropod has grown her very own emotional exoskeleton. For years she has hardened her outer shell. But now Quinn's obituary has caused her to molt, exposing a soft underbody that feels the pain she inflicted on Quinn's wife and family. It must have been great. He had left The Wife, she's sure of that. But had they reconciled? She was in his obituary, so they must have. Had she suffered? Had the daughter? Had Leslie cried? For years she couldn't imagine, but now she can. She can imagine because imagining is how she spends her days. What if she had stayed with Quinn? What if she had married any one of the other men who had asked her over the years? Why had she not pursued a family? Who would look after her as she aged? Even now, when she has a cold or the flu she is acutely aware that she is alone, with no one to nurse her back to health.

Aging is the pits. The La Brea Tar Pits. And Quinn has taken the first step toward becoming a fossil: he's died, leaving Alicia to flounder all alone in the stickiness of remembrance and regret.

Did the great woolly mammoths have regrets as they struggled in the muck? Did they pine for things done and left undone? When the dire wolves leapt on them did they think of their mammoth wives? Did the carnivores regret consuming an animal that had been trapped by its own desires? When the scavengers descended and got stuck themselves, did they understand that their hunger was also their downfall?

COMFORTABLY NUMB

Soon as Hurricane Edna quit rattling my windows, I was crazy to get to the aquarium. No question that losing air would kill the fish, crammed into little mindless boxes the way they were. Every stifling minute that passed in Florida's late-summer heat, more fish were dying. I knew that. But the bridge was out and the National Guard had blocked off the whole spit of land—no way to even get there to assess the damage. Hell, if we could've at least gotten in the building we could've set some of them free.

Margie came by my place after the storm to give me a status report. I worked for her at the aquarium, doing odd jobs mostly. She came up the sidewalk picking through the puddles in shorts and a tank top; her hair was wavy, a color halfway between red and gray: strawberry slate. Her face looked shiny and bothered.

My door sat wide open in the heat, begging for a breeze. She rapped on the doorframe and stepped in. I was at the table, shirtless and sweaty, eating up cereal before the milk soured.

"Don't suppose you've got coffee?" she said. "Even cold? I'd kill for a cup."

"Never touch the stuff."

She sighed. "Had to try."

"Come all this way to ask about coffee, did you?"

"I came to let you know it could be three weeks before we get back in the building, Jack." She kept her eyes right on my face.

"No damn way."

She pulled on the front of her shirt and it fell back, the tie-dyed swirl of it Saran-wrapping her breasts. Sweat beaded on her upper lip. "Construction crews have to rebuild the bridge."

"This is *Florida*." I tipped the bowl and drank the last of the milk, then wiped my mouth on my forearm. "Boats every-damn-where you look."

She leaned against the doorframe and let out a tired sigh. "It's dangerous. Gas lines are torn up, the phone and electricity are down…"

Before working at the aquarium, I'd had some trouble—getting a job, keeping food around, that kind of thing. It started once I came stateside; two tours in Nam'll do that to you. But the aquarium was a peaceful place. Even before Margie hired me, I'd go just to watch the fish. Like a whole bunch of TVs playing visual muzak, it took my mind off things.

"Fish don't know dangerous," I said. "They just want air."

"Still." She crooked one leg up like a heron. "I wouldn't ask you to do such a thing."

What I heard in that was, *I won't ask you, but if you're set on it, go ahead.* I said, "I follow your meaning."

"No, you don't." She put the foot back down and leaned toward me. "I'm serious, Jack. I'd never forgive myself if you got hurt."

And in that I heard, *I want you, Jack*, but that seemed to be a recurring thing with me, thinking women wanted me. I decided to believe it anyway.

My first job at the aquarium had been working the touch tank, standing beside it to keep kids from squeezing the sea cucumbers until their guts shot out. Answering a few questions, mostly the same ones all day long: *What's this? What's that? Can I pick it up?* Before long, Margie had me doing odd jobs around the place, unclogging filters, feeding the stingrays, mending maps on the mangrove trail, whatever needed doing.

After she left that morning, I got on the CB and called a buddy. Dobber moonlighted as a small-time drug runner. Three sweaty days passed before he brought his boat and dropped me off at the edge of Hutchinson Island. He kept one eye out for the Coast Guard as he trolled by; I jumped over the gunnel.

I waded to the island through chest-high water. Hurricane Edna had taken away the beach, left the mangroves clinging to life by long red taproots that grew straight down, like the bars of a cage. I pulled myself up by those roots, squeezed seawater out of my shirt, and started up what was left of the road.

The place looked like hell. The Sun Trust Bank across the street was gutted and mostly gone. The Publix was blown out. Down-island a ways I could see the gas station smoldering, a plume of gray smoke floating upward. The aquarium was a big old wooden building, and it still looked mostly sound. Windborne sand had taken her paint off and a few sheets of tin roof were gone or pulled up long and crazy, but that was all.

I tried the front doors: locked. The storm shutters were sealed up tight and wouldn't budge. But the service door around back was open.

I should say right here, that salt water gone stagnant is worse than the greenest, stillest, cow-shittiest pool on the remotest Iowa pastureland. And the minute I opened that stink-hole door, I knew there'd be no hope of finding anything alive: three days with no circulation, in *August*. That aquarium smelled worse than a ditch of rotting napalmed bodies. I leaned back for one last breath of fresh air, then stepped in out of the sunlight and waited for my eyes to adjust.

The air inside was close, jungle-damp. Moisture trails ran down the glass. When a hurricane finishes with you, the heat comes right back— sun and heat, all of it. No relief for those who lost their homes and cars and maybe even a loved one or two. In the middle of the howling wind and cold rain it seems like it'll never be warm again, but soon as the storm passes, bam, you're hot and sticky with a whole damn mess of destruction in need of picking up.

First thing I could think to do was to dump out the lighter aquariums. I picked a small one—the stonefish, a prized orange specimen now covered with white moldy slime—and carried it out the back door. I breathed through my mouth—only when I had to—and dumped him on the ground with a swishy flop, then headed back in.

I'd chosen a second aquarium—two sergeant majors and a dusky damselfish—and was lugging it outside across the muddy ground when the whump, whump, whump of a helicopter stopped me.

Maybe they were surveying damage for the TV news, maybe it was the president himself up there—hell, I don't know, but something in that vibrational whump made my blood pump fast, made my hands go slippery with sweat.

I looked at the ground to give my head a reference point, but my feet were sunk in a muddy field of black sand mud. I looked up and saw shattered palm trees and blown out, roofless buildings with fires burning in the distance. That soft sound slicing though the air was like a pulse in my body, ratcheting up. I dropped to the ground and made myself small, taking that heavy aquarium down with me. The glass cracked and split outward. A long spear of it shot sideways, stabbing through my upper arm, square through my tattoo. The sleeve of my T-shirt disappeared into the jagged hole and blood oozed around the edges. I lay on the ground and stared at it, confused.

I touched the glass. It felt solid and stuck. I reached around the back of my arm and felt the other end sticking out a couple inches at least. I sucked in a big breath of air and tried to pull it back out the front. An explosion lit up inside my skull.

The shard wouldn't budge. The helicopter kept pulsing overhead, and pretty soon I saw a rescue chopper moving through columns of red smoke, swirling into the sky above the spinning blades, Viet Cong advancing faster than we could shoot 'em and the RTO plopped his radio box down beside me to dial for backup.

I hauled myself up and stumbled over to the lobster pool, falling back against the side of it until I could feel the point of that glass dagger touch the wall. Black spots spread in front of my eyes from the pain. My gut squirmed like a salted slug.

I pressed my injured arm back against the low cement wall and the bloody glass slid slowly out through the front. It fell on the cement and broke. That's when I remembered that you're supposed to leave shit like that *in* your body until you get to a doctor.

"Godammit." Blood ran down my arm. I grabbed the wound with my other hand and held it tight. I could feel a pulse beneath my fingers. "Shit." I turned to get up and saw a spiny lobster staring up at me from that stagnant water. He must have hunkered down in his little cement casita and eaten the southern stingrays as they died. Survival of the fittest. Which is what our platoon leader, LT, used to say after humping miles of endless red clay trails: *Survival of the fittest, fellas.*

I always meant to tell him that was for evolution, not war, but I was too busy blowing gobs of red-dust snot out of my nose and taking a knifepoint to my big toe, opening that same damned perpetual blister. About the time I decided that war was *survival of the sneakiest*, a sniper illustrated that point by picking LT off on the way to the crapper, got him right behind the ear. Blew all the teeth out the front of his mouth. With his mouth closed, you couldn't even tell. LT just looked surprised.

I heard footsteps now and grabbed around for my gun—thirty-five years too late for that train. A pair of sensible shoes came into view.

"Jack?" It was Margie. "God, Jack, what happened?" Her face came into focus and the chopper faded in the distance, the smoke cleared and the sun came back out. My arm throbbed.

"Enemy fire?" I offered. "Sniper?"

"Right." She reached out a hand to help me up. Freckles spotted her arm—light ones, like a banana that's just getting ripe.

I climbed awkwardly to my feet, one hand pressing the wound; she pulled her hand away and waited.

"Inside," she said, when I'd finally struggled to a standing position. She tilted her head toward the building. "I brought a flashlight." She unclipped a crook-necked light from her belt loop.

"What a woman." Even through the blood and sweat, the sway of her body pulled me forward.

Halfway to the door, Margie turned, opened her mouth, then closed it. "Keep your hand on it," she said finally. "That's a lot of blood."

"No it isn't," I said, in a clipped voice like the Monty Python black knight with his arms chopped off. "I'm invincible."

"You're loony," she quipped back.

You got to admire a woman who can make a quick comeback in the face of a major flesh wound.

There were women like that in Nam, nurses who told us, "No" or "*Hell*, no," when asked if we were going to die, even if the asker was just so much hamburger meat. My buddy Ron swears a nurse saved his mangled leg. Said the doctor came around with a six-inch needle and shoved it in his foot. She pinched his neck so he hollered out and the doc said, "Guess it won't have to come off, then." Ron still talks about her—thirty years past, and she's become Nurse Legend, Nurse Saint.

"How the devil did you get here?" Margie's voice carried a fair bit of accusation.

"Friend dropped me off."

"By boat," she said. It wasn't a question. Then, "He'll be back for you?"

"Two hours."

"Too long." She quickened her step.

"How'd *you* get here?" I asked. "Chopper?"

She gave me a funny look. "I climbed over what's left of the causeway, Jack." A small stream of blood trickled down between my fingers, dripped off my elbow when I crooked my arm. Margie pointed the flashlight at the marble floor, illuminating the bright red drops.

"Cleanup on aisle four," I called.

She laughed, then pressed a hand over her mouth. "God, the stench." Margie opened the office door and shut it behind us. The stink wasn't as bad in there, but it was bad enough. Maybe it just clung to my clothes.

I sat on the edge of her desk. She held the flashlight and fished around in a drawer, found a bottle of Jack Daniel's. I would have hugged her if I'd had a free arm. "Sure wish I'd known that was there."

"For emergencies," she said, and uncapped it.

I took a big swig and set it on the desk, feeling the muscles of my arm rub against each other in an uncomfortable way. "Any chance you've got a needle and thread in that emergency drawer?" She gave me another funny look, then said, "Wait," and left the room with the light. She returned with a tangled gob of lightweight line. "From the *Dangers to the Marine Environment* display." She set to work untangling it. Tiny pinpricks of light floated around in the dark room. I took another swig.

"Anything that can pass for a needle?" I lifted the whiskey, put my thumb over the opening and drizzled amber liquid into the gash. "Sonofabitch." I pressed the wound and slid to the floor. Blood and whiskey oozed between my fingers.

She gave me a hard look and held up the untangled line. A fishhook dangled at the end of it. "Will this work?"

My tongue felt thick. I nodded, brain sloshing against my skull. I took another swig of whiskey, felt it burn down my gullet, then noticed that the gash was turning white. Crusted blood rimmed the edges. "Bleeding's slowed down," I said and took another swig.

"Good. You're lucky."

"Yeah, lucky." I looked at the fishhook. "I've sewn patches before.

And buttons on my jungle fatigues. Helped a guy tie his calf muscles back together, once. Ritchie...Varnish? Vanquish?... something with a V... limped to the pickup zone himself."

She held the makeshift needle over my wound and grimaced. "Good Lord."

"Go on."

She pressed the hook against the flap of skin. It slid to one side. Blood squeezed out. I groaned and gritted my teeth.

"Press *into* it," I said. "And I'll push the flap on. Like a shish kabob."

The white part of her eyes showed like a horse about to bolt. She brought the hook up, held it in the air, then set it on the desk. "I can't, Jack." She sighed and walked out of the room, taking the light with her.

I sat in the dark for a few minutes, confused, whiskey settling like a blanket over my brain. Then I finally struggled to my feet and felt my way out, my arm limp with pain. I found Margie staring at a wall of dead and dying fish, the beam of her flashlight aimed at the French angelfish we called Fred. Fred was struggling sideways, his big flat body parallel to the surface, pectoral fins waving in the murky water. His bright yellow eye band had gone grey. In my experience, the life went out of fish one color at a time. I took the flashlight and pointed it at the floor.

"Poor Fred," said Margie. She touched my wrist. "And poor you."

"Nothing we can do?"

She shook her head and wiped at her face. "How are you?"

I shrugged toward Fred and immediately regretted it. The pain radiated out from my shoulder. "I always thought the fish were happy here."

She reached for the flashlight. "I need some of that whiskey." The white circle of light dimmed as she walked away. I sat on the floor, back against the wall. Margie returned and settled beside me. She tipped up the bottle, coughed, and wiped the back of her hand across her mouth. "I'm sorry about your arm, sorry about..."

"It was the helicopter," I said. "Just the sound of it." Dark shadows hung underneath her eyes. Death floated all around us. I realized I'd gotten used to the smell.

Margie looked at her knees: freckles there, too. "I get flashbacks," she said. "Drug ones." She tapped the side of her head. "The worst stuff has to catch you by surprise to get remembered." She extended her arm, stroked the inner skin of it. "Twenty-five years ago."

"Can't say I figured you for a user."

"All that's left is the holes."

I thought about that, said, "Holes, I know. One minute you're walking along fine, and then there's the smell of rain on hot dust, or somebody's stupid car backfires and before you can stop your foot, there's this big black nothingness. Down you go."

She gave a little half-smile. "Sometimes I think, *Here we go. Buckle up, Margie.*"

"I'll throw myself in, just to get it over with. Be in charge for a change." I drank some more whiskey. Margie did the same. I shivered, despite the mugginess. She scooted closer. "I fall out of bed a lot," I said. "Girlfriend described it once, the thrashing. Never sounded like me." I played the fading light back and forth across the wall. "When she said I hit her in my sleep, I knew I couldn't ask that much."

"You never married?"

"Nope."

"Never had a special girl?"

I considered. "Once, maybe. She was all of seventeen. I was only eighteen. Didn't even know her before the night we met. My brother Doug was supposed to escort her to some dance. He got chicken pox and it fell to me. She wore the longest white gloves I'd ever seen. Satin. And her skin was just as soft as those gloves. She was Puerto Rican, in Miami for the occasion, with some crazy Polish last name I couldn't parse. But we danced and I could feel her soften in my arms. Before the night was over, we snuck out back. We were hungry, both of us. Everything we did worked. First time."

"But?"

"But maybe I took advantage? I was a kid. A kid who left for Basic the next day with the smell of her still on me. I always regretted not getting an address, not looking her up when I came home."

Margie patted my leg. "There's regrets in every life." She took a deep breath, crossed her arms like she was hugging herself. "I've got regrets. Things that wake me up at night. Who hasn't?" She seemed to consider whether or not to say more, then looked at my wound and gave herself permission. "Somewhere, out in the world, I've got a child. A baby girl. A woman now. I never told this to anyone, Jack."

"I won't say a word."

"It was 1966, I was just a messed-up kid. The father was an Army guy from Fort Eustis, married. I'd already signed up for the Peace Corps and I wanted that more than anything. But she was tiny and perfect. The nuns at the Catholic home weren't supposed to let me hold her, but Sister Catherine did. I've always been grateful for that."

"You ever try to contact her?"

"Oh, I wouldn't do that. She got good parents. Real Ozzie and Harriets. I know that much."

"You have *what ifs*?"

"Every single May 10th and most days in between. Her birthday puts me into a deep funk. But she'd look me up if she wanted to reconnect. I've got to respect that. I wouldn't force a relationship on anyone."

"Still," I said, unsure what exactly I was protesting.

Margie took another swig. "So which is worse? Memories we regret or flashbacks we can't control?"

I leaned back, stared at the ceiling, thought about it. "I can't control memories *or* flashbacks. How are you supposed to fight shit that isn't real?"

"I don't know." She sighed. "Maybe numbness? The absence of anything?"

"Comfortably numb."

She pulled her fingertips across the floor in a lazy swirl. "Yeah."

"I can't drink coffee," I blurted out, then just kept talking. "My buddy Jim and I were on rear patrol. I've thought back. I can't remember any giveaway, just silence. But there came this *whump!* and a sound like air wheezing out of a tire. I swung around to see Jim patting at the hanging shreds of his gut like he thought they needed rearranging. He didn't look scared or hurt, just annoyed by the mess, you know? Then he fell."

"You went back."

"I couldn't leave."

"No." She shook her head. "I guess not."

"They force fed me coffee till I shit myself."

She touched my arm. "Oh, Jack." It was almost a whisper.

"Can't even smell it now, without getting anxious in my gut. You know what a fucking handicap that is? Can't even smell coffee? The whole world drinks coffee. When I came back, it was the one thing my

Mary Akers

old man couldn't get over. I'd served two tours, been a POW, got honorably discharged, and he got stuck on his son being afraid of the smell of coffee. 'It takes a special kind of pussy to be scared of coffee.' His words."

"I didn't know."

"You never wondered why I don't take morning shifts?"

"I'll remember, Jack."

I looked away. The flashlight was so dim, almost out. You couldn't see much. My arm was throbbing less, because of the whiskey, maybe.

"When's your friend picking you up?"

I shone the wisp of light on my watch. The face was brown with dried blood. "An hour ago."

She shrugged. "I knew you'd come here. I let myself in the service door. I stood there and cried. It's horrible, isn't it?"

I nodded.

"Catching all those beautiful specimens only to have them die like this." She rubbed the lip of the bottle with her thumb.

I watched the knuckle bend and move, back and forth. I put my good hand over hers on the bottle. Her chest rose and fell with careful breaths.

"It was a hurricane," I said. "It wasn't your fault."

She shook her head slowly, not ready to accept my pardon.

"Margie," I said. "There was *nothing* you could do." As I said the words, I felt the grace carried inside them.

"I wanted to save them," she said.

I looked at the dead and dying fish and remembered a string of numberless days—weeks that passed captive and airless and alone. I thought of Jim and the blackness of coffee and the blackness of a night with no electricity when you can't even see the stars. "I know," I said and clicked off the flashlight. My bloodied arm felt thick, fat and numb, but at least the pain had pulled back some—back to wherever pain goes when it quits hammering at the base of your skull. "I wanted you to save them, too."

Margie leaned into my good shoulder and we sat there on the floor, side-by-side, feeling Fred-the-Angelfish struggle against death.

LIKE SNOW, ONLY GRAYER

In July 1946, the United States announced it would conduct a series of atomic tests over a ring of small coral islands called Bikini Atoll. That same week French designers launched a very tiny, very risqué line of swimwear named the 'Bikini,' reasoning that the burst of excitement generated would be like an atomic bomb.

When Leslie and her daughters landed on Kwajalein, the Base Commander's wife draped them with plastic flower leis and air kissed each cheek. Master Sergeant Manolo Stackowski transported them by golf cart to the military-issue Airstream trailer they'd been assigned as living quarters. It would serve as their home for nine months while Leslie worked on a reef impact study for a pier reconstruction on neighboring Ebai Island.

Sergeant Stackowski opened the squeaky door with a flourish and five-year-old Tabitha clapped her hands. Her younger sister Reese skipped around the fold-up table chanting, "This-can-be-our-club-house."

"You need anything at all, ma'am," he said, his deep baritone filling up the small trailer, "you let me know and I'll see to it personally." He handed her his card with a smile. "Just dial that extension. It rings right into my office."

In addition to the table, the trailer held one double bed, a two-eyed hotplate, a mini-cubicle shower and a flesh-colored gecko climbing the window above the sink.

"A gecko in the kitchen is good luck," said the sergeant, following her gaze. "They eat their weight in ants."

Outside the Airstream, on the edge of the oyster-shell-paved road, her transportation waited: a rusty rental mountain bike with attached toddler pull-behind. It seemed prophetic, somehow, this squeaky vehicle assigned to carry her into her new life as a single mom.

Their first day passed in a blur of activity, marked by the tasks she managed to complete only because she combined them: brushing her teeth while pushing accumulated sand out the door with a towel; unpacking suitcases while imagining her husband Gus getting comfortable in the home of his new girlfriend; buttering toast while very slowly spelling "Kwajalein" for Tabitha; crying while showering.

The Bikinians were asked to leave their atoll temporarily so the United States could perform atomic tests for "the good of mankind and to end all world wars." After much sorrow and deliberation, their chief announced, "We will go, believing that everything is in the hands of God."

After putting the girls to bed, Leslie took the dishes from the cupboard one by one and set them in a sink of soapy water. She stood there, hands soaking, and watched the gecko climb the window, two small eggs visible through its backlit, translucent skin. She decided she would make the gecko her totem—parthenogenic gecko gals didn't need a male to make babies, all of whom were daughters.

On day two, when the girls got fussy, she strapped them side-by-side into the pull-behind and headed to a nearby cove that had been engineered for safe swimming—meaning cleared of long-dead World War II jeep shells, big gun mounts, and other twisting, rusted, metal war detritus that poked through the waves at low tide. She brought towels, PB&J sandwiches, and water bottles. She pointed her camera at the girls, and said, "Wave to Grandma and Grampa," which they did, obediently, with cheesy smiles, *snap*. Through the viewfinder, stenciled on the bike, she saw for the first time *Department of Defense*.

167 dispirited Bikinians prepared for their mass exodus while 242 naval ships, 156 aircraft, 25,000 radiation-recording devices, and 5,400 experimental rats, goats and pigs began to arrive.

The lagoon was shallow and calm enough to let Tabitha play alone with her goggles—she'd always been a water baby—and Leslie involved Reese in sandcastle construction several feet above the shoreline. They dug until they reached water, made a pile of sand beside the hole, then lifted watery sand-handfuls and held them lightly over the accumulated mound. Rising drips of sandwater climbed into fairytale towers.

With their heads down, neither heard the approaching footsteps.

"Lovely," said a man's voice and Leslie jerked up, startled, her arm still deep in the sand hole. The man had mahogany skin and wavy black hair. From the side, his face appeared flattened, brow and chin in the same plane as nose and eyes.

"It's otay, Mommy." Reese patted her mother's lowered shoulder with a sandy hand.

"What a lovely sculpture," the man said, squatting down to their level. When he smiled, deep creases formed between the nostrils of his broad nose and the corners of his mouth.

"It's a dwip tassel," instructed Reese, her arm disappearing from sight as she reached into the hole.

"A drip castle," Leslie interpreted. The man held a small paper sack in his left hand; something about his knuckles seemed odd. She deliberately didn't stare.

"This is where I eat lunch." He inclined his head toward a nearby picnic table, its feet sunk deep in the sand. "Will it bother you?"

"I'm hungry," said Reese.

"We brought sandwiches," Leslie told her daughter, then to the man said, "Mind if we join you?" The idea of adult human company was enticing; she knew the island to be safe, populated only by approved US military employees and dependents.

Reese stood and smacked her sandy hands together. "I'm hungry."

"We'll eat at the table, honey. Go rinse off in the water. And tell Tabitha it's time to eat." Leslie waited, the plastic bag beside her on the bench.

The relocated Bikinians were shipped 125 miles across the ocean on a Navy LST landing craft to Rongerik Atoll, a previously uninhabited island that lacked adequate fresh water and sources of food.

Leslie's father, a retired professor of paleontology, served briefly in the 1950s aboard a joint Navy Task Force ship in the Marshall Islands; Quinn witnessed the test of the Bravo hydrogen bomb. He only spoke about it once, on a father-daughter deep-sea fishing trip before Leslie left for college. Being out on the ocean, with his daughter ready to go off on her own seemed to pull the story out of him.

He'd felt the incredible warmth of the explosion on his face, he said, scary and exciting all at once. He said it was beautiful. "Like," and he lowered his voice respectfully, "a genie being let out of a bottle."

Quinn had been a good father—involved and kind—she adored him, relied on him, and never questioned his easy love. With her mother, relations had been far pricklier, competitive even, in a way she never fully understood. Then, as she moved into womanhood, an uneasy, unspoken truce settled between them, these two women who loved the same man. Then inextricably, her mother, three years ago, not out of love, but of spite, finally told Leslie that she'd been adopted as a baby, then in the very next breath launched into a tirade about Quinn having an affair with a student in the 1970s, as if the two were somehow related.

Leslie has a vague memory of a long, strange time in her childhood when her father was absent and her mother might as well have been, given the long hours she spent lying on her bed in a darkened room. Her only explanation for Leslie was, "Your father's off digging in the dirt." Leslie was ten, and although that "trip" seemed especially long, it was only one of many so she never questioned it. She wonders now how her daughters will remember this trip. Will they associate it with the end of their parents' marriage? She hasn't yet figured out what to tell them about their father and this other woman. She only knows for certain that she won't wait fifteen years to bring it up.

The callousness of her mother's late-stage adoption revelation, yielded not as an act of love, not as a confidence, but as a weapon, ripped away Leslie's underpinnings; it unmoored her sense of self and created a giant rift of trust. She believed it even contributed to the self-destruction of her marriage to Gus. It also kept her from her father.

Worse, her father had been receiving treatment for prostate cancer for six months and she hadn't made it home. Affording three full-price round-trip tickets was out of the question. Her parents called and emailed but she couldn't face the surge of unwelcome emotions their voices caused in her and so she wrote the occasional bland email in reply, fighting down a toxic mixture of anger, sorrow, and guilt.

The Americans detonated a massive hydrogen bomb (code name: Castle Bravo) on a reef in the northwest corner of Bikini Atoll. Bravo turned out to be a case of accidental overkill—with a force a thousand times more explosive and destructive than Little Boy, the bomb dropped on Hiroshima at the end of World War II.

"I'm Leslie." She wiped a sandy hand on her thigh then held it out to the gentleman.

"Jonku." He offered an apologetic shrug and held out a hand with two twisted and three missing fingers. When she hesitated, he said, "It does not hurt." So she held his disfigured hand lightly and briefly. She did not shake it.

They sat. Jonku rummaged in his bag with both hands and lifted out a piece of cold, wrapped fish. He pinned it between his misshapen hands and took a bite. Leslie turned back to the water. "Come on, girls," she called and they ran toward the picnic table, Reese in the lead. Tabitha veered to one side and kicked over the drip castle as she passed.

The girls sat on Leslie's side of the bench. Tabitha stared at the man across from them. "What's wrong with his hands?" she said and Leslie nudged her foot, with a quick stink-eye follow-up.

"That's not nice," announced Reese, too loudly, and Leslie could feel the heat rising into her face.

"I'm sorry," she said.

"It is not a problem." Jonku smiled. "My old hands now are only in my dreams. That is when they tell their story."

Bravo produced a giant fireball, measuring in the millions of degrees, that shot skyward at 300-miles-an-hour while a cloud of nuclear debris rose 20 miles into the sky, generating 100-mile-an-hour winds that stripped Bikini's coconut trees bare.

"Did you get burned?" asked Tabitha. Her dripping bottom made an expanding wet circle on the wooden bench.

Jonku smiled. "What age are you, young miss?"

"Five," said Tabitha proudly. "And she's three." She pointed her thumb at her sister, who stuck her tongue out at being preempted.

"I'm *free*," Reese declared, holding up the fingers for emphasis.

"Do you know, one day when I was five years old, I saw two suns rise in the morning sky. Two suns! Can you imagine that?"

Tabitha's eyes widened. She shook her head.

"A giant tree of fire grew into the sky. Its flowers dropped white petals all over us. They were soft between our fingers." He wiggled the stumps on his hand. "We laughed and threw handfuls at each other. We pressed it into our hair and played elders. That night our hair fell away and our skin turned angry. Soldiers came and took me to a hospital, but still my fingers did this." He set his hands on the table, exhibit A.

More than 42,000 U.S. military members and civilian personnel were shipped to the Marshall Islands to witness and participate in the atomic testing.

"I'm sorry," said Leslie. "Tabitha shouldn't ask so many questions."

"It is not a bad thing to be curious. I like the honesty of children very much."

"Do you have kids?" Leslie asked.

"My wife and I could not. Three she lost too soon. Then one was born. But he was a jellyfish baby and did not live."

Leslie didn't ask what a jellyfish baby was, but looking at the man's hands she could imagine. "My father is sick back home," she told Jonku. "Tabitha was a baby when we last visited and he hasn't even seen Reese yet. Only pictures."

Jonku's eyebrows came together. "A grandfather should see his granddaughters. Should hold them on his lap. Why do you not take them to him?"

To get to Kwajalein, Leslie and the girls had hopped a military jump flight, a grueling six-hour trip strapped into C-130 jump seats. The girls pulled their ear plugs out and the C-rations were wretched, as if anyone could eat anyway, flying overnight in a big metal tube in the frigid noisy body of an uninsulated plane, butt hanging in a breezy sling.

"It's so far, so much money. I don't know." Suddenly her excuses all seemed weak. "The VA offered to let my dad use their new web cam to talk to us, but I never could afford to buy one. I wouldn't know how to hook it up, anyway."

"In the office of my boss, we have one of these. We could connect to the hospital where your father is and you could show him his granddaughters."

"Oh, my God," said Leslie. "He's at the VA in Hampton. Hampton, Virginia. That would be—he could—" she covered her mouth and spoke through her hands. "I'd like that," she said. "Very much."

In 1968, President Lyndon Johnson declared Bikini Atoll safe and a number of Bikinians came home to prefabricated concrete houses erected by the US government.

Jonku shook two Dum-Dums out of the jar on his desk for the girls. Sergeant Stackowski stood up from a half cubicle on the other side of the room and came forward, hand out. His handshake was firm and overly warm, but not sweaty, his smile a happy squint, topping two rows of large teeth that were both crooked and widely spaced. But there was something about his cockeyed smile that said *calm*, that said *kind*. He led her to his cubicle and typed an email to his VA contact at the Hampton hospital. It was late there, but a reply came within minutes. They set a time for noon the following day.

Leslie took the long route from Jonku's office back to the Airstream, past the ocean end of Kwajelein's tiny airstrip, where a giant white geodesic radar dome rose into the sky. It tracked incoming missiles and Tabitha and Reese called it the big golf ball. (*Can we go see the big golf ball again, Mommy?*) Even though it mostly followed unmanned, minor splashdowns, it was unsettling to stand with her children at a missile destination point on the military's map.

When they reached the trailer, Sergeant Stackowski was standing outside it, wearing shorts and a t-shirt and holding onto the handlebar of a child's bike with training wheels. He jingled the bell with his thumb and Tabitha's eyes lit up. "I thought you might want your own." To Leslie he said, "We keep a bunch in the warehouse, for visiting families."

Tabitha climbed on and he steadied the bike. "The outdoor theater is showing The Little Mermaid tonight. Think your girls would like to go?"

"Ariel!" cried Reese, and the adults laughed.

"I think that's a yes. Thank you, Sergeant."

"Please, call me Manny."

As the sun dropped low in the sky, Leslie settled the girls on a long bench toward the back. Tabitha held the popcorn; Reese sat beside her swinging her legs under the bench and reaching over for handfuls. During the opening credits, Manny leaned toward Leslie and said, "Your kids are great."

"*Sometimes* great. But thanks. You have kids?"

"Just the one. Martin. I was only eighteen when he was born." When she looked at him in surprise, he added, "Yeah, I'm one of those guys. He's twenty-three now, on his own already. It's kind of crazy."

"What about your wife?"

"Single for sixteen years. The marriage didn't take. Those shipping-off-to-war ones seldom do." He looked at her over his sunglasses.

There was a silence during which the sea creatures on screen sang and Leslie considered telling Manny about Gus and his new girlfriend, and how sometimes even the best attempts at love don't *take.* Instead she said, "Growing up, I used to be jealous of friends who had brothers and sisters. I knew I'd have more than one child, if I could. My ex always wanted a boy. Girls are all drama, you know?"

"Oh, I have a twin sister and an ex-wife. I know about drama. Personally, I'm not a big fan of it."

She smiled at him. "Me neither."

The following morning, Jonku met Leslie and the girls at the beach for an early lunch. Halfway through, Manny pulled up in the commander's white Ford Explorer, complete with small U.S. flag and gold insignia. The web cam, he said, leaning out the window, was ready.

"Finish up, girls." Leslie shoved everything back into the plastic PX bag. "I can't sit still another minute."

Soon her parents would be on the screen in front of her, and her girls would get to see them and be seen by them. She scanned Reese's face and made a quick swipe to remove a clump of grape jelly on her cheek. Reese squirmed away, voicing her objection.

In 1977, further testing revealed that radioactive strontium-90 in Bikini's well water exceeded maximum allowable limits; scientists recorded an eleven-fold increase in the islanders' cesium-137 body burdens. The DOE told Bikinians: eat no more than 1 coconut per day.

Leslie's mother came on the web cam first. Andrea hadn't changed—a few gray hairs, but the same quick, efficient smile, all teeth, nothing wasted, her cheeks flushed, ruddy with excitement. She put her face too close to the camera and spoke loudly.

"It's okay, Mom," said Leslie, "you can just sit back and talk normal. We can hear you fine." Jonku reached across the screen and lowered the volume.

"Is he the one that set this up?" shouted her mother.

"Yes, Mom, that's Jonku."

"Well you be sure and tell that man thank you from us. This is a gift. Don't ever let it be said that island people are not smart, because this is a special gift he's given us. A special gift."

"He can hear you, Mom."

"What?" she craned her neck closer; her face filled the computer screen.

"Hi, Grandma," said the girls in unison at Leslie's urging. Tabitha waved shyly.

"Oh, my, look at you girls! You're so big! Grandma won't even be able to pick you up next time you visit."

"Mom, is Daddy there?" Leslie wanted desperately to see her father, but when her mother rose from the chair, pulled it away and rolled her father into place, she gasped then hoped the microphone hadn't picked up the sound. He had lost weight—his neck was deeply corded when he smiled. "Daddy?" she said, uncertainly.

"Sorry you have to see me like this, honey." Very little remained of his once thick hair. The skin of his scalp was translucent, like veiny parchment, and his skull alarmingly bumpy without the hair to hide it. His making an apology for his appearance only heightened her pain at seeing him so reduced.

"When did you start using a wheelchair, Daddy?"

"A week or so ago. It's just temporary. Till I get my sea legs back."

Tabitha popped in front of her mother, stuck her thumbs in her ears and wiggled her fingers.

"Stop," said Leslie, but Quinn was laughing.

"And who is this lovely young lady?"

"Say hello to Grampa, Tabitha."

"Hello, Grampa." She wagged her head back and forth, watching her own smaller image in the corner of the computer screen.

"Last time I saw you, honey, you were a baby. Can you believe that?"

Tabitha looked over at her little sister. "How big was Reese?"

Leslie's youngest stared at the computer screen. She shook her head and pulled back when Leslie reached for her. "Come on," Leslie insisted. "Grampa wants to see you."

Most Marshallese can outline their family tree in terms of cancers: thyroid, pancreatic, liver. An uncle, a cousin, a sister, a child. There is no family that has been left untouched.

Leslie pulled Reese onto her lap. She pointed at the computer screen. "This is *my* daddy."

"Hi there, Reesy-bear. You look just like your mama. My Lord."

"Tell him how old you are," said Leslie, a reliable way to get Reese talking.

"I'm free."

"Oh, boy, when your mother was three, was she ever a handful. Once she drew all over herself with magic markers and called it clothes."

Reese giggled.

"Daddy!" said Leslie. "Don't give her any ideas."

"And gum? Well, we didn't even give her the stuff, but she'd always find it somewhere. She had gum radar. Once she pulled a wadded up piece out from under a restaurant table and started chewing it before we could stop her." Reese squirmed on her mother's lap.

"Tell Grampa bye," Leslie said.

"Bye-bye, Gampa," said Reese as she wriggled down and away.

"Daddy, I want you to meet Jonku." Leslie turned and urged him closer. He leaned in briefly.

"Good afternoon, sir."

"Hello, Jonku. This means more than you know."

"Jonku's Marshallese, Daddy. He saw the bomb, same as you. The fallout fell on his island."

"Like snow, wasn't it?" said Quinn. "Snow, only grayer."

"I have never seen snow, sir," said Jonku.

Quinn chuckled. "No, no, I suppose you wouldn't've. It's beautiful, though."

"It was a pleasure meeting you, sir. I will return you to your daughter."

"Why did you say the bomb was beautiful, Daddy?" Leslie carefully held back the tone she heard in her own head: accusing.

The hospital on Majuro, home to a number of displaced Bikinians, is repeatedly overwhelmed with radiation-exposure complaints and cancers. Hundreds line up to wait for appointments with the island's understaffed medical team.

"It *was* beautiful," said Quinn softly. "Like the awe of seeing God." He ran a bony, veined-and-spotted hand through his wisp of hair then smiled ruefully when he realized what he had done. "Force of habit," he said, looking at his hand. "You know, I still hear the clicking crackle of that damn Geiger counter. If we went out on deck it went crazy. We wore gas masks, couldn't swim in the ocean, caught giant, silver tunas we couldn't eat...it was a fouled-up world."

"You could have told me that part."

"What's to tell? I did the job I was sent to do. Served my country. Came home to start a family...except your mother never could get pregnant...we were so happy when the adoption people called and told us you were there."

The sudden pang of this first admission from her father made her stomach turn over, but his smile was soft, sifting together the joy of memory and the unease of newly spoken truth.

"Oh, my God." Leslie shook her head. "The bomb. The bomb was why you and Mom couldn't..." She clenched and unclenched her fists. *How could she have missed that for so long?*

"Most likely, honey." Another admission.

"And your cancer...?"

"That, too, I'm guessing."

She looked again at her father, at his familiar, wasted face. For years, silence had equaled protection in her parents' eyes. And now the balance was shifting. Soon Leslie would become the needed one, the one in charge. She forced a smile for her father's benefit. "Is the VA hospital treating you right at least?"

He lifted his hands from the armrests. "They try."

She stared into the web cam's tiny, electronic eye. "It wasn't *really* beautiful, was it Daddy?" She needed to hear him say it.

His eyes looked back fifty years; the shift of focus moved across his features like a wave. He shrugged, helpless before the memory. "It really was, honey. Beautiful. I promise."

In 1983, Ronald Reagan's Star Wars Project announced a feasibility study for launching "smart rocks" from space to intercept incoming Intercontinental Ballistic Missiles before they enter the earth's atmosphere. Kwajalein, it was decided, would serve as the missiles' destination point.

When the web visit ended—reluctantly, on both sides of the world— Leslie loaded the girls into the pull-behind and pedaled around the island until they fell asleep, lulled by the steady oyster-shell crackle and the bumpy ride.

The island's perpetual breezes turned her tears into salty lines that pulled at the skin of her cheeks. She stopped at the bivouac-shaped chapel and knelt before its altar, waiting for words to come. When they did, they came as pleas, pleas for her father to be spared, even though she knew it was too late to ask.

In the quiet of the chapel she heard Reese crying through the open doorway. She knew that cry—the annoying cry of *want*. Leslie stood and walked out to the bike.

"I'm here, honey. What is it?"

Reese licked her upper lip, wet from her nose, then sniffed. "I wanna see my tassel."

"Your castle?" Leslie ran a hand through her hair, exasperated. The movement echoed her father's, and she thought how he'd done it, even when his hair was mostly gone. "Honey, a drip castle doesn't last. Sand doesn't stay."

Reese plucked at the buckle on her chest. "I wanna see it."

"It's probably already washed away."

"I wanna see it."

Leslie knew her stubborn three-year-old well enough to know that she wouldn't be satisfied until she saw the castle—or what was left of it—and that no one else would have any peace, either.

Operation Smart Rocks, poetically renamed Brilliant Pebbles *by the U.S. Air Force, continues to test long-range guided missiles, firing them 2,300 miles—from Vandenberg Air Force Base in California to the Marshall atoll of Kwajalein.*

When they pulled up to the beach, the flat expanse of sand made Leslie's heart sink. Reese leaned forward, tugging at the chest straps. "Where's my tassel?"

She considered all the responses she could give: a hard dose of reality, a bewildered confusion to match her daughter's, a platitude, a lie. She had the thought that parenting was a constant daily barrage of choices, but that all the choices boiled down to one thing—how to present the world. It was a burden. A burden to have to choose how your children would see the rest of their lives, a burden to make everything about something larger.

"I don't know where it went, honey. It isn't here anymore. But you know what? We can build a better one—bigger and prettier, and farther back from the ocean."

"And make it stay?"

"We can dig a moat around it to catch the seawater. And we can make a high wall to protect it, and we'll do what we can. How does that sound?"

On Kwajalein, concrete bunkers cover the island, the mounds grown over with dirt and grass and sea grapes. A small rectangular pool holds sea turtles free to come and go as they please. The island has a water tower, a giant golf ball, and 1,000 geckos, the cleanest and most prized method of household pest control.

BEYOND THE STRANDLINE

Everything made Walt angry: the too-hot sun beating down on his bare head, the stranded dolphins in the nearby shallows, the dead one they'd been too late to save, the overeager volunteers, and now this zealous young interviewer. Fifteen months after Chelsea's accident, and the sight of a healthy woman still made him angry.

He held out his hands, thick palms facing up. "I'm no candy-ass bunny hugger," he said. "I mean look at me."

And she *did* look. Stared with her eager, shiny face all turned up to his as if he were some fount of freaking knowledge, as if he—Walt Glenny—had all the answers.

He cocked his head, gave her a sideways glance. "Where'd you say you were from again?"

"Did I? Atlanta, originally. But I—"

"No, no. Just now, I mean. Who sent you—the interview?"

"Oh." She giggled and ducked her head. "Sorry. Dolphin Shoals. The Institute there. You know them?"

Oh, Walt knew them, all right. They touted marine mammal rescue as a way to up their enrollment, but were useless during any real missions. Walt had butted heads with them on more than one occasion, touchy-feely bunch of do-gooders.

"I do," he said. "Better leave it at that." It wasn't like he wanted to make nice with a Dolphin Shoals rep, but he'd spouted off lately to enough media worms who'd twisted his words and made him out as some sort of vigilante. He'd try keeping his mouth shut for a change. Chelsea would approve—if he could ever tell her and get some sort of meaningful response again, which he couldn't.

"I'm so excited to finally meet you," the interviewer said. "I mean, I've heard so much about you and all."

So that was it. She'd come for an interview, yes, but also meant to worship at the fins of the great dolphin rescuer, maybe even offer herself up to him before the day was out.

And Walt? He couldn't care less. Oh, her flesh filled up her skin nicely enough; smooth and rounded, she was, with shiny straight hair that smelled like cooked apples. Not a knockout, no, but since when had beauty ever been one of Walt's criteria?

"Heard a lot, have you?"

"It's totally inspiring. Helping dolphins like you do—fighting for them, and all, while your wife…" Her voice trailed off.

Yes, there was that. He understood Chelsea's accident made him a tragic figure, but he'd never wanted that, never asked for it, and in the end all the sympathy did was make him angry. Just like this little girl made him angry in some way too complex to name.

There was a time—not so long ago—when he'd have had her out behind the dive shed, all quivery and tender in his hands, getting life and youth from her like some damned infusion, but not anymore. He just plain didn't have it in him.

"It's a sad fact," he said, crossing his leathery-tanned forearms, white hairs bristling between his fingers. "But they do need help. You'd be surprised what-all humans'll do just to put on a show."

She took a step closer. "I think it's amazing that you're so committed."

Walt switched to his lecture voice. "In Japan they stage huge roundups, bang hammers against steel poles in the water and herd hundreds of dolphins into pens. It's a god-awful noise." He gave her a meaningful look. "Dolphins are echolocators."

She nodded with a pretty, blank expression.

"Sonar?" he tried. "Think of the pain." He touched his ear. "Herders pick the healthiest ones and sell 'em to dolphinariums as performers, or to Swim-With programs, even if it means taking a nursing baby from its mother. The rest get bludgeoned and harpooned. The dolphins panic and thrash around—the whole bay turns red."

"Can't we stop them?"

"I've tried. And I'll keep trying, but the herders get violent if they see you videotaping—dolphin round-ups make too much money. The killed dolphins get cut up into steaks. In Japan, I'm talking about. And what the poor slobs over there don't realize, is dolphin meat's about the most contaminated thing a person could eat—heavy duty mercury poisoning." Walt raised an eyebrow. "You writing this down?"

She gave him a coy smile. "I've got a photographic memory."

"But I'm *talking*."

"I'll remember. You know, I heard that dolphins are the only species besides humans that actually have, um—sex. For fun. Is that true?"

The girl—*what was her name again?*—slipped a foot out of its sandal and swirled her bright red toenails in the sand.

Damn, Walt was tired. And this young blonde ball of sex and energy made him even tireder. "How about you tell me what that has to do with these dolphins?" He pointed to the gray shapes in the nearby shallows, draped with wet sheets, surrounded by volunteers dipping and pouring seawater, speaking in soothing tones. "You think they're thinking about sex?"

Her eyes flicked up at him and she jerked her foot back; hurt, he guessed. Not that he had time to worry about little girls' feelings. Better off, these days, if they learned early.

"No." She spoke in a closed-off, spoiled child's voice.

Amber—*was that the name she'd given him?*—well, she was mad, now, little Amber was, but better mad than courting sex from a man old enough to be her father.

And Walt wasn't *old*. He could still do more pushups at fifty-three than most men half his age. He could wrestle a panicked dolphin into calm, organize a group of hysterical do-gooders with a barked order, and sweet-talk the big money folks into donating. Everyone knew who manned the helm at The Alliance for Dolphin Freedom. The ADF *was* Walt Glenny. And he meant to teach the world that dolphin capture and use was akin to slavery, every bit as bad as the human kind.

"Didn't you used to capture them?"

He sighed. "Yes, and I've seen firsthand, the damage. That's why I work so hard to stop it. Now, if you'll excuse me, I'll be getting back." He about-faced and strode away.

As he reached his truck, the pink-skinned woman who'd discovered the stranded dolphins ran up to him. She was older than the interviewer, closer to Walt's age, but just as eager, captivated like everyone else by her own ideas of what she wanted dolphins to be. Fading blond hair hung in wet strings about her face. Her smile, big and horsy, dominated the rest of her sharp features and her bathing suit sagged at a pair of used-up breasts.

"You're leaving?" she asked, holding his door as he tried to shut it.

Walt remembered *her* name well enough: Andrea. The widow Andrea. Pronounced, she'd had the gall to say, like the *on* in sonogram. All those other *on* words (oncology, onerous, onlooker, onslaught) and she chose *sonogram*—fish finder, fetus finder, blood clot finder—the damned thing they used when they opened up Chelsea's skull to look inside, after she collapsed thirty feet below the surface and he got her—somehow—to the beach, picking her up when the water no longer supported her, dropping his own tank and resting her head on the warm sand just beyond the strandline. Then Chelsea lying slack in the emergency room, still in her bikini, sand all stuck to one side of her face—right on her *eyeball*, for Christ's sake—and half in her mouth as they wheeled her away. Chelsea's pretty face, already collapsing in on itself, told him more right then than anything the doctors would say later.

And as hard as that memory was, it was still better than the ones his brain was making now: Chelsea's wasted body after fifteen sunless months tucked under starched white hospital sheets beneath buzzing fluorescent lights, all traces of sand long since washed away, her hair thin and clumpy, white scalp showing through the coarse gray roots that had grown halfway down into the brown.

She would've hated that.

He retrieved his sunglasses from the dash. "Listen, I gotta run get the van. Can't carry a dolphin off in this." He pointed to the truck bed behind him. "Van's got a sling—doesn't bruise the dolphin."

"Bruise?" She cocked her head like a sandpiper and studied the motionless dolphin. "Isn't she dead?"

"Yeah, dead." He gave Andrea a withering look, then thought better of it and rearranged his face. "You want any bruising to be from trauma *before* death. Autopsy tells a story that way."

During the recent months of Chelsea's *illness* (as that infernally Bible-thumping sister of hers continued to call it), Walt found himself wishing that day of diving *had* been fatal. At the moment of crisis, when Chelsea looked at him through her mask, eyes big and panic stricken, he thought he was doing the right thing rushing her to Marathon, to the emergency room there, but fifteen months of limbo-hell later it seems like he should have just let her finish out her last breaths there on the sand with the warm sun beating down on her.

Chelsea always hated air conditioning. It took years of living under her rules, but he finally got used to nothing more than a ceiling fan. Now, visiting Chelsea in the meat-locker hospital for as little as ten minutes left him fighting off a subterranean chill for hours.

"It was just so strange," said Andrea, "seeing those dolphins close to the shore, all in one place, clicking and clicking like that. They must have been saying 'Get up, get up,' or something. Anyway, when I got closer I saw the dead one at the bottom. So sad. I kept thinking that my daughter—she's a marine biologist—would know what to do for them."

Walt knew dolphins. Hell, he could practically speak their language after thirty-plus years of working with them. First watching them ride the bow waves as a Merchant Marine en route to Vietnam, then helping capture dolphins and train them to perform at Ocean World, followed by a stint with the Navy teaching dolphins to place underwater charges, always looking for some way of working with them that didn't feel so wrong.

Then finally, after one of his girls—Britta, a spotted dolphin he'd helped capture and train—died in his arms, it was like the blinders came off and he could see how bad the animals missed the wild, how depressed they became when they were captured and forced to eat dead fish handed to them, how often the dolphins died. People assumed performing dolphins were happy, smiling things, but the sad truth was that performing dolphins didn't live that long and turnover was high. Dolphinariums always trotted out the odd 20-year-veteran performer who smiled and chirped for the spectators and made everyone believe it was a good life, free of dangers and disease, but that wasn't the norm. And hell, some slaves didn't want their freedom, either, even after the Civil War—begged their masters to keep them on. Some kidnapping victims came to side with their violent captors. It didn't make it *right*.

"Can I help?" asked Andrea. "I mean, I can come with you."

He shook his head, then thought, *what the hell.* "I guess there's no harm in a tagalong," he said, adding, "Other side's open," in a gentler voice. She scrambled around the truck and climbed in.

Shortly after Chelsea's accident, when the words *Persistent Vegetative State* were spoken, the women began to throw themselves at Walt. There was nothing to explain it. No change other than a name put to Chelsea's affliction. He was the same man all the time—a squat man, really, taking after his shovel-handed father who worked his life away in the coalmines of Norton, Virginia, his father with the broad, flat, Neanderthal forehead and shoulders like a damned plank.

The first woman to approach him was a neighbor, a young redheaded widow who brought him a soufflé, arriving at the door in a see-through black shirt with no bra. He'd been too shocked to appreciate the gesture at the time. Too shocked, also, when she sidled up to him and rubbed her left breast against his arm. All he could think was, *Soufflé? What kind of man eats soufflé the day his wife gets diagnosed a vegetable?* And she took her cherry-red nipples home with her that night, untouched, but by the end of the week she was back, and this time he didn't let the gesture go to waste. He knew it was pity sex, but there was something cathartic about it just the same, something cleansing about accepting this woman's offering: her body a sacrificial object for his healing. Something primitive made him feel that, yes, he was a man still, alive still, sexual still, *not* dying, not wasting away in that hospital bed on those white, white sheets beside his brain-dead wife.

It came easier after the first. *My wife's a vegetable,* the mutually acknowledged shorthand giving women permission to soothe his pain. Walt wasn't exactly proud of the long string of soothers whose offers he'd accepted, but he wasn't ashamed, either. Pain was pain, and the only way to make it stop was to give the body what it wanted. And besides, he made the women feel good. It wasn't as if they left unhappy.

And so it went. Until Chelsea's doctor finally tap-danced around the idea of removing her life support, feeding tube included. It was almost funny watching the doctor work up his words when Walt'd already decided it would be best. He agreed to remove everything, as per Chelsea's expressed wishes in life, said but never written. Walt understood—he had identical thoughts on living life as a vegetable—

but even understanding, he couldn't watch her die, and he wouldn't. He would say his good-byes well before she checked out permanently. No holding his wife's wasted, dying body in his arms for Walt. No sir. He'd been there, done that, at the time of the stroke, the time of her *real* death. No need to relive that.

And that day of decision was the turning point for him. He stopped bedding every woman with a soft eye for his predicament. He stopped using his persistently vegetative wife as a tool of seduction. Just stopped. Cold. And he couldn't say precisely why, but it relieved some sense of burden he'd been experiencing, took away the elephant he hadn't even known was sitting on his chest.

Meanwhile Chelsea's stupid, thick-headed sister continued to believe it was only a matter of time before Chelsea recovered, and she fought Walt's decision at every turn. In her eyes, he was a murderer for wanting to finally give his wife's worn-out body a little peace.

No one could say he hadn't done right by Chelsea. No one. He had been there from the beginning. He visited her every day, even sold off the furniture and moved to a dingy apartment in Marathon to be closer to the hospital. He exercised her arms and legs the way the physical therapist taught him, talked to her blank face about life outside the hospital the way the nurses said might help. But that body in the bed wasn't Walt's wife any more than that dolphin carcass on the beach was. He knew Chelsea's smile. And that once-in-a-blue-moon spasm that twisted up what was left of her face wasn't it. She couldn't even eat, for crying out loud. Couldn't swallow her own spit. Wore a diaper. And that crimped tube they squirted liquid food into, that nasty tunnel that led right to her stomach? Well, that was the most barbaric thing of all. He would've rather seen her eaten by a shark.

"It's all hinked up," Walt said as Andrea tugged and twisted at the seatbelt. "Might as well just click it in. You won't get it righted."

"Well, you be sure and drive carefully then," she said, with what passed for a coquettish—if horsy—smile. "Yes?"

He looked at her sideways. She wasn't half bad from that angle.

"Yes," he said. "What brings you to Florida?"

"How do you know I don't live here?"

He considered mentioning her pink skin and brand new bathing suit, but held his tongue. She sighed and looked out the window. "My husband died last year. One of those long, messy C-word things. I still can't say it. Then my only daughter, who is always traveling all over the world—she couldn't even make it to the funeral—got married, for the second time, and now she's expecting, for the third time, and nobody even seemed to care what I wanted anymore, so I just thought, don't I deserve to do something fun? Where's *my* adventure? So I signed up for a weeklong cruise in the Bahamas. The ship leaves in two days. I came down early to soak up some sun beforehand. Quinn never would go on one of those things with me, not for all my years of asking."

"He get seasick?"

"Oh, I don't think it was that. He was in the Navy. Besides, those big ships? They're rock solid, even in a storm, or so I hear. He just never wanted to do the things I wanted to do, that's all. So now that he's gone, I get to be me."

"Well, good for you," Walt said, not really meaning it but wanting to stem the flow of information. They passed a sign for the hospital and he thought about the fact that he needed to swing by and manipulate Chelsea's limbs today. Or no, no he didn't. The feeding tube was out. Couldn't he finally admit that moving her arms and legs wouldn't matter? But her remaining days were numbered; he needed to stop by for that simple reason, manipulation or not. He turned to Andrea. "You care if I run by the hospital first?"

"The hospital? Can they help?"

"Not for the dolphins. My wife's there."

"Your wife?"

"She had a stroke. A year and a half ago."

She brought her hand to her mouth, covering her teeth. "I had no idea. I'm so sorry."

"I figure I'm used to it by now. Still doesn't seem like her in that hospital bed, though."

She spoke to the closed window: "I guess not." Then turned back to him. "Is it horrible?"

He gave her an appraising look. "You're the first one to ask *that*."

"I just mean . . . it must be. Yes?"

He tightened his grip on the wheel and turned into the hospital parking lot. A row of palm trees clattered their fronds in a hot breeze off the blacktop. He pulled into a "Visitors" space and shut the engine. "Yes," he said.

"Mind if I come with? I've got a cover-up in my bag. It's too hot out here."

He nodded. "Suit yourself."

Outside of Chelsea's door, Andrea touched his arm. "I'll wait over there." She cranked her head toward a row of mustard-colored Naugahyde sofas.

Walt stepped into the room, moved over to the bed, and took Chelsea's hand, rubbing the fingers. "Hey, Chels," he said. "Sweetheart."

He had long ago stopped asking questions. No "How are you?" No "What's up?" The silence that followed a question was too all-encompassing. It sucked the air out of a room.

"You look good." His standard line. Really, she looked like hell. Three days without the feeding tube or even water had left her skin a pasty gray. Her lips were flaking and he reached for the jar of Vaseline and spread a greasy layer over them. "I can only come a few more times, honey, then I'll be . . ."

Unfinished sentences didn't matter either. It was all the same now. During their marriage, whenever Walt told a story that rambled on for too long, Chelsea would lean toward him and roll her hands in a move-it-along signal that told him he was losing focus. He hated it at the time. He longed for it now.

"Here, let me." He lifted her limp hands, held them at the wrists and attempted to do the hand roll. "Move it along, Walt," he said, in a high falsetto.

Not that Chelsea's voice was ever high. It was sexy-deep. Or maybe he just remembered it that way. Hard to say. Memories had a way of going fuzzy and indistinct much faster that you ever thought they could. Now he was the husband of a voiceless wife. He guessed that the underlying plumbing still worked so that technically she *could* talk. If she had the air and the will and the muscle control and the brain to back the voicebox up. The real irony was, Walt had never been the sort of husband who wanted his wife to *just shut up*. They'd talked all the time—about meaningless shit some days, but also about real, gut-wrenching stuff.

How the hell he ended up in this ridiculous melodrama of a life is beyond him. Bent on saving dolphins when he couldn't even save his own wife. No wonder women saw him as a tragic figure. Hell, it's exactly what he was. He'd be happy to quit the ADF if he could. But the dolphins were his job—his mission. He was the head and founder of the whole organization. He couldn't quit his reason for being. He just had to wait it out was all. Wait for life after Chelsea. See what that held.

Walt pinched the space between his eyes. He leaned over, gave Chelsea a kiss. A slime of Vaseline—he hated the stuff—smeared against his lips but he lingered an extra moment, then wiped the back of his hand across his mouth and turned to leave.

When he pulled the curtain aside, Chelsea's sister Bea was standing there. Her face, with its sad echo of Chelsea's, startled him every time.

"Murderer," she said, by way of greeting. "Come to finish the job yourself?"

"Fuck off." Walt wiped his nose. Vaseline smeared across his cheek.

"I want you to know, I've filed a motion to stop you from killing her."

The words took a moment to sink in. "You what?"

"Tomorrow, expect a court order to replace the feeding tube. I won't let you do this. You don't own her."

Walt wished for a moment that he *were* a murderer. Bea would be his first victim. His fingertips twitched with the terrible urge to encircle her throat and squeeze. "Chelsea never wanted this. It isn't natural."

"Don't you tell me what's natural—you want to starve an innocent woman to death. Your *wife*. That's natural?"

Bea's voice was shrill. Walt wondered if he could have her physically removed from the hospital. Would security do that for him? Would they be on his side? Would he be the ultimate bastard if he did that? Did it even matter anymore? His ties with Chelsea's family had long since been broken. "How 'bout we don't do this in front of Chels," he said, trying like hell to take the high road.

"Wouldn't you like that? Don't think she doesn't know you're trying to kill her. She does. I've told her and she knows. Just look at her face." Bea swung her arm in an arc that ended at Chelsea's bedside. "Look."

Walt looked, and what he saw was the same thing he'd seen the first time he visited her, and the same thing he'd seen every day since: a shell. Not a spark of his wife. Nothing.

~ ~ ~

"Who was that woman?" Andrea asked when they were back in the truck.

"Sister-in-law."

"She didn't look very happy."

Walt pulled the truck up close to the warehouse and cut the motor. The air in the cab began to get hot immediately. He turned to Andrea. "She's got a court order to replace the feeding tube that the hospital finally removed." He ran a rough hand down his face. "She wanted to die peacefully. My wife, I mean."

Andrea turned her hands over in her lap and pressed them between her knees. "There's no hope?"

"None. Unless you ask her sister's freako-religious cult of a church. They do chanting and laying-on-of-hands in the hospital and expect a miracle any day. It would have driven Chelsea mad. She'd kick 'em out before they even got their Bibles open. Instead she just lies there while they pray and sprinkle holy water on her. It's all for themselves. A fat lot of good it does her. She can't even tell them to fuck off."

Walt opened the truck door and stepped out. Andrea didn't move.

"You don't believe in God?"

He sighed. "Not Bea's God." He drummed his fingers on the top of the truck then leaned back in. "You coming?"

"Should we be getting back?"

"Key to the van's in the warehouse. I've got in-water volunteers for the next three hours. The only thing left is to cart the carcass to the lab; I'll wait on daylight for that."

Inside, Walt flipped the light switch; the bulbs hummed then flickered to life. Andrea blinked in the sudden brightness. He moved deeper into the warehouse, guiding her by the elbow. She reached across and placed her hand over his; her fingers were cool.

Damn Bea for getting the lawyers involved. Walt didn't have the money to fight her in court and, frankly, the possibility that he would have to do such a thing in order to let Chelsea die a natural death hadn't even occurred to him. What was worse, he sure as hell didn't have the money to pay for another year of hospital care at three-hundred-plus dollars a day. Which begged an even bigger question: How the hell had *life* come down to *money*?

"You okay?" Andrea leaned forward to look into his eyes.

"Fine," he said, though his throat felt like it was locked in a vise.

"No you aren't." Her eyes were big and blue and they welled up with the tears that he should have been shedding. "It's okay," she said.

"You're the one who's crying. I should be telling you it's okay."

She sniffed and worked up a smile.

He reached out and took her hand. "Look, I didn't mean—"

At the touch of Walt's hand, she crumpled. Her shoulders dropped forward and shrugged with sudden sobs. "It's just—" she choked on the words and swallowed hard. "It's just, I can't picture—I mean if it were me—even though—and Quinn—I just. I'm sorry." She wiped furiously at her eyes. "God, I'm so stupid."

"It's all right," said Walt, stepping forward, secure again in what was required of him. He knew this one, at least: the woman cries and the man holds her. He could do this much.

She moved gratefully into the embrace. "I'm sorry," she mumbled, scrubbing her face into his shoulder. "You don't need this." He felt the wetness seeping through his T-shirt.

"Shh." He cupped her more tightly. He hadn't held a crying woman since Chelsea and it felt good suddenly, to be on the other side—moving from the *comforted* to the *comforter*. It felt right. He put his palm against the back of her head and brought her in close. Her hair felt thin and soft beneath his fingers.

She leaned back. When she opened her eyes, he saw that they were red-rimmed and puffy. Streaks of color spread down her cheeks. Ragged breaths made her chest rise and fall unevenly. She smiled but her eyes kept searching his with the look of a cornered animal.

Some desperateness in her face, some rawness of emotion washing over her, just inches from his own face, broke through Walt's calm and he leaned forward to give her a kiss, just a light press of comfort. But when their lips touched she grabbed his head and pulled forward greedily, opening his mouth with her own parted lips. He felt the blood pounding in his temples.

With a handful of hair in his fist he moved her head toward his, mashing their mouths together. Their teeth scraped awkwardly. It was more a move of unbridled energy than passion but she moaned and pressed into him, pushing him against a row of high drawers. The knobs dug into his back. She tore at his clothing with a grunt of frustration.

Despite his discomfort, he felt himself growing hard. It felt good—in the way of a cold beer on a hot day—a liquid filling-up. He slid a hand beneath her bikini top.

He didn't want this woman, he hadn't lusted after her, but at the same time he did want her. He craved the wild, bucking nature of her, the roller coaster, the crazy abandon, the release. It was like a drug surging through his veins, this insane, angry desire.

Andrea mumbled into his open mouth. Her breath was hot; she tasted of peaches.

"Mm?" He didn't really care what she said. Didn't care what might be spoken. What could she say at this point but yes? There was no going back.

She pulled away, gasping. She took a deep breath and he watched her face soften.

"I saw you with her," she said. "I looked in while you were there." Her eyes were heavy-lidded, her cheeks flushed. "It was amazing. So beautiful. So—"

She took another deep breath and brought her mouth back passionately to Walt's but he kept still. For the briefest moment it was a parody—the ready female pressing herself against the male, the male standing like a stone, refusing her.

"You can come up," Andrea repeated, not opening the van door. "I would let you stay the night. You know that. Yes?"

He reached across in front of her and pulled the handle. The door swung open with a creak.

"Yes," he said. "Enjoy your cruise."

When the hotel door closed on her retreating back, it was fully dark; a halo of night insects banged their heads against an outdoor globe. He pulled away from the parking lot and returned to the stranded dolphins. His job. He knew he shouldn't have been gone so long, but Nick, his main volunteer, was a smart kid, trustworthy.

Traffic on Route 1 was minimal; Walt made a U-turn and parked on the side of the roadway. Nick met him halfway to the beach.

"Mimi and Ralph are gone."

"What?" Walt shook his head. "Dead?" The two older dolphins—a mated pair, he suspected—had been gaining strength over the course of the day. How had they deteriorated so quickly?

"No." Nick laughed. "I mean gone. They swam off."

"Off?" Dolphins rarely left a sick or stranded pod member. They usually stayed to the bitter end, even becoming casualties themselves. "They just left?"

"Well, yeah. Amber and Stacy were in the water and the dolphins started making noises and then they just squirmed out of their hands. They eased off like they'd planned it, then surfaced farther out. They're getting around okay, too."

"Good. One for the record books. How about Lulu?" Lulu was the youngest and sickest of the dolphins; she had suffered a case of severe sunburn prior to being covered by Walt and his volunteers. Most likely the sunburn—a deadly condition for dolphins—had further weakened her.

"Lulu's not doing so hot. She's breathing, but it's slowed way down. She's pretty unresponsive."

"Damn. All right. Thanks, Nick." Walt clapped the younger man on the shoulder. "You look beat, man. Go home—all of you. I got it from here. You guys get some shut-eye. I might need you tomorrow."

"Who'll take Lulu's watch?"

"I'll stay with her."

"All night?"

"Yeah, I got it."

"And that one?" Nick angled his head toward the carcass on the sand.

"We'll have enough volunteers in the morning. I can deliver it anytime after first light." Walt returned to the van, donned his wetsuit and booties, then trudged through the waist-high water.

"I've got it from here," he said, placing his palms under the dolphin and nodding to Amber.

"Thanks." She dropped her shoulders and rolled her head. "I'm stiff. And cold."

"Get some rest," said Walt.

"You don't need me?"

"Nope. Come back at first light. I can use you then."

"Can we finish the interview tomorrow?"

For a moment Walt was confused. Had that really only been today? "Sure, sure," he said. "We'll finish, no problem."

Amber waded to shore. With a protective hand at the small of her back, Nick guided her up the beach. They walked to the road together. *Good*, thought Walt, she'd found a far better receptacle for her considerable affections.

After Nick's beat-up Volkswagen roared to life and moved off down the road, Walt was alone with the ocean. Exactly where he liked to be. Soft waves pulled at his legs then moved on, small ribbons of phosphorescence sliding onto the sand. If there were sounds other than the water lapping against Walt and Lulu, of water rolling over itself to shore, he couldn't hear them. Being alone in the ocean felt like moving back through time to meet the origins of life. Walt could be a one-celled phytoplankton, or a floating jelly, or an intertidal fish using its fins like feet for the first time.

And Walt was with Lulu. He could feel the faint pulse of her heart against his palm. Her blowhole opened and closed laboriously in intervals that were much too long. Each exhalation was a blast of moist air; he could feel the effort as her lungs pushed old air out and pulled new in. The dolphin was giving up. The accrued weight of her body had increased, like a baby slipping into sleep, its mass heavier for the slackness. His shoulders already tingled from the strain.

Was she suffering?

He had no doubt that animals suffered, that wasn't the question. No. He wondered if Lulu was suffering, here and now.

Only one side of a dolphin's brain sleeps at a time—one side rests, the other side keeps watch, stays alert. So was there a portion of the brain devoted specifically to suffering? Could the suffering section sleep all the time? Was there a neurological setting for near-death that allowed a body to feel no pain?

If Chelsea's brain had worked independently, functioning side-by-side with itself, would she, after the stroke, still have had one good side left? Would she even now have a waking side for Walt?

He had held a dying dolphin in his arms before. He knew the signs. What to do about the dying was the question he faced. What to do? Did he owe Lulu some sort of *death duty* as a compassionate fellow creature? If so, what was it? Stay with her and keep her company as she died? Pet her? Talk to her? Offer solace? Was he obligated to try, stubbornly, to keep her alive, despite her obvious instinctual attempts to die? Or was the better course to leave the dolphin completely alone, and let Nature take its course in a way that Walt—outsider—could never comprehend?

In the end, he talked to the dolphin. He stroked the smooth area under Lulu's pectoral fins, beneath which her fragile heart stammered on.

"You're a pretty girl, aren't you?" he murmured. "I bet you love to swim and catch fish and play with your family. You're a smart girl, too. Yes, Lulu's a smart girl. A smart girl and a pretty girl." He pulled one hand away, keeping her blowhole above the waterline by a light touch on her underbelly.

"But I think it's time. And I should let you go, shouldn't I, Lulu?" He pulled his remaining hand away slowly. "Hmm? Do you want me to?" The water slid up the gray sides of her flanks and edged toward the blowhole. "Do you, Lulu?" Walt put his head close to hers and whispered, "Yes?"

¡Vieques!

It was May of 2000. And we were beautiful.

We were fierce.

We were Boudreaux and Rothschild, Miller and Stackowski, O'Toole and Greene. We were Dani, Alyx, Rickie, Carlita, Jaz, Sam. We were butch. We were femme. We were *bois*. We were a tribe. *Una familia*. We pitched our tents between a bombing range and an ammunitions dump. We slept on sand still hot from the sun. We fueled our righteous indignation with campfire speeches and furtive tangles in the dunes. Our voices ached to be heard. *We are here! We are queer!*

In clumsy high school Spanish we planned to rescue *la isla nena* one sign at a time: Vieques Libre! Bomba no mas! Latin@s Para Paz!

They told us where we could not go.

They told us who we were supposed to be.

We did not listen.

We were solid and ready. Our ankles were strong. We were floating seaweed, pale as a neap-tide moon. We were blue-blooded crabs, armored in the shape of luck. We were double rainbows. We were thirsty. We tied our salty dreads. Our scalps burned in the blazing sun.

We had fathers. We wanted fathers. We wanted to *be* fathers. We hated our fathers for cheating on our mothers. We had alcoholic fathers who stayed and Navy fathers who left and crazy fathers who had no choice and congressional fathers who made the laws. Our fathers did not speak to us anymore. We had never heard our father's voice.

We named our patch of sand: Camp Peace and Justice.

We sent out scouts for fresh water and meaty *pastellios* and waited for word from our adversaries, Los Norte Americanos and their local thugs the *Grupo de Choque* who carried jointed truncheons and smoke bombs and righteous indignation that matched our own. They held their positions. And *dios mio*, did that one *wave?*

We were sure-boned and steady-kneed. We tested our mettle. Our flesh shimmered in the heat, jostling between linked elbows.

We were strong; we were invincible.

We did not ask. We did not tell.

But the *Grupo de Choque* pushed back, pressing their guns into our breasts, the only yielding part of us. They called us *monstruosidad, hermafrodita, fenómeno*. We were marooned. We were Ginger. We were Marianne.

"*Santa Librada*," a mustachioed thug whispered and his comrades underarmed their rifles to free a hand for the sign of the cross, protecting their immortal souls from the long-crucified saint standing before them wearing both beard and breasts.

When I turned seventeen, I told my mother I was born to love women. She cried. She yelled. She took me to a psychiatrist. An old man with a scaly forehead and strings of food in his teeth. Very helpful, that. He told me, categorically, that I had mother issues.

My reply: *Tell me something I don't know.*

An Oedipus Complex, according to Dr. Brill, caused me to fixate on my mother. And *my fixation*, I said—of course—had nothing to do with the mornings she drove me to school and leaned over the center console while I unwound the curlers from her hair and lacquered them in place with a can of hairspray she kept in the glove compartment. It had nothing to do with the two jobs she worked, or our Sunday dinners, a shared can of SPAM glazed with grape jelly and baked by me, ready when she came home from cleaning the church. It had nothing to do with me left home alone at the age of twelve while she went to bars and picked up men, nor the loud sex they had in our small apartment with the bedroom door wide open. It had nothing to do with the fact that my mother, on hot nights, wore only her slip, her body outlined beneath the satin in all the right ways.

No, it was the unsuccessful resolution of my Oedipus Complex, the shrink was certain. All good students of Freud knew that such a complex led to homosexuality and—in the case of girls—penis envy. Oh, if the old goat only knew. In the years since, I have out-Freuded Freud.

But my mother, Rosarita, Rosie, Mami, god-rest-her-soul, she loved me, even if she was, put kindly, *inconsistent*. At fifteen, I might stagger in, hours after curfew, reeking of alcohol while she feigned sleep on the couch and said nothing. Then the next night she would stand in the doorway, smoking a cigarette, backlit in her nightgown, waiting to ground me for a month for returning three minutes after midnight. She would stay home thirty nights in a row and then go out three times in one week, bringing home a different man each night, shooing them out in the morning in time for early Mass. A mountain of dirty clothes rose in the bathroom until I was forced to dig and find the cleanest of the dirty underwear. Dishes festered in the sink, stacks of cups and plates that filled the house with that peculiar smell—that unwashed odor that is always the same after three days no matter what you've cooked or eaten. Then, without warning, she would blow through the apartment armed with a rag, a bucket of bleach water, and a mop, a Mr. Clean hurricane, descending into a screaming fit if she found so much as a sock on the floor after.

Mami could live with the dirt she made only until she glimpsed her life from the outside in. She couldn't keep up with that woman she longed to be. It was the tragedy of her life, born to Maria Santiago and Bart Stackowski—pious Puerto Rican mother, gruff GI father—and then mysteriously pregnant when she was only seventeen, shipped off to Miami relatives for the birth and follow-up. No good island girl could come back from that shame, not in 1974.

The same year I came into the world, Mami's twin brother shot the final arrow into my grandparents' collective heart. Tio Manny took a girl he barely knew to the Justice of the Peace, bedded her all night then shipped out to do his patriotic duty. When Saigon fell, he returned home to an infant son and a wife he did not recognize or love. By all accounts the feeling was mutual and his wife of eleven months left, leaving little baby Martin to my grandparents to raise while Tio Manny, who had decided he liked the Army life, continued his career around the world. Seven years passed before he came home long enough to file for divorce. Ever an island boy, he met his second wife fourteen years later on an atoll in the Pacific, a woman named Leslie who was already raising two daughters. They married and promptly had a third, the final froth on our already messy family frappe.

In 1998, the Universidad de Puerto Rico accepted me to graduate school and I made the stoplight parrotfish the focus of my research. For the first time in my life, I visited my grandparents in their little cement block home with the statue of the Virgin in their dusty front yard and a painting of her Suffering Son bleeding above the plastic-covered couch. I wore my hair in a crew cut that year. I fit no notion of what they thought a good *nieta* should be, but they were boisterous and affectionate and said their home had been too quiet after eighteen years of raising twins followed by eighteen more of my cousin Martin. Plane fare to Miami was expensive so I joined them for Thanksgivings and passed Puerto Rican holidays at their table. When he could, Tio Manny flew in and surprised us. My mother never came, *la paria* that she was.

Camp Peace and Justice lulled us to sleep at night with the shushing of the waves against the sand and the million *coqui* trilling in the trees. (*Eleutherodactylus coqui*, the Puerto Rican tree frog, songstress of the island.) By the end of the first week, the coqui drove us crazy and we vowed to kill every last one (except Carlita, who loved every animal, even spoke to the feral goats wandering on the other side of the high chain-link fence). We slapped our arms and legs and grumbled out a new name for the place: *Puerto Mosquito*.

At least the vocal *coqui* ate their weight in bugs.

We slept in sight of the Navy's fenced-in burial ground for depleted uranium, the skull-and-cross-boned signs the artwork of our outdoor living space. We slathered DEET on our bodies to keep the pesky bugs at bay. We hoped our children would not be born with two heads.

If we wanted children. *If* we found a way to have them. In my earnest voice, I told Carlita she would make a good mother. She tossed her hair and laughed; her hair, roasted in the tropical sun those many weeks, had turned red-orange like the flowering tree the islanders called *flamboyan*. I told her this. She laughed again. We, her bois, began to call her *Flamboyan*.

Flamboyan: flamboyant, flammable boi. It suited her.

In every group, one person holds the whole together. That person was Carlita, our sexy femme. She made us strong. She made us brave. With a glance over her sunglasses, a furtive smile, a toss of her hair, a touch on the arm, she could make you want to hold her nestled gently in the crook of your arm, drop whispering caresses against her collarbones, then open wide and devour her. When Carlita pressed her body against mine, I felt my shoulders broaden for the embrace. Her sweet smile gave me an ache in my jaw. My hand, rested on her softly curving hip, sharpened my angles, brought every cell in my body to a point.

Jaz and Alyx had spent the fall and winter performing as drag kings. The pay and tips were good. They encouraged me to join the troupe, knowing money was tight and sensing, perhaps, something I had not yet recognized, but truthfully I never longed to don that muscled, tool-belt-wearing cliché of manliness. My persona, had I chosen one, would have been a Cary Grant, a gentlemanly Jimmy Stewart. Me, in coat and tails, offering my arm to an elegant woman with swishing skirts. A handkerchief-in-the-breast-pocket man. But drag was burlesque. It did not appeal to me, not even as an easy income stream.

Here's one reason: Jaz's stage name was Buster Hymen. Alyx called himself Richard Cranium. They decided, in honor of my uncle, that I should be Manny Nuff.

I do my best to avoid spectacle. And what *is* drag if not spectacle? The wild transformation. A few hours of inhabiting a mysterious other. They said they were Doctor Jekylls of gender. I did not ask them if they remembered how that story ended.

And somehow, aside from the spectacle, I knew the drag kings in that troupe did not desire to *become* men. They mocked and imitated them. They were not avoiding mirrors, ashamed to look at their own naked bodies. They did not stare down at their strange, pillowy flesh and think *pervert*.

No, they were proud dykes, disdainful of the base desires of men. To have the strength of a man was good. To want to *be* a man was a betrayal. Alone in bed at night, I rehearsed my confession. In the dream response, my friends stood in a ring, tribunal-style, horrified butches tut-tutting my *Coming-Out 2.0*.

There were no winners in my imaginary arguments.

Meanwhile, they spent their weekends dressed as men. They spent the workweek vilifying them. Never was this seen as ironic. Never like white actors performing in black face.

Nurtured as I was on the logical inconsistencies of my mother, I've grown acutely sensitive to hypocrisy. In the end, my dear friends helped me understand that the lesbian community was simply one more place I did not belong.

A beach is a terrible place for a standoff. Even the ground will not back you up. And yet, how many beaches have been launch pads for invasion? How many a spot that armies storm? In Tio's war, men stormed the mud-clay jungles and waist-high rice paddies. He carried home a toenail fungus that he has nurtured to this day; twenty-five years and Tio's fungus survived Y2K.

Carla—*mi Carlita*—she was the standout on the beach. The *Grupo de Choque* stared at her body, which was—and still is, more than ten years later—magnificent. Taut brown skin, breasts as generous and sweet as coconut jelly, just the right amount of push and give.

The forceful guards that day excited her. The giveaway? A sheen of sweat on her forehead, aggressive curls at her hairline that rose in the breeze, the wide stance of her brown legs, the heave and fall of those glorious breasts. She was waiting for the first Something Big of her life to happen.

Carlita must have been a combative child. In her sleep, she mumbles challenges and threats, confronting the stalkers of her unconscious hours, never backing down. At twenty-two, half 50s pinup beauty, half footloose hellcat (*mi Madonna-Monroe*), she was searching—always searching—for a worthy adversary. And those face-shielded fellows on the beach, those magnificent *compañeros* shimmering in black riot gear, were only too happy to oblige.

On the morning of May 15th the air flashed with heat and tension. The ocean roiled against the beach. Carlita was alone, on still-wet sand at the edge of the water, doing yoga stretches in her bright yellow bikini. The *Grupo de Choque* lifted their binoculars. They moved closer. Between poses, she paused to converse with a feral goat grazing on the other side of the fence. *Buenos días señor cabrón. Do you want to pose with me?*

He was white, a shaggy thing, good-sized, with two thick horns, a billy goat who smelled—even at that distance—sharp, like rusty iron and wet musk. As I watched, he backed up to the fence and unleashed a stream of hot, defiant, billy goat piss. Carlita let out a surprised bark of a laugh and the billy jumped away, pogoing on his front legs, popping up and down, stiff with surprise. Carla made a few hops of her own, in solidarity or imitation. For a moment, they were in perfect synchronization, the randy billy goat and the laughing pinup.

When the goat was ten feet away, his front hooves came down with a metallic *bong!* In that same instant, an explosion cut the air and the goat was gone, parts flying in all directions. Carlita was knocked back from the blast and fell into the sand, her hands covering her face. The goat's head and haunches flew over the fence and landed in the sand between us, hitting with a soft thud. The heavy horns pulled downward so the head of the poor beast stuck solidly into the sand. The chest was a bloody maw of shredded meat and pink hair. My first thought was that the crazy guards had blown up a goat to intimidate us.

Carlita looked at her hands. She screamed when she saw the blood pooling in her palms.

We had camped for weeks before the billy goat exploded and the *compañeros* decided to arrest us and cart us off. What had we done that day? The answer was never clear, but an explosion had happened, a goat was dead, a woman was injured, and the rest of us were guilty of witnessing it all.

We spent two difficult nights in jail, Carlita a bright spot in her yellow bikini all the while. We were harassed, but in very different ways. I still get angry when I think of her treatment, how they "fixed" her split eyebrow with a butterfly clip, how she was denied clothes, how she remained dignified even as the guards took their breaks beyond the bars to better ogle her. She kept her smile and her lovely laugh and she made them look like fools.

These days, Carlita sports a small crescent moon of pale skin that cuts through her left eyebrow. She wears it as a decoration, a badge. A year after the Vieques encampment, she had the head of a billy goat tattooed on her right shoulder. She is an Aries. It works, reminding her of fight and loss.

For me, I will always remember the night before the raid, when we left Camp Peace and Justice and poured out through the gates beneath a full moon. We walked to Bioluminescent Bay and entered the water amid millions of microscopic dinoflagellates whose bodies lit up in response to every swimmer's stroke. The whole bay was alight with shooting-water-stars. We were happy. We were milky-way safe. We were in love.

I took Carlita's hand beneath the water, our joined fingers aglow with life. I was only twenty-five but I knew enough to know that such moments were fleeting. That this was the woman I wanted to spend my fleeting moments loving.

She stretched her arms above her head and leaned back lazily to float, breasts rising above the waterline, face toward the stars. I put my hands beneath her; her weightless body hovered just above my palms. The warmth of her skin traveled through the saltwater and into my forearms, my wrists. "I've got you," I said in a whisper.

She laughed and dragged against the water with her arms, creating a shower of fireless sparks. "*Mi Dani*, my darling, are you sure?"

I repositioned my hands and pulled her gently back onto my arms, an underbody hug. "I've got you," I said again.

She turned her face to mine, one ear dipping below the surface. Her *flamboyan* hair spread across the water catching tiny creatures that sparkled through the length of it. She sighed and I felt her weight drop into my arms as her lungs emptied of air. "I feel so safe," she said, suddenly serious, draping her wrists atop my shoulders.

I looked toward the darkness of her face, searching for her moonlight eyes. "It's real."

She walked her hands along the back of my neck and the touch sent a ripple through my collarbones. I was as alight as all the creatures of the sea. "Oh, *mi amor...*" She paused while her hands found each other and her delicate fingers slid together. "...a false sense of security?" She smiled a melancholy smile. "That is the only kind there is."

TREASURES FEW
HAVE EVER SEEN

WHAT THEY CALL ME: One-armed Jack.

NUMBER OF ARMS I HAVE: Two. One that's 100%. One that's about 75.

WHAT THE OTHERS THINK HAPPENED: The Battle of Phnom Penh.

WHAT REALLY HAPPENED: Hurricane Edna, a helicopter, and a rogue aquarium.

WHERE I LIVE: In a tent. Without a rain fly when the weather's good. A solid fix on the sky helps me breathe. In bad weather, with no stars, I sleep restless.

WHERE MY TENT LIVES: The Florida Everglades. Hot as the bars of hell, and humid, too. Buggy. But it sure beats a highway underpass.

WHO ELSE LIVES HERE: Shorty and Train. Goodlow and Maurice. And Ripton, too. Shorty comes up to my shoulder. His face is pink and round with a beard that grows in stubbly clumps. He's a pervert with an ankle monitor and can't live within a thousand feet of a school or a bus stop or anywhere else kids gather. Train's a vet, same war as me. He's the skinny one. Says he hasn't touched a razor in ten years. And not a comb, neither, from the look of him. He's hiding out from his old lady, an angry Seminole who tried to kill him with a pair of hedge clippers. There's a long scar above his temple on the left side. *His* left. Goodlow and Maurice set up camp before I got here. Goodlow might be a last name. He's got a vigilante face and is twenty years older than Maurice, easy. Maurice's skin is darker than the rest of ours, and not just from the sun. His elevator don't go all the way to the penthouse. The lights are on, but nobody's shopping. They could be father and son bank robbers. Or Boy Toy and Sugar Daddy. I don't know their stories or what brought them here. Goodlow likes it that way and so do I.

WHO RIPTON IS: My dog. Some fool dumped him in the everglades and he found his way to me. He's a chow. And yeah, before you ask, it's hell for him, the heat. I saw off hunks of fur with the bowie knife I keep sharp. That helps, even if he looks like a sled dog that got pulled through a tractor combine. After a haircut, he's cooler. He spends less time showing me his black-spotted tongue.

WHAT WE ATE LAST NIGHT: Grilled alligator. Goodlow has a gas grill. A regular set up. He lets any one of us use it if we ask first. The tail meat was greasy and gamey but there was a lot. Train ate a piece then rubbed his beard and said how lately he'd been thinking of becoming a vegetarian. I laughed loud and Ripton's hackles rose up. He barked at the edge of the dark until Goodlow yelled *shut the hell up.*

WHO I USED TO WORK FOR: Arthur Finder.

WHAT HIS NAME IS: Ironic.

WHAT WE LOOKED FOR: Sunken treasure. Spanish Galleons. I joined Art's search crew late in 1990 and we combed the east coast of Florida for six long years. We fed on excitement, shook off the dead ends, started calling ourselves *The Finders.* Hell of a way to live. I slept on-deck-only, even in the rain. People called us crazy.

WHAT WE FOUND AT FIRST: Mostly junk, crazy stuff. Pulleys, grommets, shoe buckles. Bits and pieces of life. A gold tooth, once.

THE ONLY THING I EVER KEPT: An old pocket watch, engraved in Spanish. Crusted up and dead. Took me years of fiddling, gentle sanding, soaking, and oiling to get it ticking again.

WHAT WE FOUND TWO YEARS AFTER ART'S SON GOT KILLED LOOKING: The mother lode. An acre of gold bars we pulled out like a baker pulling loaves from the oven. Each loaf forty pounds. There were giant crosses we called *skull crushers* after Art held one overhead and said it was like the cross in that movie where a priest's skull gets smashed by a demon he's casting out. We pulled up fat rubies with barnacles on them and heavy chain necklaces slimed with seaweed and still-rough emeralds as big as a fist. There were golden goblets, too, just like *Indiana Jones* would find. And Spanish doubloons. Thousands of doubloons. Doubloons by the bushel-full.

WHO WAS HAPPY FOR US: The newspapers. The television. Our families. Our friends. Everyone.

WHO THOUGHT THE TREASURE BELONGED TO THEM: Art and The Finders. The State of Florida. Dade County. The Maritime Museum. The IRS. Spain.

WHO CAME OUT OF THE WOODWORK: An ex-girlfriend who wanted help making rent—just the one month, she promised. My former boss, Margie, who said I should sponsor a new exhibit at the aquarium. A neighbor whose cat needed belly surgery or he'd die. A war buddy without a dime to his name. A whole bunch of friends I didn't remember, who said I still owed them for this or that. My brother, Down-on-his-luck-Doug desperately in need of dentures. Lucy in the Sky with Diamonds. Maryjane. The Tax Man.

WHO OF THOSE I TURNED AWAY: The Tax Man.

WHAT I KEEP UNDER MY SLEEPING BAG NOW: A forty-five.

NUMBER OF DOUBLOONS I HAVE LEFT: Zero.

WHAT RIPTON NEEDS FROM ME: Occasional food. A daily pat on the head. A place to sleep. Water to drink. Barbering.

WHO CAME INTO THE SWAMP: A man I'd never seen before. He'd been trying to find me, he said. How did you, I asked. Mister Finder told me, he said. Ripton growled.

WHAT I THOUGHT HE WANTED: Money. There's nothing left, I told him. Why you think I'm living in a tent?

WHAT HE SAID: I think you knew my twin sister.

WHERE HIS TWIN SISTER IS: Six feet under.

WHO HE TOLD WHERE HE WAS GOING: Nobody. So I could kill you, I said, smiling, and nobody would know. He pointed to the guys, said, they would know. He ate a piece of alligator jerky, holding it delicate like, two-fingered. He said alligator meat was stringy and he hadn't known. He wiped the greasy fingers on his socks.

WHAT THE MAN CALLED HIS SISTER: Rosie.

WHAT I WONDERED: If one twin dies, is the surviving twin only half alive?

WHY HE CAME: To tell me I fathered Rosie's baby who is all grown up.

WHERE IT HAPPENED: At a debutante cotillion.

WHAT I REMEMBER: Being a replacement escort, filling in for my brother after he got chicken pox. We wore almost the same size.

WHAT I LEARNED ABOUT TUXEDOS: Baby blue is not my color.

HOW OLD I WAS: Eighteen.

HOW OLD SHE WAS: ...Seventeen?

WHAT ELSE I REMEMBER: A puffy dress that sighed like a pile of snow. Long white gloves. A glittery bracelet overtop the glove. Slow music. A clumsy waltz we giggled through. Stolen kisses behind the building. Pushing my hands through the layers of her snowdrift dress. Her eagerness. *That.*

WHERE I WENT AFTER: Basic Training.

WHAT I SOLD AFTER THE DOUBLOONS RAN OUT: My house.

WHAT I'M WAITING FOR: The court to rule in our favor.

WHAT THE SHUSHING TENT WHISPERS IN THE DARK: Finders keepers, losers weepers. Be patient. Be payyy…shunt.

WHAT I HEAR THE MAN SAY WHEN I ASK THE CHILD'S NAME: Danny.

HOW IT'S SPELLED WHEN HE WRITES IT OUT: Dani.

WHAT I THINK: That's a damn fool way to spell Danny. And then, *wacky Puerto Ricans.* And finally, *but what can you do?*

WHAT I THINK NEXT: If he'd had a father figure, he'd spell his name Danny.

WHAT I THINK AFTER THAT: I have had a son for twenty-eight years and no one told me. When I was held as a POW, I was a father. When I came home and the hippies jeered, I was a father. When the sound of a helicopter took me down and wrecked my arm, I was a father. When I told all those women that I never wanted to have a family, I was a father.

WHAT MY BUDDY TRAIN SAYS: The math don't lie.

WHAT ROSIE NEVER ASKED: If I wanted to be a father.

WHAT I HAVE FOR BREAKFAST THE DAY AFTER THE MAN LEAVES: A can of Budweiser and a cigarette. I chase that down with some leftover jerky, a can of Budweiser, and a cigarette. I read a little Vonnegut in my tent. So it goes.

WHAT I DECIDE: I want to make it right. My father was an asshole. I swore I would never bring a kid into the world only to neglect it, taunt it, and call it pussy. Note to self: promise your son you will never call him pussy.

WHAT I FORGOT TO ASK: Am I a grandfather?

WHAT I EAT FOR LUNCH: Maurice pulls out a giant bag of hot dogs. No one knows where he got them. We pay him a dollar and he gives us four hot dogs each. I make him cook mine extra. I give Ripton one. He gulps it down whole, like a seagull.

WHAT I DO WHILE I CHEW: Make plans to visit Danny. Think about what I want to tell him. Offer to take him fishing. I picture just how it will be, the look on his face. I make a lot of plans.

CHRISTMAS IN PHUKET

L eslie sits cross-legged on a rickety wooden dock at daybreak, snorkel and mask on her lap, waiting for her research team to arrive. After navigating the morning market—crowded with vendor carts and rainbow pyramids of hairy eggplant, dragon-striped melon, bok choy, and papaya—and passing through its humid, curry-scented haze, she's hungry. Oh, to have another shot at yesterday's Christmas dinner: spicy Thai noodles with shrimp and red chilies. The usual gauzy shroud of international travel had mucked up her senses so that she hadn't appreciated the meal at the time, but now her jet-lagged stomach reminds her that it's dinnertime in Norfolk, Virginia. And it's Christmas there, still.

She leans against a piling and lets the early morning sun burn its rays through her closed eyelids. It wasn't easy leaving her family over the holidays, three kids and a husband panicked and angry at the thought of being the only adult in charge, but her shot at tenure depends on this trip. The good-old-boy ceiling at Old Dominion University and a dearth of scientific publications had put her job on the chopping block yet again. She had little choice in the matter if she wanted to keep bringing home a paycheck. And as the primary wage earner now that Manny had retired from the Army, she couldn't afford not to.

Today is sure to be exhausting—jet lag and the newly erupting symptoms of what her doctor has called *early peri-menopause* are no help— but a prompt start will put them ahead of the throngs of holidaying tourists, at least. And morning, with its yellow sunlight slanting into the ocean at a wistful angle, has always been her favorite time to slip beneath the waves.

The pier shakes as her research assistants arrive loaded with gear and plop it down beside her. Two ODU faculty follow: an oceanography professor named Don Killington, a heavy smoker with a rheumy cough and a basketball paunch who finds a way to horn-in on her research trip every year; and Killington's illicit lover, Benita Gonzalez, graying and tanned, spry and small, an expert on sponges.

"Morning all." Leslie stands as a hollow chugging sound signals the approach of their new research boatman. Everything in Thailand could be had—for a price. When asked his name, the boatman proudly offered a string of vowel-rich syllables then pointed to his chest and said, *Sam*.

Sam's dive platform is a recycled cooler lid connected to the boat by a section of nylon fishing net on each side. It has a hand-lettered plywood sign that reads, "Easy door to Thailand under world." He professes to know the reef *like his own feet* and promises he will take them to the very spot where the ODU team has been taking measurements for years.

Brendan, the taller of her two assistants, will join her. He's blond and wiry, with a build like Leslie's ex-husband Gus. Handsome, for a kid, he fights as a featherweight in the competitive ring at ODU. Brendan attends on a boxing scholarship and is careful not to damage his bite or deviate his septum. "You good to go?" he asks.

He's referring, of course, to the fact that she spent half the night dancing—it was Christmas after all—with a bar full of giddy, happily tipsy revelers. She'd even broken one of her cardinal rules and slow danced with Brendan, reveling in the sweat and tang of a young male body in a way that she hadn't for ages. It was innocent, just an earnest student indulging his middle-aged professor—she would never cross that line, would never be *that* professor; she'd suffered enough from her own father's indiscretions to know she would never—but the dancing was heady nonetheless.

Brendan catches the bowline as Sam cuts the motor and ties off the stern. Each armload of gear he receives with a, "yes, yes" or a "no problem" until the boat is loaded.

Leslie gives the shore a final look as they pull away. Lush vegetation springs up in a line at the end of the beach. In the expanse of white sand that precedes the rising hillside, a lone palm tree leans toward the sea. "Ready?" she asks the group.

"Born ready," says Jake, her other assistant. He's buff and talks big, but is also the one most likely to have trouble in the water. He'll have difficulty clearing, or a fin strap will break, or his regulator will free flow. Jake reminds Leslie of her daughter Melody when she was three years old and nothing was ever quite right. Her sock was always "funny" or her shoe was "too tight," or her pillowcase too scratchy, or the tags in her shirts felt like bugs crawling up the back of her neck. Leslie calls her Pea, for "The Princess and the Pea," since she can feel the tiniest grain of sand in the toe of her shoe.

"Got everything?" Killington asks.

"We'd better," she says. "*Four weeks* I've been labeling, bubble-wrapping, and shipping supplies, arranging carpools for the kids, cooking and freezing pre-portioned dinners for my father-in-law, lining up caregivers my mother will recognize through her budding Alzheimer's, lecturing my teens on what *not* to do while I'm away, and re-explaining to Manny that this is not a pleasure cruise."

Killington's eyes cloud, he takes a step back. "Right. Glad it's under control, then."

And still they end up trolling back and forth while Leslie searches the bottom, the boat's platform creaking with each swell. There are GPS coordinates, but a transect has to be in exactly the same location to be accurate. Somewhere a pair of ten-penny nails has been driven into the coral and she can't find them.

They're here to study the effect of rising temperatures in the Andaman Sea on once-thriving coral colonies. Massive beds have bleached out, the symbiotic algae abandoning the host, leaving behind a forest of brittle, colorless skeletons. Increases of only one degree Celsius can cause massive die-offs and the local colony of staghorn coral—a staple of Thailand's once-virgin reefs—has been hard hit. The lush reefs are what first drew her team to Phuket, a place that's as colorful above the waterline as below, unlike the North African desert, sere and empty, its rich extravagance all lavished on a ballroom at the bottom of the sea.

Desert dryness. It's something she understands all too intimately these days. She can't even remember the last time she and Manny had sex. Their anniversary? August? Could it have been *five months?* God, there were no simple parts to her life anymore. Certainly not her trio of daughters: Tabitha and Reese, two teenage drama queens from her first marriage, and eight-year-old Pea, product of her and Manny's union. Nor Martin, her now almost thirty-year-old stepson who had made her a step-*grandmother* two months after she married his father. Not her helpless, widowed, half-blind father-in-law Bart whom fortune had dropped into the small apartment attached to their house (the one they *used* to rent out for additional income). Not her mother, with her aging, Swiss-cheese mind that could still remember the names and symptoms of her various ailments, outlining them in great detail during her daily phone calls. Not the pull of an irate ex-husband full of demands that she parent the girls *his* way while remaining elusively *in absentia* himself, calling by cell phone from remote locations (Beirut, Greenland, Afghanistan) always with the buzz of foreign voices and loud machinery in the background. And least of all not that damnably strange thing that the gynecologist had found inside her body, the thing growing right there in her uterus, exaggerating the already annoying symptoms of peri-menopause, that thing the doctor called a *polyp*—as if Leslie were turning into a coral herself—and insisted she schedule an appointment mid-January to remove.

The *sandwich generation* is what popular culture calls this stage of her life. *The Shit Sandwich* is how she thinks of it. Leslie, a woman who loves nothing more than solitude and time to think, has somehow managed to accumulate this chaotic, embroiled life.

The week before she left Norfolk, her father-in-law celebrated his eighty-third birthday, still in mercifully good health, except for the macular degeneration that for three years has been overtaking his vision like a creeping fungus. Evenings with Bart passed in an exciting succession of spilled, broken, and dropped things, followed by hasty but breezily casual clean-ups intended to keep him from feeling bad about his limitations. At least he can't see when she rolls her eyes.

On outings with Bart, it's as if she has a toddler again, shooting for that ideal mix of independence and assistance, focusing her gaze two steps ahead, hyper vigilant, prepared to intervene if the curb drops off too steeply or the table corner extends too far.

The one thing no one ever warned her about? Toenails. She has to cut Bart's toenails. He can't see to do it himself and he doesn't have the hand strength, anyway. If someone doesn't cut them for him, he slices up his shins at night and bloodies the sheets. The nails grow so thick and tough and yellow that she has to have him soak his feet in a pan of hot water first. Sometimes, when she stands in front of a lecture hall full of students, she looks out over their young heads and thinks, *I cut an old man's toenails last night.*

It's a form of penance. She knows this. Penance for being out of the country eight years before when her own father died. She was newly separated from Gus then—divorce pending—and working in the Marshall Islands on an environmental assessment for a replacement pier on Ebai Island. A recent typhoon had taken out the whole port and the island had no resources of its own. Everything had to be brought in by boat, so, as they told her, they needed the pier built *yesterday.*

Intermittent military flights were the only ones that came to Kwajalein, and so she couldn't get back to the States in time for the funeral. The girls, whom she'd brought with her, were too little for such a sad whirlwind trip, anyway, but he was her father, her one true advocate and the only parent who'd ever made her feel loved. She was dating Manny by then, and sometimes the guilt would swamp her, as if she'd made a deliberate choice—to trade a father for a lover. *Could she have made it if she'd tried?* Eight years and she still felt the shame of her empty spot in the pew as acutely as if she'd been there and witnessed her own failure to appear.

However, none of that changes the fact that she would happily trade in an aging relative or two these days. If only. She's picked up additional dependents at an alarming rate in the past ten years and now that blasted sandwich—that stupid, stupid sandwich—has morphed into a towering Dagwood monstrosity with her as the soggy, wilting lettuce squashed at the very bottom. Just thinking about it brings on a hot flash. She leans over the side of the boat and scoops up water to splash her neck.

When she first started having symptoms six months ago, she couldn't figure out why she was suddenly angry *all the time.* She could feel a rage storm coming, sense it way off in the distance, barreling across the landscape of her psyche. She had plenty of warning as it approached, and still she couldn't stop it. When her doctor asked her to name her most distressing symptoms, she said, "Everyone's stupid."

"Yep," said the doctor, "that's menopause." He scribbled in her file and she wanted to punch him.

"What's a hot flash *feel* like?" her ever-clinical Tabitha asked when Leslie passed along the diagnosis.

"Power surge," corrected Leslie. "I've decided to call them power surges. And it feels like…like you've suddenly been transported to a dense swamp…and taken with malaria." She elected not to mention the bursts of sadness, the feeling that all her life had been a waste of time and now here she was, after years of raising children, of pursuing a career, of *having it all,* and she had nothing to show for it, nothing to live for. Some days, especially around four in the afternoon, the black void positively beckoned, promising elusive quiet, a sort of surrendering relief. She'd stood on the curb one especially bad afternoon and actually considered which truck she would step in front of—she calculated fenders and grills for a good ten minutes trying to decide which would put her into a nice restful coma. She didn't want to *die*, not so long as her children still needed her, but she figured six or eight weeks of unconsciousness would do the trick.

They've circled the same buoy four times. She's so hot she feels nauseous. "This is fine, Sam. Just hook us up there." She points to the bright orange float.

"*Mai pen rai*," he offers, the Thai version of *no worries, mate.* Once the boat is tethered, Leslie and Brendan suit up and drop over the side. The water is warm for late December and the current strong—a receding tide—with enough turbulence to hamper visibility. As they descend, a blue-spotted stingray shakes off his grainy mantle and swims away in a trail of cascading sand. A stray plastic bag floats past; Leslie plucks it up and shoves it beneath her weight belt to keep a turtle from mistaking it for a jellyfish and dying of a clogged intestine.

To her left, a colony of soft corals waves its fuzzy, frondlike polyps in the current. A week after returning from this trip, the gynecologist will fill Leslie's uterus with saltwater, suspending her own feathery polyp, and then carefully clip its tiny anchoring stalk. The old method had been a dilation and curettage, or a D&C as the pressed-for-time doctors euphemistically referred to it. She prefers this newer method—flood the area, target the problem, and snip it away—rather than having the whole area brutally swept clean.

Brendan locates the first nail and raps on his tank to alert Leslie. She ties off the transect line and swims to the second nail, ten meters away, securing it in the strengthening current. Brendan holds the T-bar over the line while she records the incidence of disease on her dive slate.

They're halfway through the transect when a sudden surge of water moves them sideways. Currents often change in unpredictable ways, but this one pulls and keeps on pulling. It rips the dive slate from Leslie's hand. It drags her sideways across the substrate. A staghorn coral snaps under her elbow and a thin stream of blood floats away from her arm. *Damn.*

The water pressure builds, pressing at her temples. Brendan stares, wide-eyed beneath his mask. He clutches a brain coral, digging his fingertips into the grooves, trying to hold his position on the reef. A residue of fine white grains rises up from his scrabbling fingers.

Then suddenly the current comes at them from all directions. Leslie reaches toward Brendan as she's spun and sloshed around, but he's too far away. The sea churns like a giant washing machine and she sees his bright yellow fins crash into a giant barrel sponge, just before a cloud of black water envelops them. She bumps along the reef, backward and forward, elbows and knees slamming into rocks, corals snapping beneath her as she's tossed and turned helplessly. The underwater sounds are a strange mixture of gurgling and roaring that is as disorienting as the crazy dark water.

She grabs the buckle at her waist and drops her weight belt. Just as she thinks to hold onto her regulator, its tubing snags and the whole thing is ripped from her mouth. She sweeps back to retrieve it, but there's only a severed black line, air pouring out. She pinches it shut and holds her breath, feeling around for her auxiliary regulator. *Thank God.* She pops that into her mouth and takes a deep breath, hoping to calm her racing heart. The torn end of tubing she clumsily ties into a knot while she tumbles along the reef.

In the churning black water, she has no clear sense of which way the surface lies. Panic swirls inside her chest, pulses against her ribcage. Past the panic, her limbs move slowly; they take on weight as if absorbing the heavy darkness. Time slows. She feels a flash of solidarity with her father-in-law; she has slipped into his foggy, clumsy world, darkness creeping inexorably in from its edges. Unidentifiable objects bump against her and scrape past in the crazy current. Soft things, sharp things, moving things, things that wrap around her feet and neck. She shakes her wrist free of a ribbon-like substance and reaches out. Brendan? Her chest tightens. Is he here? Is this what it feels like to die?

Keep breathing, Baxter. Whatever you do, do not stop breathing. You can't go out like this.

An image of home flashes into her mind. Her daughters. Two of them almost women now, but weren't they just babies nursing at her breast? And who will fix Pea's socks? Braid Tabitha's hair before soccer practice? Talk boy-crazy Reese down from the ledge? Oh, and Manny! Her Manolo *muy guapo*. They hadn't been married long enough to lose each other. She can't be a casualty here, not like this. She cannot.

The sloshing slows, finally, and she stares hard into the dark water. A gentle rocking sways her body back and forth as strange swirls of muck move all around. The weightless black-water churning has left her disoriented. *Which way to the surface?* She forces herself to breathe slowly, deliberately, then presses the button to inflate her vest and lets its buoyancy carry her upward. She surfaces and scans the ocean, paddling in a circle. Where is Sam's boat? The buoy? Brendan? The shore? How far has she been pulled? All around there is only swirling black water and surging, floating debris.

The trunk of a palm tree spins to the surface beside her. She moves away and bumps her head on a bicycle tire, trash wound through its spokes. Busted lumber and bright-colored cushions pop up all around. To her left, the body of a woman rises to the surface. Leslie gasps and inhales a mouthful of seawater. Coughing and gagging, she moves to help. Then she sees a long metal pole running through the woman's abdomen and out her back. There is a young child floating with her, tied to her waist by a flowery fabric; the baby stares at Leslie, eyes wide and wild.

A mother's instinct moves her forward but she can't seem to make headway in this unpredictable new ocean. The child's big dark eyes close as Leslie struggles through the spooling water. The impaled woman's hands clench the iron bar running through her body. Leslie tries not to look.

She grabs the naked child—a baby girl—and pulls her free of the encircling fabric. She is limp and heavy. A thin pulse beats in her tiny neck but she is not breathing. Leslie pulls her close and breathes into her mouth.

Brendan surfaces. "What the fuck?" His breath is short and choppy; he bobs up and turns himself in the water to look in all directions, flailing his arms and striking the water. "What the fucking fuck? Where's the boat? Goddamn it!" A woman screams to their left and struggles in the water.

"Help her," Leslie says to Brendan. She blows another breath into the child's small mouth. From the beach, a distant wailing rises on the air. From the other side of the island, a boat chugs into view, moving toward shore.

Brendan continues to tread water and stare at the floundering woman. "Fuck," he says, with a sighing breath of disbelief. "Fuck, fuck, fuck."

"Brendan," Leslie says. "She's drowning." He moves off to help.

The baby girl vomits seawater then wails a high, thin cry. "Shhh," Leslie says. "It's all right." This child—who can't be more than fifteen months old—probably doesn't understand English, but a soothing tone might reach through her panic. "Shh, baby. Shh. It's all right. I've got you."

Leslie cradles the child's tiny buoyant body. The woman Brendan is rescuing screams and grabs at him, clutching his head and neck while shrieking a string of sounds that have no meaning other than abject terror. The fishing boat retrieves two motionless bodies. With a grappling hook, a man pulls them toward the boat while two others reach down and grab whatever appendages will help them land the bodies. Leslie hears the slap of limp, wet flesh landing against the deck like so much sea bounty.

She waves an arm in the universal *help me* sign. "Please," she says as they approach. She doesn't know if they understand, but—like uttering soothing words for the child—hopes they recognize the tone. "Please," she says again, holding up the baby as proof that she is worthy.

Instead of reaching for her, the men bend down into the boat and straighten up with a limp body between them. They dump it over the side. It's a woman. She lands face down and her long hair floats free on the surface, swaying in the shifting water.

"No," says Leslie. "Stop!" But the men are already hauling another body over the side. Before it hits the water, she sees a crushed forehead, eyes canted crazily. "Please," she says again.

"The boat's too heavy," Brendan says from behind the men. "They've got to lighten the load."

Finally a man takes the child then drags Leslie up the side of the boat, smashing her breasts and scraping her stomach. She barely has time to drop her dive vest before being pulled over the gunnel. She lands with a flop on the deck, surrounded by hollow-eyed survivors and corpses with limbs splayed in all directions.

She lies there, breathing hard, staring into the face of a dead woman until the men lift the body and drop it over the side, too. She hears the baby crying and moves on her hands and knees toward the sound.

The boat shifts heavily as Brendan lifts another survivor into it. Now that she's safe, Leslie doesn't want them taking on any more people. "Let's go," she tells the captain. "We're too heavy." She stands shakily. The ocean is filled with floating bodies. Debris rises to the surface all around: a mattress, a plastic chair with a squawking, flapping chicken on it, some sort of wooden bowl sitting upright like a tiny ship. A child clutches a red gas can like a life preserver, which it is. Brendan hauls the child on board then pries the can away and tosses it into the ocean. The boy reaches out as if his favorite teddy has been thrown into the sea.

The boat barely moves, and the engine chugs, belching out a thick grey smoke. They pull toward the beach as more survivors reach up from the sea.

A wet, dark-skinned man hands Leslie the baby and the child clings to her shoulders. She hugs her tightly. The weight of tears is heavy behind her eyes. Her mouth is dry from saltwater. The boat scrapes against the sand and the captain urges people off. Leslie stumbles over the side with her burden and topples onto the wet sand. The child begins to wail again.

On land, she hears the word *tsunami* and realizes what has happened to the beach, the reef, the people of Thailand. Palm trees are snapped, uprooted, bent over. A red car perches nose down, wheels against the side of what used to be a building. A narrow alleyway has become a rubbish heap, piled with objects and bodies and fragments of buildings. Human remains are caught in the branches of trees, slung over concrete slabs, entangled in twisted metal, crushed beneath unmoored stairs, sometimes with only a hand sticking out for the living to find. Trails of blood crisscross the sand. Everywhere there is wailing, everywhere grief, freshly discovered.

She stumbles forward. The child whimpers at her shoulder. A frantic woman, bleeding from the head reaches out and grabs the face of the child, staring intently, then releases her with a cry and walks off. A warm wetness spreads along Leslie's hip. The child has wet herself. Not a concern at the moment, but she has no diapers. Would she be able to find any? And what to call her? "Baby" will not do. "Mai," she thinks. Mai, pronounced My, as in My Child Now.

Leslie thinks of her children still at home, of finicky Pea, of Reese and Tabitha whom she too often links together as one entity: her teenagers. But they are discrete individuals, outdoorsy Tabitha who still calls her "Mommy" and always says, "Love you!" before leaving the house, and Reese, reigning queen of the double dangly earring and French manicure with her pudgy, bookish boyfriend. She longs to hear their voices, make sure they're okay, even though it is *she* who has almost died. Would they hear of the tsunami and be worried? Thailand was a world away from Norfolk, Virginia. Maybe a tsunami in Thailand wouldn't even make the news and her family wouldn't know. Could she locate a working phone?

Up ahead, against the side of what had been the Red Star Hotel, she sees a boat similar to Sam's and thinks of her fellow researchers. Did they get underwater in time? Had they, too, ridden out the wave by going beneath it? How would they ever find one another again? What if they never did? She leans against a palm tree and hitches Mai higher onto her hip. A sudden exhaustion seeps up from the soles of her feet, still squelchy-wet but protected. Thank god she hadn't lost her dive booties in the wave. Some people were stumbling around completely naked, disoriented, bleeding. The force of that crazy mindless water stripped them of everything.

Brendan appears, his arms hanging at his sides. A fair-sized chunk of shoulder skin has been rubbed away and the area oozes with a pink, painful-looking, sand-encrusted slime. His face wears the expression of a lost puppy scanning each passing face for its owner and best friend.

"Jake?" he says to no one in particular, and then louder, "Jake?"

Leslie loosens Mai's clutching fingers and shifts her to the other hip. "I think we're on our own, Brendan."

He focuses on her and clenches his fists. "You saying they're dead?"
She shakes her head. "We'll find them. I'm sure they're all right."

"Look around," he says. "Nothing's fucking all right." He pulls his
fist back and punches the trunk of a palm tree, then shakes his hand
and flexes the fingers. Mai whimpers.

"Shh." Leslie pats the little girl's back. Her fine hair lies against her
skull, clumped in sweaty lines. Leslie fluffs it up and blows air into it to
cool her down. The child pulls away and stares at her, eyes wide. She is
beautiful, with soft skin and fine, black hair. Her eyebrows pull together
as she examines Leslie. The girl's left temple sprouts a swelling goose
egg that Leslie hadn't noticed before.

"Why don't you go and see if you can find the others," she tells
Brendan. "We can meet back here." A white line of salt has dried along
the ridge of Mai's hairline. "Be careful," she tells his retreating back.
She watches him leave, his bare feet pushing through standing water,
blood streaked down his back, the outlines of his body soon blurred by
the piles of broken cinder blocks, shards of shredded timber, matted
reeds and palm fronds, twisted sign boards, and ragged strips of cloth.
It's a dizzying array of mud-colored rubble.

A group of *farang*—foreigners—begins to gather nearby; Leslie
approaches them.

"We are not *alive* for here," laments a man in broken English, half
of a couple from the Netherlands.

His wife—still wet, with a nasty cut to her forehead—nods as he
speaks, then weaves dizzily. "Our child," she says, cradling an imaginary
baby, then throwing her arms wide and sobbing.

"We were on holiday," begins a woman with a thick German accent.
"The wave came, *und* Rolfe, he grabbed for me, but he—and I—" She
moves her shaking hands to her face as if to keep them still.

Then someone screams and the panic spreads up from the beach
like a wave. A couple runs, frantically, away from the coastline, and
soon everyone turns to flee, thinking only of escape, screaming and
shouting and running.

"Another one!"

"*Allez! Allez!*"

"Go! Go!"

"*Schnell!*"

"Run!"

It turns out to be a smaller wave, an aftershock wave, but the survivors keep fleeing as best they can through the debris and muck, eventually slowing to a walk, collectively moving toward the tree-covered hills, a mournful herd in unspoken agreement. *Higher ground.* The group stops climbing when a safe height is reached and Leslie sits against a large tree, her legs burning from the effort of the climb and from carrying Mai.

A naked man with a thick trail of dried blood on his thigh sits beside her and shakes his head. "We only arrived last night." He laughs with an edge of hysteria. "We slept in. Woke to *this.*" A white-haired woman in a torn nightgown settles herself cross-legged on the ground beside him and puts her head in her hands. She wears one sandy slipper. "We've got to call," she murmurs into her palms. "We've got to call home."

Yes, home. Leslie stares down at the coastline. How is it that she feels so frantic about home when there is so much suffering, so many lives lost, so much at stake here? The yearning tugs at her, a visceral, physical need. She will not feel as if she has come out alive until she hears the voices of her loved ones at the other end of the line.

And now she has lost Brendan.

She has sand in every crevice. She could hike back down and bathe in the ocean, but even from here she sees it depositing and retrieving mounds of debris, some of it human remains. Instead, she unzips and pulls her wetsuit partially down and brushes off what sand she can. Then she goes to work on cleaning Mai, who is still diaperless, but she's clearly bright. Perhaps Mai will be—as Pea had been—one of those children who potty trains early.

Sweet Pea. Where would she be right now? On her way to gymnastics? Leslie conjures up an image of her bright, fidgety, spandex-clad daughter and smiles at the memory. And the older girls? Surely off somewhere, Tabitha perhaps at work at the ice cream shop, Reese with her doughy boyfriend, both oblivious to the other side of the world. Had she hugged them before she left? Had she told them that she loved them?

She needs to find her coworkers, someone, anyone. Back home, it's Christmas break. The university would be a ghost town. If she could even reach the school, she has no news of how the others fared. What would she say to the person on the other end of the line, *I'm* okay?

They sit in the shade of the hillside vegetation and stare down at the coast. A few brave survivors head back down to help, but Leslie holds Mai and rests. The little girl fingers the ring in Leslie's bikini top as if it's a puzzle in need of solving. She stops mid-tug and Leslie follows her gaze to the road below. An elephant is walking toward the leading edge of the destruction. A man sits astride the beast and the late afternoon light casts long shadows across the piles of debris. The huge mammal picks its way gingerly but surely along the littered ground. At a command from its mahout, the elephant reaches its trunk into a small space beneath a beam, lifts it, and gently sets it aside. Mai squirms to get down, but Leslie pulls her to her lap. "Oh, no, baby girl," she says. "You stay with me."

Behind the elephant, a truck comes into view and a man leans out of the passenger seat calling, "Hospital! Hospital!" Injured survivors who had been limping along the road climb aboard, quickly filling the bed to overflowing.

How could there be a truck—so soon? *Ah, of course*, the devastation was complete within the wave zone, but there must be a line, a line *past which* everything remained untouched. Just a little ways away, beyond the reach of that brutal wave, life is still normal, buildings still stand, people who had been breakfasting or relaxing are not swept away, hundreds—thousands—are not suddenly missing.

She watches a van edge as close to the chaos as the clogged road allows. An official-looking woman steps out holding a clipboard, and survivors gather. From her elevated perch in the trees, Leslie sees Brendan and calls to him, then picks her way back down the hill, Mai at her hip. They join the thronging survivors and form a ragged line, patient, even in catastrophe. When they reach the front, Leslie accepts a water bottle and asks, "Is there a way to call home?"

"We can take your name," says the worker. He has an Australian accent and points with his head to a woman beside the truck. "Tell Isra. She'll write you down."

Leslie and Brendan approach the young woman holding a clipboard. "Can you help us call home?"

"You are American?"

They nod in unison.

Isra looks at Mai. "And her?" Mai grunts and pulls her arm away when the woman tries to touch her.

"She was drowning. I'm looking for her parents."

"The lines are too busy to call out," Isra says. "But we are making a list of survivors."

"My family won't know to call," says Leslie.

Isra looks at her strangely. "They will know," she says. "It is all over the American news."

"Thailand?" says Brendan.

"Not only Thailand. All of Sumatra. Thousands have died."

Leslie feels numb and suddenly exhausted. Behind Isra, the owner of the Tsunami Hotel—a Dane expatriate—adjusts his battered hotel sign atop a mound of rubble that had been an outer wall. Surviving diehard surfers congregate, dazed, in the wet, jumbled lobby.

"I heard there's a cruise ship," says Brendan.

"Ship?" Leslie watches as a man holding two large, green coconuts walks up to them. He holds one out, its top lopped off, open to the watery milk inside. Mai reaches for it and he smiles. Leslie gives her a drink, takes a sip herself, then hands it to Brendan. She turns to thank the man but he is gone.

"They say it's anchored nearby," says Brendan, wiping his mouth. "God, that's good. An American ship that missed the tsunami completely—it'll ferry us to the airport."

Leslie thinks about her passport, swept away along with the hotel wall that contained the safe in which she had locked it. "What if your passport's gone?"

"The Christmas trip," says Brendan, "from hell."

Christmas, thinks Leslie. *What a concept.*

"You want to stay and keep looking for the others?" she asks, "Or hike into town?"

"Keep looking," says Brendan. "They've got to be here somewhere."

"We can camp on the hill." Leslie points. A few survivors have already built small fires for comfort. "Then find a better spot tomorrow." Mai's breathing slows; a spot of drool spreads on Leslie's shoulder. They hike back up and settle between the roots of a banyan tree just before the sun dips below the horizon. Darkness descends with coastal suddenness.

Brendan scoots closer. "Where do you think the others are?"

She shakes her head in the dark. "I don't know."

Traditional night sounds surround them: the buzzing of insects, chirping geckos, trilling tree frogs, but tonight they are interspersed by the eerie keening of distant sorrow. "Do you think you could...?"

He sniffs. "What?"

"Put your arm over me?"

They scoot closer until their bodies touch. She feels Brendan's chest spasm as he cries silently. He falls into sleep before she does, his breath still catching with residual spasms. Back home, in the Stackowski-Baxter-Downy household, that after-crying catch is what they call The Snubs. Tabitha was the queen of sleep-snubbing when she was little. The day of her first birthday party Leslie hadn't been able to get her down for a nap and when they put her in the high chair and set the tiny cake in front of her on the tray, hoping for some adorable icing-fingered pictures, Tabitha had simply looked at them in alarm. Still holding the video camera, Gus reached out and pushed her hand down into the icing. Tabitha jerked her hand back and screamed, sobbing until she finally fell asleep against Leslie's shoulder, a red icing rose melting in her tightly clenched fist.

Sleep was one of those things that when you're young you assume will always be the same. But the relationship with sleep changes throughout a lifetime. As a child, Leslie regularly dreamed that she could fly. When those flight dreams stopped, she missed them terribly. As a teenager, she could sleep through a marching band crossing the foot of her bed but dreamed that she was naked in school or had forgotten her locker combination and woke mortified. Once she had kids, the slightest whimper or sigh had her awake and checking on them anxiously; when she did sleep, she sometimes died in her nightmares—the great horror of that scenario being not her own death, but her children left motherless. After the girls became toddlers, they often crawled into the adult bed in the middle of the night and Leslie learned to sleep with chubby arms and legs draped akimbo, with small knees pushing into her lower back, with a chorus of gentle snores as a lullaby. Then overnight the girls morphed into teenagers and the sounds she listened for changed again: the quietly closing door, the tiptoeing footfall, the muffled whispers that meant they were up to no good. Most recently, with the onset of menopause, she has finally surrendered any hope for an amiable relationship with sleep. She drifts off each night, knowing she will soon be awake, throwing back the covers like a madwoman and stumbling stiff-legged into the kitchen to stand before the open freezer, face pressed into the icy fog that drifts past the glowing interior light.

There will be no freezer relief tonight.

When she wakes in the morning, Brendan is gone. He returns carrying two water bottles and hands one to Leslie.

"They need people to collect bodies," says Brendan. "Thought I might help. Maybe look for—" He stops himself, touches Mai's arm and walks off.

The day progresses and Leslie walks to a nearby mobile aid station doling out cold Red Cross rice. Mai learns to hold a water bottle by herself. When, mid-afternoon, she feels suddenly heavier in Leslie's arms and her head begins to bob, Leslie heads to the temple-morgue to find Brendan and pass Mai to him for a spell.

A swelling need pulses just below her breastbone. *Home*. Her husband. Her children. *Home*. Her life. *Home*. How had she been so anxious to leave it?

The temple sits on a rise, just beyond the reach of that awful, killing wave. The devastation ends right at its doorstep. It could be a picture postcard with its old walls, lush greenery and high trees. A box of surgical masks sits just inside the doorway, and Leslie grabs one. It does little to hide the stench of blood gone stale and of the soil a body releases at the moment of death.

She moves slowly down the line of corpses, fearing that she will step on something, on some*one*. So many of them are children—were children. A mother mourns at the feet of a small boy, handsome except for his mouth, eyes, and nose filled with dark gray sand. Beside him are two young girls. Twins? One reaches out in death, still, as she had in the final moments of life, fingers yet grasping for anything that will save her. The other stares, eyes wide and teeth bared in an eerie smile, the strange rictus of sudden death.

The odor in the temple is unbearable.

She pulls off her mask and rushes outside to the fresh air and sunlight. So much death.

A bull elephant and its mahout work outside the temple. The animal's great gray bulk is soothing; she watches it lift an uprooted palm tree— a slow, prehensile, front loader. Pea wrote a report on elephants the year before. Leslie thinks back to what they learned. Elephants are social. They walk hundreds of miles a day in the wild. Gestation takes twenty-two months. Babies are nursed for two full years and kept close for many more. Had these elephants lost loved ones in the tsunami? But no, she'd heard that animals move to higher ground *before* a tsunami hits, their own complex early warning sensors saving them from death.

She remembers that elephants have their own graveyards, too. They go there sometimes, even when they are healthy, to caress the bones of their ancestors. Researchers had run tests and found that elephants recognize the bones of their dead loved ones and pick them out from the piles of others.

Concerns of heat, disease and the vast number of dead override the need to identify remains and a mass grave is prepared at the edge of town. Before burial, each corpse is photographed with a Polaroid camera. The pictures are stapled along the temple wall so that relatives might still search for answers. This wall reminds Leslie of the photos of the missing after the 9/11 attacks. Except those photos had been questions, still, representations of a slim hope, desperately nurtured, and they were taken of the living in the midst of happy lives—the missing man smiling with his arms around two friends, the mother proudly bearing the birthday cake to her child, the bride and groom smiling for the camera. Those pictures had somehow spoken of hope even as they tattered and faded in the sun. But *these* photos are a horrific gallery of gruesome, hopeless answers.

Because there is so very much to do, the person behind the camera had no time to pretty up the corpses. Shirts have not been pulled over bruised, bloated stomachs, bloody faces are left bloody, eyes are not closed, sand not removed from mouths. Could it be that the mark of injury is some small comfort to the family? The photos of unmarked children—who look to be simply asleep—are surely the more disconcerting.

God, Leslie needs to find a phone. She needs to talk to her family. She needs to contact ODU and let them know that three people on her research team are missing. What if they are never found? Would she return home without them? She would have to, and yet, how could she?

And she would be leaving without the data she had been sent to collect.

A small thing, perhaps, in the wake of disaster, but the destruction of the reef is tied to this human tragedy. In a healthy coastline, reefs and mangroves buffer giant swells and surges. Nature designed her shores with built-in shock absorbers, but human impact and overdevelopment has depleted the buffers and here, *here* was the awful result.

Back at the upended boat, she finds Brendan struggling to comfort a restless Mai. Leslie sits in the sand beside them and Mai reaches out in the hold-me signal understood by parents the world over. Leslie soothes her with a gentle rocking motion. Already the sun is dropping toward the water, an apricot and cream-colored postcard swirl.

"Shall we make camp here, then?"

"Under the boat?" Brendan's voice carries an edge of panic. He slaps an insect from his leg.

"Good a place as any. Maybe the others are still looking for us."

"It wasn't even twenty-four hours ago."

"I know." A woman's body hangs tangled in the branches of a nearby palm tree, too high to have been removed yet. Leslie imagines it there later, in the darkness, falling to the ground, reanimating.

She rests Mai gently on the sand. Leslie strokes her arm and her eyes droop, then open, droop, then open, before finally surrendering to sleep. Soon she lies sprawled in the way of sleeping babies everywhere.

"Think there'll be another one?" Brendan asks.

Leslie hears the fear. A corresponding voice keeps ticking off concerns in her head: *family, phone, food, water, disease, desperation, home.* And the ocean, *her* ocean, the one place that had always been her refuge, her ultimate source of solace, has mutated without warning. It has morphed into a murderous lover. It has betrayed her.

In the morning, day three, when the sun rises above the horizon, Mai reaches up and touches Leslie's chin. Her fingers are soft and tiny and Leslie cups the little hand under her own. She gets stiffly to her feet, lifts Mai, and steps outside their meager shelter. An elephant works nearby, still searching for survivors. She sets Mai down. "Go shee-shee." The girl responds with a weak stream of urine. Smart child. She smiles at her. "Good girl."

Leslie lifts Mai to her hip and bends down for their last water bottle. The little girl spots the elephant and holds her hands out, gurgling in appreciation.

"You like the elephant?" Mai reaches as far as Leslie's restraining arms allow, nearly toppling them both. "Hold on, baby girl." It's the first time Leslie has seen Mai excited. She moves toward the elephant then looks up at the mahout atop it. "May we come closer?" She inclines her head and gestures toward the animal.

The lines of the driver's face soften when he sees little Mai. After a short command, the elephant stands still. When it spots Mai, it reaches its trunk toward her. Leslie pulls back in alarm, but Mai jabbers happily and reaches out.

"Chaang," she says, *elephant*, the first word Leslie has heard her speak.

The rider continues to sit erect, a statue atop an elephant. He stares as the elephant moves its trunk over little Mai's hair, snuffing and circling around her head. The baby giggles and reaches up to touch the elephant's trunk with both tiny hands.

The rider, shocked into action, calls loudly over his shoulder. Again he calls, his voice urgent. Leslie looks around, confused. A man hurries from behind the elephant and freezes when he sees them. She holds Mai tighter. His mouth forms words, but no sound comes out.

The two adults stand in frozen silence until he finally whispers, "Su-ay," and puts a hand over his heart. His eyes shine and he steps closer, holding out his arms; Mai bounces against Leslie, reaching toward the man. Before Leslie can even think to stop him, the man lifts Mai from her arms. He is crying and laughing, first holding her close, then lifting her high in front of him. "Soo thong khloong jai," he says. Leslie understands only *jai*: heart.

As he croons over the child, Leslie stands there, uncertain. The man smiles at Mai in a way that only a father could. He pets her hair and cries, tears sliding into the creases of his smiling cheeks. When he finally turns to Leslie, he says, "Khorb koon," over and over. "Khorb koon." *Thank you.*

Leslie has no words to offer in return. What could she say that would touch this simultaneous sudden loss and sudden gain? No words will do. A gesture then? She remembers the water bottle and holds it out to Mai who grabs for it with two hands, then brings it to her mouth and tips it up, the top still on. When nothing comes out, she puts a hand over the lid and with intense concentration tries to twist it off. The man watches, his face broken wide open with happiness.

Leslie steps closer and lifts a hand to stroke Mai's fine, dark, hair. "Baby girl," she says. Still clutching the water bottle, the child looks back and forth from the man—her father—to Leslie, her interim mother. Mai—Su-ay—is where she belongs, Leslie knows this, but her arms feel suddenly useless. They hang against her body, bereft and heavy. She moves in to kiss Mai's tiny forehead and the baby tips forward in her father's arms, closes her eyes and leans into Leslie to receive it.

WHAT LIES BENEATH

Eight days before you leave for the Sinai Desert, Dr. Simon cuts a flap into the skin of your lower back and inserts twelve subcutaneous pellets of synthetic testosterone. The area swells, red and hot to the touch.

That should hold you, he says. For the next three months.

Let this serve, you think, as he swabs and needles and tugs at your skin, *as my ritual scarification, my tribal transition into manhood.*

Later, you pack, certain you will forget some essential tool of masculinity. Research gear makes up the bulk of your luggage—sixty plastic collection jars for specimens and a lightweight field microscope. When the jars have all been filled, you will return to your lab in Miami and create a series of RNA microarrays for *Cetoscarus bicolor*, the parrotfish you received a grant to study.

The parrotfish supermale—the most potent, sexually mature and sought-after mate—begins life as a female. You plan to search for observable changes in gene expression especially during a female's transition from initial phase to terminal phase. You hope to generate a more complete picture of the physiological processes of gender transformation. You are aware that this makes you a mildly humorous figure, like Dr. Byrd, the ornithologist whose hobby is flying small planes, or Dr. Butz, the proctologist who is also an asshole.

You will find your specific parrotfish in the Red Sea, and Salim Mohammed, a Bedouin of the *Muszeina* tribe located near Sharm-El-

Sheikh, will be your host along with his extended family. You do a Google Earth search for their camp (near the point of the peninsula, on the western side), but nomadic tribes are tough to pin down. You learn that "Sinai" translates roughly as "teeth of the moon."

Testosterone—or T as your doctor affectionately refers to it— involves no special molecular pyrotechnics. Its formula, fairly simple, contains three basic elements in unique combination: Carbon, Hydrogen, and Oxygen, as $C19H28O2$. Simple like water. Like air. T, your simple savior.

You first took T as a dermal patch, several years ago, supplemented by a cream. The increased T coaxed a scream from your cells, roughly the equivalent of *Well, all right!* as if they had been waiting on the correct hormone and could finally get down to business. Your voice deepened, your libido went through the roof, you relished every hair that sprouted from your chin, every vein that bulged on your arms. Your shoulders broadened, you stopped menstruating. You sweated more, a metallic tangy sweat that you relished. You felt, at long last, swollen with confidence, with lust for life.

Dr. Simon prescribes subdermal pellets for the research trip. They will not wash off in the ocean. They will not melt in the hot sun of the desert. They will hide beneath your skin and send out daily messages to reaffirm your identity.

Six months before the trip, you get your top surgery. One reconstructed nipple remains persistently high but you are thrilled to look down and have an unobstructed view of your abdomen, which you work on toning after the mastectomy drains are removed. You face the fact that you may never have a bottom surgery. For even the best, most perfect penis, you cannot imagine spending 50,000 dollars. Also, the mechanics of said operation make you queasy.

On the day of your trip, during a security pat down, the TSA worker feels a series of suspicious lumps at the back of your waist. He lingers there. He orders you to untuck and questions what you have beneath your shirt. You try to explain that the pellets are not beneath your shirt, but beneath your *skin*. The wand, passed repeatedly over that portion of your body does not reassure him. The security line behind you comes to a standstill. Two more TSA employees gather to render an opinion. All eyes are on you. It has been only four years since nineteen men with box cutters changed the shape of the world. A supervisor is called. When you try to quietly explain, they decide there is something not quite right about you. You are whisked to an interrogation room and subjected to a humiliating barrage of questions followed by a strip search that reveals what you had not wanted to reveal. You nearly miss your flight and board at the last minute, breathless and burning with shame from the past two hours and the angry glares of your impatient fellow travelers.

An interminable trans-Atlantic flight follows, the hours of which evade calculation given the forward leap in time, the backward feeling in your brain, and you land in Rome, only to then endure a barrage of leading questions from El-Al, questions that never end in the interrogative. ("You have smuggled something on this plane!" *I have? Wait! No, I haven't.* "Someone has put something in your bag!" *They have?* Et cetera.) Finally you land in Tel Aviv and your Egyptian travel agent stands at the bottom of the escalator holding a placard with your name misspelled (Mr. Starchonsti). You find yourself so grateful for the "mister" that you smile and grip the hand of Ali with gusto. He sneaks furtive glances at you as he drives you and your bags to a tour operator with whom he holds a long, gesticulating conversation until the operator throws his hands in the air and tosses your luggage atop a rickety bus filled with hot people of all nationalities whose amorphous hate you feel emanating from behind the bus windows. You adopt an unconcerned air and hold your jaw in a way that you believe makes it appear strong and square.

Ali stands on the cracked sidewalk beneath a scruffy date palm. He waves good-by as the tour operator drives to the border at the edge of the Sinai desert. The Israeli side is manicured and lush. The Egyptian side is bare and dusty. Border guards enter carrying black assault rifles. They move down the aisle checking passports. They linger over yours. It says you are Danielle even though you now look nothing like a Danielle. You hope they assume it is a variant of Daniel, French perhaps. You do your best to affect a fey, European air.

After an endless bus ride, during which the sweaty, swarthy businessman beside you snores and mumbles, the bus stops somewhere, you know not where, for food, in the middle of the night. You hold out your map to the businessman with a questioning look and he points to a spot roughly halfway down the peninsula. There is no dot on the map for this place where you are. At a small stand, you buy a shish kebab of meat that must be goat and are surprised by its deliciousness. Fatigued and body-sore, the pellets in your hip aching like a fever, you are herded back onto the bus for the ten-hour final approach into Sharm-El-Sheikh. To pass the time, while you are not sleeping, you consider the many ways one can die in the Sinai, all of which seem equally plausible this night: a fatal head-on collision on a sharp switchback; a tire slipping off the edge of a cliff, the top-heavy bus rolling over and over before landing upside down in a dry wadi and catching fire; a monstrous avalanche of rock that crushes everything in its path, including you and your fellow passengers; the driver forgetting to top off the fuel tank at the last stop, causing the bus to run out of petrol and you to wander aimlessly in the desert before dying of dehydration or possibly a puff adder strike.

And it occurs to you with a frisson of shame on this crazy, dark night, as you stare out the window through your own reflection, that you are a biologist who cannot be certain if a puff adder actually makes its home in the desert. You have made an assumption, using only the dusty sounding words *puff* and *adder* as your guide.

In the early afternoon, the ramshackle bus shudders to a halt and the driver unceremoniously deposits you in a cloud of grime at the end of a dirt road. He points to a group of tents in the distant beige sand and says, "*Muszeina.*" He plops down bag after bag of your clothes and supplies as you watch, curiously calm, thanks to your recent subdermal infusion of T.

When he is done and gone, the brakes of the bus sighing and spewing that familiar smell of road and travel, you sit on your bags and prepare yourself for lugging everything to the tents. A man walks down the sandy road toward you. He turns and gestures to two young men behind him. You heft your heaviest luggage so as not to appear weak and they move faster, taking up the other bags and smiling. They wear long *djellabayas* over white, loose-fitting trousers and the older man, who introduces himself as Salim, wears a red-and-white draped head cover held in place with a shiny black cord. You marvel at how anything could shine in all this dust.

"My sons." He points. "Yusef. Zayed." You further marvel at his English accent. The sons wear off-white head covers, no cord.

A group of children drawing elaborate designs in the sand look up when you approach. They stand for a moment and then run behind the tent, laughing.

"Noora," says Salim, pausing beside a woman with beautifully lined eyes that crinkle when she smiles. "My wife." Faded blue tattoos cross her forehead and flow down her cheekbones, swirling in curlicues that sweep toward what you can see of the graceful curve of her jaw. You establish this through a series of furtive glances. You do not stare. You are a man in a man's culture where the men do not look at women. Physical contact must also be avoided. Accidentally brush against a young woman's hand while being served and you could bring great dishonor upon the family. You keep your hands in your pockets just in case.

Your belongings are carried out of sight around the back of the tent while you are ushered through the front, with great ceremony, into a wide-open area. A large welcome rug, banded with swaths of purple, red, and ochre, stretches across the dirt floor. You remove your sandals and sit with Salim, Yusef, and Zayed. You sweat profusely even though the air inside the tent is not hot in the way you had imagined it would be.

Yusef's wife brings out tiny glasses of exquisitely sweetened tea. The men are anxious to practice their English; they make halting inquiries into your trip while urging you to rest your back against a pile of rugs. The rugs are rough, they scratch against your incision site even through the shirt you wear. They smell like a wet dog that has rolled in a rotting fish, drying beside a woodstove. You have been warned about the odor of camelhair rugs by a veteran of Desert Storm: *whatever you do, do not get them wet.*

After you have been honored with sweet tea, Salim says, *"Mihbaj,"* and Noora brings out the largest mortar and pestle you have ever seen. It is made of wood and filled with coffee beans and cardamom seeds. The oldest daughter, Farah, who wears a purple dress and headscarf, grinds the beans and seeds filling the tent with a dark, flowery smell. The seated men breathe deeply as if to inhale caffeine from the air. Farah pours the grounds into a brass urn with a long spout and Salim brings the mixture to a boil three times.

After the grounds settle, Noora pours a bit of the thick brew into a cup incongruously made of china, as delicate as an eggshell. She hands it to Salim. "Al Heif," she says.

He sips and turns to you. "The first cup. I drink so you may feel safe."

Noora pours another cup. "Al Keif," says Salim, "The second cup. For you to taste."

You sip, smile, and nod. Noora pours more and says, "Al Dheif."

"The cup of the guest," Salim interprets, cupping his hands and lifting them toward you so that you will drink, drink. Anxious to please, you tip the cup back and receive a mouthful of grounds for your enthusiasm. They swell in your cheeks and the family watches intently for your approval. The grounds fill the crevices between your teeth, they settle onto your tongue, drift back toward your soft palate. There is no option but to gamely swallow and smile, hoping your teeth are not still holding the black grounds, but feeling grit everywhere in your mouth. "Delicious," you say past the crumbs of coffee, and then rub your stomach enthusiastically, delighting everyone.

"Now," says Salim, "you are one of the family. If the family is threatened, you will have protection."

Over dinner—a celebration of stewed lamb and spices, served on the floor on a massive metal plate—you speak with Salim about the Bedouin household and about your work. You describe the parrotfish, how he sleeps in a transparent spit bubble of his own making, a caul of mucous that encases him like a loose-fitting womb, how spit cocoons move and sway and blur the edges and colors of the fish, working as a hedge against predation, how they mimic a decaying strand of bleached-out seaweed and mask the scent of the parrotfish and the electromagnetic signals it emits. You describe your plan to enter the water before daylight and capture genetic material from several fish still in their spit bubbles, how you will effectively have *swabbed the cheeks* of sixty or more parrotfish before the end of your research trip. Enough to keep you busy back at your lab in Miami for the rest of the year.

Salim proves a wise and curious host. His English is excellent. When asked a direct question, he thinks long and well before offering an answer. He places a high value on metaphor and allegory. You ask him how many are in his family.

"I have two sons and their wives, my three daughters not yet married, my mother, and the six children of my sons. We will have another soon." He does not mention his wife.

"And Noora," you add, without thinking.

"Yes." Salim nods. "We are family. We all eat from the same bowl."

You like this description of family: all who eat from the same bowl. You envy him his large, extended family, but have no words to convey this. "My mother died three years ago," you say, surprising yourself.

Salim frowns and you remember from your research that Bedouins rarely speak of emotional issues directly.

"You have a father?"

"He is..." you pause, considering how best to answer. Fortunately, a silence, even a long one, is not a bad thing in Bedouin culture, where careful words are believed to indicate a sharp mind and poetic turns of phrase are highly valued. You think of the things Tio Manny has told you about Jack, this man, this *father* you have never met: a veteran, a prisoner of war, a treasure hunter, an aquarium handyman, but you could not pick him out of a lineup. "He does not know me well. I only learned I had a father after my mother died."

"Everyone has a father."

"But not every father stays for the raising."

"This is a shame. The father must teach his son the ways of men."

"My mother kept the secret from us both." You think about the secret you are keeping even now, beneath your clothes. Would your host be so hospitable if he knew?

"I do not wish to speak ill of your mother. But the child and the father should know one another." He crosses his legs and rearranges the fall of the long white shirt. "You have a wife, Mister Dani?"

"Yes." You smile. "Her name is Carla." You stop yourself from saying *Carlita*, not diminutive anymore, but the forty extra pounds have given her curves and creases that you love. She remains feisty, and has decided she wants—no, *needs*—children. She craves the mayhem of her Puerto Rican childhood, of loud relatives that bustle in and help themselves, of children scooting through the house trailing toys, dripping liquids, layers of women wedged tight in a small hot kitchen, *como sardinas en lata.*

Even though you ran around the neighborhood without a shirt until you were eight, at nearly thirty you are shy about your body. Your friends know this. They will never find you discussing surgical procedures at a cocktail party. You will not be offering tours of your reconstructed body. When Salim shows you the rug where you will sleep it feels wide open and conspicuous. In lieu of goodnight, he leans toward you and quietly says, "When you sleep in a house, your thoughts are as high as the ceiling. When you sleep outside, they are as high as the stars."

You wake up at 3 AM to get to Na'ama Bay while the parrotfish may still be found asleep inside their spit cocoons. This does not appear to be a problem for Yusef. You rub your eyes and he hands you a cup of coffee and a piece of hard flat bread, loads a camel with your supplies, saddles another, then helps you on and leads the beasts across the dark desert to begin the first day of your research.

There is something exciting about the promise of new fieldwork. The possibilities stretch before you and your job at first is only to be open to them all. This is a feeling as wide as the desert sky, as rippling with promise as the stretch of windblown sand before you.

You are not prepared for the cold. Or, rather, you have an intellectual understanding of cold desert nights, but the steamy breath of the camel surprises you. You alternate tucking each hand into your armpit for warmth, keeping hold of the saddle horn with the other. You look up and see the vastness of a dark, wide sky. Every star is visible and there are millions. From the western sky a satellite moves briskly through the stars and you think of Carla and the time you fell in love with her, camping in the Caribbean, so earnest and idealistic. But against all odds you have lasted, your long-time love and you.

The desert is quiet. Yusef is quiet. The rhythmic shushing of the camel's hooves sliding across the sand relaxes you like white noise and you fight to stay awake even as you rock in sync with the animal's awkward, lurching gate.

Over dinner, Salim asks more questions about your research.

"Your fish, it has the name of a bird."

"Yes. Parrotfish have hard beaks like birds. They're brightly colored. Each supermale guards and watches over a harem of females." After you have spoken, you feel a flash of anxiety, but Salim smiles and nods. The word *harem* does not faze him. "But what's really strange is that each supermale starts out its life as a female. For some reason, it changes. This is what I want to study. Why and how that change takes place."

"Why *would* an animal start one way, only to change later? What you tell me does not make sense."

"Nature can be very confusing. Your questions are what I want to know, too."

"I do not question Allah's wisdom in creating this fish, I wish only to understand."

"Maybe being a female *first* somehow makes the male a better male." You smile in case Salim would only accept such a statement made in jest.

By bedtime, you both agree that the ways of God are mysterious. They are not for men to question, only to accept. And to study.

As this night's pre-sleep missive, Salim offers, "Only three things in a life are certain: birth, death, and change. I will think about your changing bird-fish of the sea. Goodnight Mr. Dani."

Two weeks into your research, the pellets begin to work their way out of your skin. Two at first, and you cannot push them back in, although you try, causing no small amount of pain. Briefly, you wonder what would happen if you swallowed the pellets instead. Or inserted them in some other orifice, anywhere they might yet be absorbed. You put them in your pocket, instead. The following day, another pellet works its way out. You stare uneasily at the bullet shape of it in your palm.

The day the final pellet reemerges, you worry that menstruation might follow. The idea appalls you. Your body is betraying you. Again. If you menstruate, will you still snorkel? Will you bleed in the waters of the resident hammerhead who patrols his reef wall every morning? You leave open the possibility of harvesting a small sea sponge to absorb the flow. Fortunately, the blood does not arrive but a dark cloud of estrogen depression does.

The evening before your final day of research, Salim approaches with a serious face.

"Tomorrow," he says, "Farah will join you. She has asked Yusef to go along. It is not customary, but Noora agrees that you are family enough."

You hesitate. The girl is beautiful and delicate, maybe fourteen years old, maybe fifteen. The hesitation shows on your face.

"Farah is most intelligent," Salim says. "She has always loved the sea. She considers it an honor to help with your important research."

At 3 AM the next morning, Farah is there beside Yusef helping without hesitation. She moves with grace and confidence.

At Na'ama Bay, you search the reef for specimens while Yusef tends to the camels and Farah gathers driftwood for fuel. When you are done with collection, you linger, this is your very last day in the Red Sea. The sun, rising above the flat edge of the horizon, tints the ocean pink in a wide V that opens toward you. You float on your back and breathe deeply. The sky is cloudless and deep blue. You watch it lighten, then finally, reluctantly, you exit the sea and move behind a large rock to change out of your wetsuit as you have done every day.

But today, after you have removed everything and are reaching for your dry clothes, Farah rounds the rock carrying an armful of wood, only three feet away by the time she sees you and stops. She starts in surprise, but does not look away and you stand there naked, mercifully breastless, although scarred, and empty between your legs. You cover the area with your hands, but not before she sees. Her eyes have a question in them and she stares openly. You stare back, frozen, exposed, aware that this is a terrible taboo. You hastily pull on trousers. You have no words to explain your body to this young woman.

"Operation," you say, pointlessly, only to fill the gaping silence. She draws back and you pull on your shirt and gather your things.

"I'm sorry," you say to her retreating back. You emerge from behind the rock shortly after and Yusef is there, holding the reins of the camel in his hand. The driftwood is tied in two bundles and draped over the beast's haunches like saddlebags. At a word from Yusef, the camel begins a four-point movement that folds its front legs until it kneels and drops its haunches into a squat. The physical awkwardness of the camel mirrors the clumsy swirl inside your head. *Is now the time for you to speak?* You look to their faces for some clue. Yusef says nothing but gestures for you to climb atop the kneeling camel and so you do.

On the ride back, you watch Yusef and Farah closely, surreptitiously. You cannot tell what they know. How could Farah describe what transpired? *What did?* Of all the thoughts racing through your mind, you understand this: Farah, a young unwed female, has seen you, an older male, undressed. Though your downstairs plumbing may be female, you have surely dishonored her with this one brief, careless act. Will the family's honor require retaliation? A spate of scenarios runs through your mind. Most of them involve violence. Would the men be more forgiving if they knew you started life as a female?

You have dishonored your kind and generous host. You have betrayed his trust. Shame begins as a sweating in your feet and travels up through your legs, pressed against the swaying belly of the camel. Shame radiates over your scalp, spreading down each strand of hair until your whole head is lit up—a fiber-optic show of shame. It overtakes you like a sickness.

You must meet with Salim and explain. You must tell him you are different, not exactly a man, not yet, not in the truest sense of the word. You are still finding out who you are, who God has made you to be, to become. That maybe it does not need to bring shame on his family if he knows this about you. Maybe Farah is still pure, only seeing other women. You are willing to call yourself a woman again, if only it will make things right for Farah, for Salim, for all of you. Without your friend T to back you up, you feel unstable, emotional. You are certain you will cry.

You try to stay calm when you talk to Salim, but you blurt out, "I've ruined everything."

He holds up his hand. "One moment, Mister Dani." The lines of his face are deeply creased. You think the words: *He knows*.

Noora emerges from a slit in the curtain and Salim asks her for tea to accompany your conversation. The two of you sit cross-legged in the silence and wait for what feels like an hour. You attempt to formulate the words that you will say but your head is a swarm of locusts.

Noora brings two tiny glass cups on a tray. The tea is black and steaming and sweet and it burns your mouth but you drink it anyway, welcoming the pain.

Finally Salim drains his cup. "Tell me who you have harmed."

"Farah." You shake your head to release the insects. "Dishonored her."

"You have touched my daughter?" His face is stern.

"No." You feel sweat move in a trickle down your back. The air inside the tent is still. It is stifling. You choke out the word, "Worse."

"Come, Mister Dani. I saw your return from the sea. All were happy. I have no reason to suspect insult."

You explain the incident as briefly as possible. Everything. Your temples pulse and burn. You stare at the sweep marks on the floor.

Salim is quiet for so long you wonder if he has fallen asleep. You look up and see him watching you. You understand he has been waiting. "I believe you are in pain, Mister Dani," he says. "Pain inside the body is bigger than outside pain. It is trapped."

You nod. You do not trust your voice.

"For a just man, mercy must prevail over wrath. This is what Allah decrees."

Your eyes, so tired, are crusted with sand. Your tongue swells with the anxious words you do not say. "I never meant—" You stop short, unsure what you meant or didn't mean.

"I will give my daughter time to think. I will ask her when she is ready. But I believe there is no one you have harmed today."

Words leak past your swollen tongue. "I don't *know* why God made me like this. I've never understood." If only you could speak in parable. There is so much to explain, so much to ask forgiveness for.

"You think it is *not fair* of God to make you like this." Salim spreads his hands open between the two of you. "To be fair, to find fairness, you must only desire for others what you desire for yourself. That is all. What is it you desire for yourself, Mister Dani?"

You stare at the wall of the tent. It flaps gently in the hot afternoon air; a thin line of sand rolls beneath. "To be understood." Your traitorous voice cracks like a teenager when you speak but Salim nods his head.

"Many want this." He presses his fingertips together. "Because of you, I understand that it is possible to start life one way and change to another. You were sent to teach me this. You and your bird-fish, designed in a way that only Allah, Wise Creator, can understand." He rearranges the white *djellabaya* over his knees with a deliberate tug. "Is it possible you have the same purpose, Mister Dani? That this is why you study the changing fish?"

You stare at your hands and attempt to parse the meaning from Salim's words. "You think God made me this way?"

Salim's mouth turns down and he is still for a meditative moment. "No. You are changing how God made you." He looks out of the tent flap and considers the desert beyond. "My beautiful wife has ink drawings on her face. God did not put them there, but they add to her beauty. They make her happy. It is important to be happy."

"Even when what makes you happy makes you different?"

"We are already like the fingers of a hand, Mister Dani: all are different. You are welcome here. We will not speak of this again."

The distant mountains reach unevenly toward the sky, the *teeth of the moon*. Their jagged tips glow orange, lit by the falling sun. They are the sides of the great bowl. The giant bowl that sustains us all. The fingers of one hand: *Us*.

Your eyes sting. A stupid rush of emotion that is not you, but is, is also you, rises.

Salim rests a hand on your shoulder. "Mister Dani, the weight of the burden is known only by he who carries it."

Mister Dani.

Burden-bearer.

The sun's bloody outline wobbles in the heat. Breath rises and falls beneath your ribs.

My ribs.

Me.

Salim searches my face for understanding and I hide my overflowing sentiment so as not to embarrass my good host.

COLLATERAL DAMAGE

All this time. Only one hundred miles apart.

Manny, on Route 41 in the Everglades, just past Forty Mile Bend, early September, bleary from a red-eye flight. Top down on the rental, a Jeep, roll bar whining overhead. Blacktop stretching out for miles. Like driving into a stretch of shiny swimming pool. Crushed lovebugs in a hundred black-and-gray smears on the windshield. Stale morning breeze lifting off the canal. Swamp air.

Swarming with creatures: alligator, coral snake, snapping turtle, red-tailed hawk, turkey vulture, black bear, panther, raccoon, gar. And boa constrictor. Slithering and slinking, swallowing up birds, mammals, household pets, small deer. Boas on the lam. Thank you, exotic pet fanciers. No, really, thank you so very much.

Or hurricanes and blown-over mobile homes with cracked aquariums, dead heat lamps, owners gone. *Fancy a boa?* Nothing stays in a box forever. Not memory, not life, not animals, not stuff. And wasn't there such a hell of a lot of stuff.

Parents and a twin sister never able to come together. A baby, a son. Who names a kid Martin—in 1975? *Your ex-wife, buddy, that's who.*

Always feeling so *apart* from his son. A tiny baby. Helpless and needy, but foreign, somehow, not a part of Manny at all. Frail. Little bigheaded alien son. A lifetime of guilt born right along with him. Weighty package, that. Then, with the same people raising him *and* his son, more like a bug-eyed baby brother. But Bart, his father, so much softer as a grandfather-father, unrecognizable from the stern, disapproving parent he'd been to Manny. To Rosarita.

And then, a do-over. Miraculous. Manny, at forty, a real father, finally.

Echo. Rewind. Children accruing like the military alphabet. Melody his Echo. Alpha-Martin. Bravo-Tabitha. Charlie-Reese, and now Delta-Dani, his child, too, by virtue of his sister dying. Drinking herself into oblivion. No, literally—oblivion.

But Martin had done all right, hadn't he? A geologist. Head of a research station in Dominica. Nothing shabby about that. A college boy—Manny had raised a college boy. Or not raised him—sired him, paid for his raising. Supplemented his own parents as *they* raised him, as he listened to accounts of Martin's life transmitted from halfway around the world: Little League games, Boy Scout patches, choirboy honors, whatever kids did back then in the seventies and eighties. Whatever kids raised by grandparents did.

Now Danielle—Dani—his de facto daughter. Son. Never will get used to *that* change. The big change. Dani, same age as Martin. His twin sister's dark child and he'd hardly been there for her. *Him.* He could have done so much more. Little Dani, loved to suffocation by her mother. His mother. The constant motherly narration as backdrop.

At ten: *All good little girls paint their fingernails, honey.*

At twelve: *Dani, my goodness, must you walk like John Wayne?*

At thirteen: *Would it kill you to wear a dress to church* once?

At sixteen: *Trust me, you loved those frilly things. You would twirl and twirl.*

Looking back, he sees it now. Twirling was Dani's escape, and Rosie a twirler, too, with him. Twins, they twirled together. Two as one, coltish, early. Front teeth missing. First grade? Second? Different teachers—they divided twins back then—same recess. Holding hands to spin together, faster, faster. Tandem spinning. Spinning till your hands broke apart and you staggered around, drunk with the swirl in your ears.

Years later, thinking *that was the start*. The start of Rosie's fatal love affair—the altered state, the boomerang consciousness, the Bill W struggle. The thrill of the twirl. Swings and gymnastics and the Merry-go-Round and boys and booze. Definitely a pattern. If only he'd seen it, been a better twin. An older twin.

Ridiculous. An *older* twin.

There is no parallel.

And yet. Martin and Dani. Son and niece the same age. One parent each. Would Dani's father have stayed if someone had taken the time to say, *Jack, you have a child (yes, you!)?* Would everything have been different?

Rosie only remembers having a daughter. A lesbian, but a daughter. Would she recognize her daughter now? In heaven, someday, what sex will Dani be?

He should have chaperoned his sister's debutante ball. Oh, sweet irony! She got pregnant with Dani at a *coming out* party. There's some Karma. If he had chaperoned, Rosie's whole life would have been different. No Dani, no banishment, no family rift. He should have been there for her.

One-armed Jack-in-the-Swamp and Dani. Quite a pair. Motley crew. Bringing them together was an act of genius—or foolishness, he isn't sure—but it should have happened years ago. Rosie refused.

He wonders, did she want it as she took that sip-too-many? Was her final bottle filled with truth serum? Elixir of honesty. Did she slip away thinking *Lord, what have I done?*

Hoping and driving.

Jack better have the sense to clean up. September, still beastly hot in Florida. Hopefully he's shaved, at least. Put on what passes for a clean shirt…when you live in a tent.

Top down, the wind encouraging Manny to believe in possibilities. *Cautiously optimistic.* That spineless phrase, coined by… Reagan, was it? To keep from disappointing either side. We need a catch-phrase. Let's go, fellas. CYA all the way. Something long-lived. Useful. Something a Press Secretary can throw about during a future war. *We remain cautiously optimistic that rebels will take out a weakened Saddam Hussein.* Ass hats. Fucktards. A meaningless straddle: *We, your government, want credit for having believed a good outcome was possible, but no culpability when it all goes to hell.*

Cautiously pessimistic, the better phrase. Cautiously pessimistic that Shrub will be a better president than his father was. Manny had survived Clinton's draw-down, his Don't Ask Don't Tell, Bush Senior's thousand points of light, his Read My Lips and wouldn't-be-prudent finger wagging, Reagan's Tear Down This Wall and Ollie North thrown onto his own grenade, Carter's oil embargo and sandstorm-foiled hostage rescue, Ford's post-*involvement* recession and a wacky Helsinki Accord.

Career Army, he'd served under six Commanders-in-Chief. Respected the title? Absolutely. Respected the men? Not so much.

Jack is dressed and nervous. Fidgety. A good sign, frankly. Shaven, good, good, all good. Then he calls his shaggy mutt over to the Jeep.
    —You've got to leave the dog, Jack.
    —Ripton goes where I go.
    —You want to see Dani? Or you want to take your dog on a tour of Miami?
    —He'll stay in the Jeep. I'll tie his leash to the roll bar.
    —It's a rental. And a college campus isn't safe. And a rope isn't a leash. It's a *rope.*
    —All the more reason.
    Jack lifts himself in, whistles and the dog loads up. He ties Ripton with his good hand doing the moving and his bad hand holding the rope. The mosquitoes swarm around the dog's patchy fur.
    —He's got mange?
    —Nope.
    —Fleas?
    —Nope.
    —Hope to hell he doesn't hang himself.
    —He's a smart dog.
    The dog opens his mouth and starts panting, a smiley face with its tongue stuck out.
    —What's on his tongue?
    —He's chow. Part, anyway. They've got black tongues.
    Manny watches drips of dog saliva. One, two, three. At least it's a rental. Jesus. A dog.
    —You ready?
    —As I'll ever be.

Manny doesn't speak for most of the drive. so Jack sits in silence, watching the heat rise up off the highway. After what seems like an hour, he checks the time.
    —That a pocket watch?
    —Yep. Gold.
    —I see it?

—Found it in the ribs of an old shipwreck.

Manny holds the watch with his steering hand, flips it with his free hand. His eyes track between the road and the watch.

—Still works?

—Took a while, but yeah. I'm patient. Some might say stubborn.

—You seen the inscription?

—Course I seen it. Can't read it, not in Portuguese, or whatever.

—"Tú eres mi corazón, no dejes nunca de latir."

—And?

—"You are my heart, never stop beating."

Huh. Romantic watch. Jack never figured. Seems fitting, carrying a sappy Spanish watch to meet the son he made by a Puerto Rican mother.

They enter the campus gates—each brick column nearly as big as Jack's old house in Stuart—and he stares at the manicured grounds, the grass so green it hurts his eyes, the coconut trees, each one precisely trimmed, concentric chevrons climbing the trunk. As he's taking in this Eden, this oasis of green smack in the scrub of South Florida, small sprinkler heads rise up all around them and shoot water in crisscrossing arcs across the grounds. Manny pulls into a parking space and Jack notices that the sprinkler closest to the Jeep has malfunctioned. Water is bubbling onto the sidewalk. By the semicircle of yellow grass, it appears to have been that way for a while.

—Ready?

—You keep asking that, I'm going to change my mind.

Jack pulls out a pack of Marlboros and lights one. He takes a long drag, feels the nicotine buzz spread to his extremities.

—Your dog going to be all right in the heat?

—He lives in the Everglades—in a tent. What do you think?

He blows out a long plume of smoke.

—I just don't want some animal rights activist suing me for leaving a dog in a hot car.

—In a hot *convertible*.

—Point taken.

As they walk past the malfunctioning sprinkler, Jack stoops to examine it. He puts the cigarette between his lips and his hand into the bubbling water, turns the head a quarter turn and then smacks it with the heel of his palm. The sprinkler comes to life, spraying a wide arc of water across the front of his shirt. He removes the cigarette and grins like a maniac. Manny shakes his head and they continue on. At the steps he drops the butt and steps on it. With a vacuum-sealed swish of doors they enter the Cox Science Center. Cool marble squeaks beneath their rubber soles, still wet from the sprinklers.

Jack looks up at the high ceiling. A giant, hanging mobile sways in the upper air-conditioned reaches; he lets out a low whistle of appreciation and his discount-store shoes make a scrunching sound on each step of the grand, wide, glass-and-metal staircase.

Manny locates the biology listing and runs his finger down the menu. *Dr. Dani Stackowski*. At least it doesn't say Danielle. Or worse, a leftover *Ms*. He struggled over whether to tell Jack about the whole gender thing. Leslie urged him to, but how the hell do you bring up such a thing? *By the way, there's this thing I've been meaning to tell you. You know that son I've told you about? Well, he used to be a girl. But don't worry, he's packing now.* Not that Manny knows for sure, although there does seem to be a bulge. He tries not to look, doesn't want to ask. Like seeing a breastfeeding mother out in public, first there's the automatic double take that you try to turn into a casual sweeping glance at the last minute, followed by the overly self-conscious refusal to look by becoming intensely interested in something off-stage, something that is definitely not a breastfeeding mom, a dwarf, a cripple, or a transgendered individual.

Jack touches the name on the board, too.

—Hadn't thought about that. Just assumed.

—Assumed Rosie knew your last name? Or assumed she'd give you credit?

—Deringer.

—Say again?

—My last name. Back then. I go by Dell now. Deringer was a spiteful old man's last name, a weak woman's assumed last name, a pistol I couldn't carry around one day more.

—You go by *Jack Dell*.

—Yup.

—Sounds like a nursery rhyme. Dani Dell's not so hot, either.

—No, I don't suppose it is.

It was a relief to be blunt. To be matter-of-fact. Leslie always wanted to *discuss*. Wanted to drive every subject to its knees with *talk*. Since retiring from the military, the only male left in the household, he'd been overwhelmed by words. And, *damn*, he'd forgotten to call Leslie and tell her he landed safely. He checks his cell phone. No bars. She's a worrier. Ever since the tsunami, being stranded like that, she'd been a lot clingier whenever either one of them traveled. *Call me when you get there. Don't forget to check in this time. Give me a second number where I can reach you.*

Leslie supports this father-child reconciliation mission of his—more or less. She'd never searched for her own birth mother. And there had always been a whiff of jealousy over the time he spent with Rosie, or maybe it was the time spent with Dani. He didn't ask for clarification. She was definitely jealous of Martin, at least in the early days of the marriage. The precise wellspring of her jealousy was never clear, but she would sigh loudly when he told her he'd written another check to Rosie, or wonder aloud why he made so much effort to stop and see Rosie and Danielle on his travels, while his own daughter sat at home.

He'd asked Leslie if she didn't wanted to find her birth mother. "Sure," she said, a little too casually. "But she'd come find me if she wanted me to know who she was. I wouldn't want to force myself on anyone. She made her choice. I'm sure she had her reasons." He suspected it wasn't as matter-of-fact as all that, but refrained from any platitudes about how time changes people. The circumstance of her birth was her personal demon to wrestle. He had his own.

And yet here he is, pushing two other people to confront their histories. Spending more time reaching out to his sister's kid, even though Rosie was gone and the "kid" was thirty-two years old.

People assumed that losing a twin was a terrible blow. In some ways it was, but they'd been fraternal twins, no more alike than any other brother and sister except for being the same age. No, it was his father's death in May that had been the bigger blow. Not because he didn't see it coming, he did. And not because they were close. They weren't, not particularly. It was a blow because his dad's dying took away the last line of defense against his own death. As long as he still had a father alive in the world, he had someone between him and the grave. He was still somebody's kid. And that somebody kept him from stepping into the gigantic shoes of The Family Patriarch. It caught him by surprise that a person could be fifty years old and still feel *orphaned*.

Manny knocks on the frame of Dani's office door and then looks around it and inside.

Tio Manny first suggested a meeting back in February, after Grandpa Bart's funeral, when family was in the forefront of his mind. September had seemed a long way off and Dani said yes then, thinking he would have time to adjust to the idea. Except here the day is, and here he hasn't. How does one suddenly just *have a father* after not having one for thirty-two years? How is that change made? Where is the manual for that?

Bart had been the closest thing to a father Dani had, and still he'd only visited his grandparents in Puerto Rico during the years of graduate school.

Everyone seemed to want this reunion more than he did. Carlita pushed him, saying it would help him understand his past, get in touch with the masculine side of his heritage. Tio Manny pushed for it, probably because he was tired of feeling responsible. And Aunt Leslie, too, for who knows what maudlin reason. Even Martin, who turned out to be a surprising advocate and an awesome cousin once they got to spend a little time together, said he should do it. Martin joked that since he was three weeks older, Dani had to take his advice.

Still, there was something decidedly *off* about sitting and waiting for them to arrive. What *should* he call him? Papá Jack? He stands and paces his office, such as it is. There's only a small space for a chair on the other side of the desk, and behind the desk are stacks of peer-reviewed journals, a box of dive weights, a knee-high pile of final papers from last semester that he had read, graded, and forgotten to return the last day of class. Even now, the odd student would pop in and ask for last semester's hard copy and he'd have to shuffle through them. It wasn't like him to be so disorganized, but the funeral for his grandfather came suddenly, during finals week. He'd had to pay a substitute to administer the exam.

There's a knock and suddenly, the two men are standing outside his office door.

—Come in, come in.

He says this before he remembers that the space is barely big enough for him. The three of them stand awkwardly, shoulder to shoulder.

—Go out, go out!

He hopes for a lighthearted tone, but his voice cracks like a fourteen-year-old boy and he feels his face flush as they move into the hallway. At least their backs are to him for a moment and he can make a quick assessment. Jack is a good three to four inches taller than him. He's got long wavy hair, brown with thick gray streaks, tied back in a ponytail and there's a ring of grime at the collar of his Red Cross blood donor t-shirt. His right sleeve hangs funny, hovering just above some indistinguishable tattoo, cut through by a long white scar. His jeans are faded with a hole at the corner of the back pocket where a wallet has rubbed. He smells like an ashtray. He looks shaky and younger than expected and when he turns, his face is leathery tan, creased with a starburst of white squint lines at the outside corner of each eye.

—Danny. Good God. I'm looking in a mirror.

Dani doesn't think he's looking in a mirror at all. He doesn't see himself in the older man's face, and is disturbed that Jack does. He holds out a hand and they shake. Jack's grip is strong, forced. His smile doesn't travel past his teeth and his lips give a slight tremble. Dani grips harder; there's a crunching sensation as the bones in the older man's hand shift under the pressure of his grip. He winces, shakes his hand when Dani lets go.

—I can answer any questions you have.

—Same here.

Jack turns to Manny, who tilts his head slightly and shrugs.

—My mother never talked about you. When I agreed to Tio's suggestion that we meet, I didn't think beyond that. I didn't want to have expectations.

Although he does wonder now how much Jack knows about the gender reassignment. He must know. Did Tio Manny tell him? He would have liked to have been a fly on the wall for that conversation.

—Expectations.

—Expectations that might not bear out. This isn't a Disney movie.

—Good thing.

—Are you married?

—No. And I should probably get this right out in the open: I sold my house six months back and I live in a tent in the Everglades.

—Right. The treasure ship. I read about that in the paper. And that was you. Go figure.

—Settlement is in the courts right now. They're hashing out my share. I expect to come into some money soon. That could be your inheritance. Although the lawyers will get the biggest payout. Ain't that ironic?

Inheritance. This scruffy man offering up the potential spoils of some ill-gotten gains. *That's* ironic.

—That gold was probably slated to fund a military conquest for Spain centuries ago. Paying for modern litigation must be slightly better than paying for ancient blood.

Manny coughs into his hand and leans into the conversation.

—Is there a coffee shop nearby?

—I don't drink coffee, says Jack.

—The student center is a few blocks away. We can walk, if you don't mind.

—Ripton, says Jack, his hands shaking.

The two men exchange a glance and Manny seems to understand the one-word objection.

—There's a faculty lounge down the hall. I can't vouch for the coffee, but the chairs are soft.

My son ushers us into the lounge. We pick seats that form the points of a triangle. The dark, burning smell of coffee fills the room. My hands start to shake and my gut clenches. He doesn't say anything so I do.

—Tell me about your mother.

I'm not even sure I want to hear about his mother. It just seems like the right thing to say.

—She was a beautiful person. She loved me. She accepted me. What else is there? You knew her.

—Thirty-two years ago I spent one evening with her. Why do you think she never told me?

His eyes turn hard and I understand I've said the wrong thing. But what the hell is the *right* thing? What am I even doing here? How can someone make amends for thirty-two years of silence?

—You didn't have to come. My life is fine the way it is.

—I thought you wanted me to come.

—Me? I thought you wanted it.

We both turn and stare at Manny.

—Someone tell me how this is a bad thing, Manny says. *You* (pointing at Dani), now you know where you've come from. And *you* (pointing at me), now you know you have a son. Where's the harm?

—The harm is all the years my mother worked two jobs to put food on the table, got up nights when I was sick, worried all alone—

—She didn't tell me. How could I know? She made that choice. She could have put you up for adoption.

—What choice? The choice to have sex with you? She was seventeen. Her parents kicked her out of the house. She never got to go home again.

—I was eighteen. My father was an asshole. I didn't know. We were just a couple of stupid kids.

—And she paid the price.

—Look at you. Smart, successful. You're not anybody's *price*. You're the best thing I've ever done.

—I'm not something you've *done*, for Christ's sake. You can't take credit now. The hard work's already been done—by others. Me, my mother, Tio. You can't bask in the glory of a five-minute sperm donation.

Silence.

—I don't know what you want from me.

He looks into his Styrofoam coffee cup, swirls it around, and studies the whirl of liquid. The hot black smell fills up my brain and the walls close in.

—I want what I've always had—nothing.

Manny watches Jack's back all the way to the door of the science building. He's even more agitated than he had been when he was waiting in the Everglades. They step outside. He lights up a cigarette, sits on the step.

—He's a twink, isn't he? That's what nobody's telling me. I've been trying to name the eggshells everyone's walking on and it's that I've got a queer for a son. I knew right away there was something off. Him saying his mother was *accepting*. I should have gotten it then, but I'm slow.

—He's got a live-in girlfriend, Jack, not that it should matter. He's your son.

—Still, he's not a man like you or me, is he? He's different. I can tell he's different.

Manny sighs.

—I guess.

—I could tell first thing.

Jack looks toward the parking lot. He lasers in on the Jeep.

—Ripton's sleeping?

—That, or he's hung himself.

Jack glares and spits on the sidewalk. He walks faster and blasts a short, sharp whistle that goes up at the end like a question.

—What? It's a joke. He's down in the floorboard where it's cooler. I'll bet you.

Except he isn't. The rope dangles loosely from the roll bar, still tied firmly at the upper end. The bottom curls like a squash tendril looking for support. Jack lifts it and lays it across his palm. He swallows hard and stares at the frayed end of rope.

—Ripton?

—We'll drive around. We'll look for him, Jack.

—Ripton!

—We'll find him.

—Rip-Ton!

They drive around for two hours, then eat dinner at a drive-up barbeque joint and drive around some more, Jack calling out, insisting Manny pull over every few blocks so he can question the homeless, the bag ladies, the prostitutes. But the dog is gone, Absent Without Leave. Or captured, Missing In Action. No one knows anything. No one has seen him.

Finally they stop at an underpass and Jack gets out. He sits on the sloping cement and the vehicles *whump-whump* overhead. He puts his forehead on his knees and slides the coil of rope over and over through his hands. Then he carefully places the rope on the ground, adjusting the circle just so. When it is perfectly round, he whistles one more time, then brings his hands to his face and cries like a baby for the dog he has lost, for the son he has not gained.

WHO OWNS THE MOON?

Leslie wraps the last doll in tissue paper and stacks it like cordwood atop the others in the box.

"Be careful with Scarlett. She's my best girl," Andrea instructs from her new gold, brocaded loveseat, recently shipped to the house for only forty dollars, an exclusive perk for valued QVC Gold Club members.

Leslie answers her mother with the screeching rip of packing tape unfurled across the top of the box.

Each turned-under foot of her mother's loveseat sits in a small square coaster intended to save her beige carpet from unsightly indentations. Each coaster holds a layer of dust even though the seat is new. How can that be? Her mother cares about the surfaces of things, only. She sets doilies under every vase, insulated pads under the dining room tablecloth, decorative drink coasters on every flat surface. She doesn't seem to see the other intruders, the pink slime at the bottom of the shower curtain, the dark ring inside her coffee cup, the hair-strewn tiles surrounding the foot of the toilet, the furniture coasters filled with dust.

Andrea continues, undeterred. "Scarlett was one hundred and fifty dollars plus shipping. I was the last one to get a signed birth certificate from the doll maker, number two hundred and seventy-five. She is hand painted and lovingly crafted."

Frankly, thinks Leslie, *I don't give a damn*. But she labels the box "Mother's Dolls" and adds it carefully to the growing pile of boxes that will travel with Andrea to her new apartment in Newhaven Woods, a retirement community with continuing care. Andrea believes they paid for the larger condominium, though they didn't, only the apartment, which was still a pretty penny, and she anticipates more space than she'll actually have. The move is two months off, and her condition could easily deteriorate before then, in which case she wouldn't remember what she packed or most of the things she's ever owned.

This is when a sibling would really come in handy. Being the sole decision maker in regards to her mother's failing faculties sucks the life out of Leslie's weekends. She arrived last Sunday to find her mother energetically unpacking everything they had packed the weekend before, muttering about where she was ever going to put all the junk. This week, Leslie plans to hide the boxes in the basement before she leaves.

"You talked just like Scarlett when you were little," continues Andrea. "My favorite was when we would climb into the hot car in the summer and you would fan yourself and declare, 'I need some ay-uh.' Do...your girls ever talk like that?"

Leslie tries not focus on the fact that her mother can remember the names and "birth dates" for each of her two-hundred-dollar dolls, but her three granddaughters' names elude her. At least she remembers they're girls. That's something. Two weeks before, on their regular Sunday visit, Melody was first to enter the house, hoping to surprise her grandmother. Unfortunately, Andrea was napping on the couch and instead of a hug Melody was met with a hard, suspicious stare followed by screaming.

"Get out! You get out of my house!" This is what Leslie heard streaming from the living room, even after poor Pea had reemerged shaking, with tears pooling and wobbling at her bottom lids.

Andrea had never been what one would call *warm*, but for most of her life she seemed to understand that she was expected to at least fake it.

Reminder, Note to Self #47: *Mom doesn't fake it anymore.* (Revised to add, sub-article F: *Be sure to enter the house first, just in case she's got her crazy-face on.*)

Leslie was so damn tired of revising. Tired of evaluating and revisiting each of her mother's failings as her faculties either slid away—fading (*despair...?*), resurging (*hope!*), fading (*despair!*), resurging (*hope...?*)—or dropped out of sight, right off the edge of the cliff and disappeared, never to return. Here's an example of the infuriatingly selective nature of her mother's illness: Andrea could cut her food fine with a knife and a fork, but give her *only* a fork, and she was helpless. She had no memory of turning a fork to the side to cut her food with the edge of the tines, and once gone, that knowledge never resurfaced. Where had that simple self-instruction to *turn the instrument* gone, when the entire knife had stayed put? Her mother's brain, always a mystery, had lately become a maze that she laboriously worked her way through (the convoluted, ever-narrowing tunnels, the false leads, the dead ends) only to find that what should have been the open end and freedom, was instead a giant, neon question mark, buzzing and spitting its light through a dense fog.

Of course, her mother had spent most of her life being deliberately vague, living in fear of being pinned down, inventing impenetrable and conflicting stories to back up whichever bizarre punishment or restriction-du-jour she managed to convince herself to enact in the guise of ensuring *Leslie's proper upbringing.*

By the time Leslie turned sixteen, her bullshit meter had become a finely tuned instrument—at roughly the same time that the needle on her tolerance meter got stuck deep in the red zone. This coincided, unfortunately, with her mother's sudden irritating stock rebuttal for everything from a grounding to refusing to buy her new jeans: "You should be grateful you *have* a mother." Followed by reminding her (for the thousandth time!) that Andrea had lost her own mother when she was only four (to some event, dark and sinisterly mysterious but never explained).

Later, when Leslie was in her twenties and her mother told her about the adoption (smiling, no preamble, no hesitation), her mother's *you should be grateful* refrain took on an even more incendiary tone in Leslie's memory. It became an ember that smoldered and burnt deep into the core of her heart.

"We're all done with the dolls, Mom. I think I'll do the papers in the roll top desk next, all right?"

"Psh, papers," says her mother and turns up the volume on the television, a show in which a man talks to the dead on behalf of the living. Leslie tries not to listen. That show makes her think of her father *and* it makes her cry, right along with the onscreen loved one, as if she'd known the deceased and couldn't believe the miracle of hearing from

him or her again. Watching that show makes her feel like the Cowardly
Lion desperately clutching the end of his tail, eyes closed, incanting,
"*IdobelieveIdobelieveIdobelieve.*"

The desk is a mess, each cubbyhole stuffed with papers, letters, bill
stubs, receipts. Surely none of this needs keeping. She pulls the trashcan
closer and glances at her mother who stares, heavy-lidded and droopy
at the television screen. Leslie pulls out a stack of papers and fans them
like a deck of cards then drops them into the trash. And another. The
third stack includes a business-sized envelope, postmarked 1982, with
handwriting that she recognizes: her grandfather's. She slides it out of
the stack and drops the rest into the rubbish can. The envelope is
addressed to her. Somehow her mother had gotten hold of one of the
many letters Leslie traded back and forth with Grandpa Rolando, her
father's father. She folds the letter and stuffs it into her pocket, then
pulls it back out and decides to reread it, all these years later.

May 30th, 1982

My Dearest Leslie,
Thank you for the birthday card. Your paper doll sailor is very creative.
I stood it up on my buffet, wearing the dress white uniform, always my
favorite. Did your father help you? Even the ribbons and insignia are
correct—I confess, old salt that I am, I pulled out my magnifying glass
to check.

But honestly, dear child, I cannot believe that you are 16! Driving
your mother's Pinto back and forth to your first real job. What an
adventure! I do hope the *residents* (as you have taught me to call them) in
the nursing home are good to you. We oldsters can be a cranky lot.

I loved your story about holding the hands of the old men in order
to keep their wandering hands still. And about the morning you made
87 pancakes. I hope Beulah the Cook appreciates you.

Most of all, I cannot believe that I am 82. It is an age I never imagined
I would reach. And yet here I am—lucky enough to have a granddaughter
who still writes to me and sends me handmade presents. This old man
is very grateful.

Can you believe we have a president who is nearly my age? I do
admit to liking that. He carries himself well, this former movie star,

born the same year I turned eleven. Your great grandmother Miranda called me her century baby—always as old as the year. How the 20th century must have seemed like a miracle to her, a time so full of promise and modernity. This is how the year 2000 seems to me now, shimmering off on the horizon.

Whatever will we call it? Double O? O-Naught? The Year Zero? I mean you, of course. Whatever will *you* call it. I cannot imagine I will see that year, but I'm quite sure your father already has clever plans for New Year's Eve 1999.

Did I ever tell you that Quinn was your father's middle name? An old family surname that he adopted in honor of your grandmother's favorite actor, Anthony Quinn. He changed it officially just before you came to them. I struggled with the change, but not Sarah. She always loved the theater. I miss going with her. Have you seen *On Golden Pond*, yet? If not, save yourself and we will go together when you visit. I think that you would like it.

At the very least, my delightful sunny granddaughter, *you* will surely see the 21st century. I take comfort knowing that. And if you study hard in school, you can be the first female Baxter to graduate college. Wouldn't that be something? Becoming a marine biologist is NOT too high a dream—I don't like it when you write that. *You* must believe in your dreams in order for them to come true.

Do you know the name Sylvia Earle? A female aquanaut—the first!— she even set a world record for deep diving. You can achieve great things like that. Never doubt it.

Remember, I know better than most what you are capable of. You have been my reliable co-captain aboard the Sea-Ray many times. I cherish those Sundays with you, out in the Bay, tooling around, eating our tuna-salad sandwiches together. Sometimes you remind me so of Sarah, her sparkly eyes, her tossing laughter, her sun-kissed nose after a day on the boat.

At any rate, it's not too soon to start thinking about colleges. William and Mary has a very strong Marine Biology program, and so does Old Dominion. You could live with me if you came to Norfolk. It would give me a reason to *keep things up*. Think about it at least. Your father would be happy to know you are being kept close watch over. You would think he had never lived a day without you.

And don't worry about the recent fight with your mother. I believe she's having a hard time accepting you as a young woman. It sounds like you handled it in a very grown up way. These things have a way of blowing over. Your mother has always been a prickly sort—it only follows that she would be a prickly parent, too. (DO NOT tell her I said that! I don't want Andrea's prickles turned on me.)

...I sat here (I'm at the old kitchen table as I write this) and stared off into space for the longest time after writing that last line. Of course, you can't see that in a letter that reads straight through, but I was thinking about grown-ups and their younger selves. At sixteen, you are already so grown up. I was that way, too, when I was even younger than you. I think of 1911 as the year I stopped being a child. That was the same year Orville Wright made a nine-minute flight in his aeroplane and gave us all big dreams.

I know 11 seems awfully young from your wise 16-year-old perspective, but kids worked harder then than they do now. Boys drove tractors and tilled the field. Girls picked cotton and cooked meals. They helped support the family. The Great War began three years after I turned eleven, and three years after that I was aboard the mighty USS Jacob Jones (proud Destroyer), steaming toward the Western Front.

In 1911, women marched for the right to vote, temperance was the big issue of the day, and the spongers of Key West were under attack. I don't think I've ever told you about our little war in The Keys. You weren't old enough to tell this story to before. But I believe other people's stories can help us understand ourselves—that's why your grandmother loved the movies—so maybe it's time.

By the time I was 11, I'd been sponging for my father and his boss, Mr. Gundt, for a year already, sculling and hooking both. We used a rake and a glass bottom bucket to harvest the sponges. Through that bucket I saw underwater plants waving back and forth and fish floating on leisurely strolls between them. It was a dream world.

Until the Greeks sailed into our waters and took over. They brought newfangled air suits with heavy boots. They walked across the sea floor cutting sponge after sponge like harvesting cabbages. I told my father I wanted to tie a knot in one of their fat hoses, but truthfully I longed to walk below the surface, too, breathing underwater like a fish, inhabiting that world for as long as I could. You will do this someday, my little SCUBA-doo.

Anyway, sponging was a good living back then—one worth fighting for—and I overheard my father and Mr. Gundt plotting to make the Greek spongers pay for stealing from our waters. *It's got to be done*, they said. *An eye for an eye and a tooth for a tooth.*

To this day, I don't believe it was prejudice. Our family tree has many branches. My father's father-in-law—your great-great grandfather—was a businessman with a large cigar factory in Key West and his wife was a society lady from Cuba. She taught Mami (the name my mother insisted I call her) to carry an umbrella to keep her half-Cuban skin fair. Mami complained when we toiled and browned in the sun. My father would counter that it was a good enough job when it was buying her fancy dresses. Miranda was her name, but he called her Mira, the same word she used with me to point out a thing of note: *Mira*, Rolando. *Look.*

My mother's voice was like soft water rolling against the side of a boat.

We filled the dinghy with sponges—some as big around as my head— then laid them out on deck to dry in the sun. Cook watched the boat. He was Cuban, too, and lived in a shack by the water with a wife and seven kids, all skinny and brown. The child that was my age had a misshapen head and could not talk.

The odor of rotting sponges has stayed with me for years, its own sort of memory, attached to the memory of what came later. Such a singular smell. I found an echo of it, six years later, aboard the German U-Boat that picked me up in the waters off the coast of France, after our beloved ship was torpedoed. She sank in eight minutes—eight minutes!—her own depth charges exploding and killing men even as she sank. A Destroyer to the last. Oh, how I wanted to hate the miserable Kraut who rescued us. *Kapitänleutnant Rose.* But he radioed coordinates to our American base so they could retrieve the 66 sailors who survived. The last gentleman's war.

You probably know this already, smart girl that you are, but sponges are animals, not plants, and the part used for cleaning is the skeleton, so we were removing the *rotten meat* from the *bones.* I tied a cloth over my nose to help with the stench. My father said it was the smell of money.

We moved the dried-up sponges to a floating kraal and soaked them to soften the skins. We beat them with wide, flat paddles. Father called it *batting practice*. We beat them until the sand and slimy skin fell off. We beat the stink out of them.

Short Key was our favorite soak spot and Mr. Gundt piloted us there. Once the island was in sight, he let loose a string of curses. A big boat flying a Greek flag was there already and my father pushed me toward the hatchway. I resisted. *I know about the Greeks*, I said, and both men looked at me. *They cheat. They steal our sponges.*

Mr. Gundt's belly was hard and heavy. It hung over his belt. He liked to scratch it with both hands when he was thinking. Father stared long and hard. I tried not to fidget and to look him in the eye. He turned to Mr. Gundt. *I wouldn't send him on his own, Carl*, he said. *The boy would come with me.*

You'd have to swim a long way, Roland, he said. *In the dark.*

I stood as tall as I could and said *yes sir.*

Cook served beans and turtle eggs for supper. Turtle eggs were my favorite but I could only stomach a few. When my father gave me a hard look, I forced another mouthful in. Cook slapped my back. Atta boy, he said, sounding jolly. I prayed I wouldn't throw it up later.

After dinner, we retired to our bunks. Father checked his pocket watch every few minutes. My father's father, your other great-great grandfather (are you keeping all this straight?), settled the Keys as a salvager. He had a giant warehouse for goods that he rescued from wrecked ships. People bought whatever he saved, sometimes even the captains of the wrecked boats, hoping to salvage some of what they'd carried across the ocean.

I wondered if my father was lying in his bunk thinking about his father, too. It seemed like he might be. Granddaddy died on the water at night, taking his boat through a storm on a salvage run. Many a Conch called him *privateer*, or even *pirate*, but he didn't *make* the ships wreck, he just salvaged the goods that would have gone into the sea, anyway. These days I suppose they would call it *recycling*.

Anyway, when it was time, I took off my shoes and shirt and went topside. My father and I climbed into the dinghy and pushed away. There was no wind. The waves were small. A little piece of moon sank toward the horizon. My father handed me an oar and we skulled around Short Key till we saw a boat-shaped hole in the blue-black sky. I remember staring into the water expecting a sea monster to emerge and swallow us up in one enormous gulp. Tiny sparkles lit the surface. My father's oar shoved a jellyfish back toward me and it glowed several colors before pulsing off into deeper water.

The slap of our oars was the only noise. A slew of stars hung in the sky and there were no lights on the Greek ship at all.

We climbed out and pulled the dinghy onto the sand. We moved into deeper water holding the grappling hook together. Suddenly I didn't care if the Greeks took all the sponges there ever were. Did we *own* the sponges just because we picked them? Because they grew near where we lived? We hadn't planted them any more than we planted the moon up in the sky. Maybe the sponges belonged to everybody, too. I kept thinking and following my father until the sand bank slipped away beneath us. My throat closed up and I could barely breathe. I knew more than anything that I did not want to die.

We swam to the hull. Rough-edged barnacles cut into my palm. Below the barnacles, the boat was slimy with algae and the water slapped against us. My father pulled his arm back and stove in the hull with the sharp end of the spike making a sound like a rifle crack. Men started shouting from the other side. Feet were running, I saw lantern-light come toward us from behind the hole. We swam away. A shot was fired. We swam faster.

Back at the boat, I leaned over the side and heaved. Father rested a hand on my back and said I'd done a good job. I went to my bunk and lay down. When I awoke, we were anchored at Dove Key, a barren island of gray rocks crowned by white drips from thousands of bird droppings. Mr. Gundt dropped the kraal into the water and secured it to the side of the boat. We threw the sponges overboard, then poured seawater across the deck. I got the brush and scrubbed away the slime. Father called me Swabbie. It felt good to have a purpose.

Cook made conch salad with key limes and garlic—a prized dish I now know as *ceviche*, but to young me, it was a slimy, sour mess. After lunch, we brought out the paddles, climbed overboard, and began to beat the sponges clean. I squeezed them, watching the water run brown, then yellow, then clear. The sun was low when Mr. Gundt whistled. *Heads up!*

There must have been ten Greeks on the deck of that ship, all staring in our direction. With Cook and me, we were four.

The Greeks came close and shook their fists. They yelled. Father and Cook and Mr. Gundt yelled and shook their fists, too.

We kept watch all night. In the morning there was nothing left of the kraal but a loop of dangling rope. The Greeks floated everything away without us even knowing. They hadn't hurt the boat, but had hurt us another way. Father was furious. We set about hatching a plan to get the sponges back and cripple the Greek boat. No one shooed me away. Mr. Gundt scratched his belly. It's got to be something big, he said. And we've got to get our sponges back. He seemed to be adding numbers in his head.

Fire, said my father, his jaw set in a hard line.

The rest of that day we made bottles filled with lamp oil, a pinch of gunpowder, and an oil-soaked rag stuffed into the top. We used three of Cook's spice bottles and two liquor bottles. To this day, the smell of cinnamon reminds me of gunpowder and guilt. We put the loaded bottles in the bottom of the dinghy and coiled rope around them to keep them upright. As the afternoon shadows grew longer, I grew more and more nervous. Firebombs could kill. I understood that. Still, I told myself, the Greeks had taken our hard work. We had to send a message. No one wanted to *kill* anyone.

When the sun went down, we put lampblack on our faces. The shadow that crossed Cook's face told me he didn't approve. He was glad to stay back with the boat. The darkness deepened and we climbed into the dinghy and set off. We rowed for what felt like an hour.

We tied off to a stand of mangroves at the edge of East Key and hiked across the middle of the island. The sky was pitch black and a thousand mosquitoes thought I was dinner. They swarmed my head and flew into my ears. They flew at my eyes and into my mouth. I thought I would go crazy from the buzzing and biting. There were prickly and sharp plants everywhere. I wondered why the mosquitoes didn't just drink the blood that was already dripping down my arms and legs. Father gave me his bandana to tie over my ears. The mosquitoes bit through the cloth.

Finally the mangroves opened back out onto ocean, and there was the outline of the Greek ship against the stars. Her sails were folded but their whiteness stood out. There looked to be three men on deck. One at each end and one portside, facing the ocean with his back to us. They hadn't bothered to post a lookout toward the island.

Mr. Gundt held two bombs, my father two, and I held one. We lit them all, then threw them as hard as we could. My arm was strong from fishing and sponging and my bottle made it onto the ship, of that I'm sure. In all the confusion, though, it was impossible to tell whose bottle landed where. One hit the mast and shattered high. Burning oil sprayed all over. One landed squarely on deck and burst into flames, one hit the side of the ship and failed to break, and one went into the sea.

The fifth bottle landed at the feet of a Greek sailor and caught him on fire. He screamed and ran around the deck while two other men chased him and tried to beat out the fire. It rose up his legs. He yelped like a wounded dog. Finally he jumped over the side, or maybe fell. Come on, my father said, and we took off. There was the crack of a rifle. Mr. Gundt groaned and fell down. My father helped him up and we kept running. At the shoreline, we grabbed the boat and scrambled in.

Mr. Gundt pressed a hand to his shoulder and moaned in pain.

Somebody was burning, I said. They had certainly seen it, too.

He jumped in the water, Father said.

His crewmates will rescue him, added Mr. Gundt. *He'll be all right.*

We returned to the ship and Father cleaned Mr. Gundt's shoulder wound in silence. I washed off the scratches and mosquito blood and put my shirt back on, my thoughts turning the night's activities over in my mind.

Cook never asked how our raid had gone, but he banged pots and pans in the galley long after he would normally have stopped for the night. The banging made me feel a strange deep exhaustion—the sort of soul exhaustion that I have only re-encountered lately, in my older years.

I avoided my bunk and instead lay on deck for a long time, listening to the banging, but I didn't fall asleep. I thought about my father saying, *an eye for an eye,* but the only picture I could make from that was a whole roomful of people, all blind. As I lay there, that little piece of moon burned on the horizon and fell out of sight. And every time I closed my eyes, I saw a man on fire.

So, my dear, why have I told you all this? I have read over it myself just now, and find I cannot say why. Perhaps to offer a parable that tells you to follow your heart. Perhaps to show that mistakes can haunt us but they don't need to define us. Perhaps only for me, and I will not even send this after all.

In any event, I am suddenly exhausted, dear girl. I will sign off now, but do remember that you can accomplish whatever you set your mind to, and please consider my offer of accommodations. My door is always open to you.

Love Always,
Grandpa Rolando

Leslie looks to the loveseat where her mother has toppled over to one side, sound asleep, head resting on the plush arm. Had she read this letter? She must have. Someone had opened it. Leslie had never seen it before, she's sure of that. She would have remembered the story of the boat and the fire and her poor grandfather at eleven years old learning the hard facts of life.

Her grandfather—as a boy even younger than Melody is now. How could he have ever been a boy? Or her mother a little girl? Leslie had come into the world never knowing life without them, even though they existed before her, had lived whole lives before she was ever born. Even though they did not share blood.

And why had her mother not given her this letter? She kept it for twenty-six years. Why? Was it the one sentence about *when you came to them* that she'd wanted to censor? That hardly spelled out an adoption. At sixteen, Leslie would not have even questioned that her grandfather simply meant *home from the hospital.*

Was it because he said his daughter-in-law was *a prickly sort?* Had that angered Andrea? If so, why not throw the letter away?

Was it the graphic story with the fate of the Greek sailor unknown? Had she tried to shelter Leslie from the violence? Or protect Rolando from his guilt? Had Andrea ever protected *anyone?*

She looks again at her mother, her blue-veined eyelids twitching and jerking in sleep as if watching a bird fly across the backs of her retinas. What did Andrea see when she closed her eyes? Did her own indelible movies play there? Were those regrets that flew across her subconscious eyelids? Or pleasures? And what would happen as the deterioration of her brain progressed? What would her mother see when she closed her eyes a year from now? Two? Five? Would there be some solace available in unconsciousness? And what, at the end of a life, would be the greater solace? Memory? Or the blank page?

Leslie folds the letter and closes her eyes. She tries to imagine.

VIEWING MEDUSA

Josie's passions were strange to me.

She studied jellyfish: the stinging, tentacled, shadowy things that drift through the deepest oceans and sometimes wash ashore, resting flat and flaccid on the sand, ready to sting the unsuspecting beach-walker. Deadly box jellies, specifically. Phylum Cnidaria, Class Cubozoa. Although, as she'd tell you, Josie's happy to study any stinging thing that lives its life in the water: jellyfish, anemones, hydroids, fire coral. All related organisms, all painful, all part of Josie's world.

My mother was a tropical marine biologist and my childhood memories reliably included one reef or another: the impossible vastness and variety of the Great Barrier Reef; the lush purple and magenta giant clams in the Red Sea; the overpopulated and dying Florida Keys; the mysterious tank-and-big-gun-mount-strewn Marshallese beaches; and the shark-rich Caribbean islands with their flat, dry, limestone bases, or lush rainforest topographies. I have stepped in the waters of every warm sea, learned to swim before I could walk, and seen my mother disappear beneath the waves more times than I can count.

So Josie's work was not what I found strange, but rather her fondness for her subject. From my earliest childhood, I had learned to fear *Chironex fleckeri*, also called box jelly, fire medusa, sea wasp, or indringa, according to the local nomenclature. In Australia's waters my mother protected my sister and me by covering our arms and legs with pantyhose worn beneath our swimsuits. Reese was two years younger and hated the hose, but I was glad of the protection, having witnessed a lifeguard's vain attempt to save a man who foamed at the mouth, arched his back and popped off the sand like a jumping bean, gurgling in a way that was horrible to hear.

The summer I met Josie, she was a field-biologist, approaching thirty, still idealistic, except also bitter, if you can imagine two such traits existing side-by-side. You could have asked her what she was like, and she'd have told you; her answer would have been accurate, too, since she couldn't escape the need to be analytical and objective, even when it was her self being put under the glass.

"I'm a mass of contradictions," she'd say, calling me *Tabby*, even though I had never gone by anything but Tabitha. "I like fast food French fries and boiled ground provisions. I eat to feel happy and smoke to feel alive. I drink and dive, with no local recompression chamber. And you wouldn't think it—from looking at squalorous me— but I'm independently wealthy, with a fat inheritance from my conservative, dead, Irish Catholic father. I send money to the IRA in his honor. Oh, and I'm also a committed communist who beds down with a black man."

My stepbrother Martin, older by fifteen years, held the position of field station director at the Rainforest and Reef Preserve in Dominica the summer I met Josie. The RRP was open year-round to visiting scientists, feeding and sheltering those who desired to conduct on-island field research. Dominica was a diverse island, with several 5,000-foot volcanic peaks, a boiling lake, and a tropical rainforest in its interior. It had fringing coral reefs in both Atlantic and Caribbean waters. As such, one could find many topics discussed by the scientists seated around the dinner tables: black band coral disease and bleaching; the feasibility of long-term ecotourism for Dominica; long-line fishing and its benefits to fishermen versus its detriments to the ocean; the effect of the herbicide paraquat on the nesting habits of endangered Sisserou parrots; the ethics of collecting indigenous rainforest orchids for greenhouse cultivation; declining iguana populations and the dangers of habitat encroachment for the great boa; and always the geology of volcanic islands and plate tectonics, Martin's fascination.

I had just been accepted to Duke University and planned to attend in the fall with Jane-Goodall-stars in my eyes, to study primate behavior.

Martin paid my airfare to Dominica in exchange for a summer's worth of work around the station. I planned to list it as a *field assistant internship* on my scientific resume. I had always known I wanted to be a scientist.

The box jellies were what attracted Josie to Dominica. They were rare in the surrounding waters—nothing like the giant schools found along the Great Barrier Reef—and Dominica shouldn't have had them at all, but they were there, they were virtually invisible, and they were deadly. So Josie planned to study box jelly migration patterns, and what that might mean globally, as well as to the free-diving fishermen of Dominica. Already there had been six sightings, two severe stingings, and one death. The fishermen were beginning to panic.

I first encountered her at a meeting of the local fishermen, a meeting she had called. Although I had been on-island for a few days, her presence at the field station had been scarce, and so our paths first crossed at that gathering, where anxious, weathered Dominicans sat behind tables in the Ministry of Fisheries—a new building in Roseau, the capital city, equipped with modern conveniences and "donated" by Japan, along with three new Nissan SUVs, in exchange for Dominica's vote to preserve whaling rights in their waters.

With the lights down, Josie projected images of the box jelly along the white stucco wall while the slide projector fan hummed and the fishermen shifted and cleared their throats. The window facing the interior of the island let in sounds of the Saturday market, and from the other side, waves slapped rhythmically against the high seawall, another, less recent, Japanese whaling gift-incentive.

"'Scuse me, Miss. But what does it do? When it attacks?" A dusty-skinned older fisherman I recognized as Raymond asked this question, calling Josie *Miss*, despite her wincing objection to the title.

"Well, Raymond, I know you've seen firsthand what they can do. I'm sorry about your son."

The room murmured its agreement. The one fatality had been Raphael, a boy of twelve, out with his father, working the seine nets. No one even knew he had been stung until they drew in the net with a drowned Raphael tangled in it, blackened welts on his legs. The whole island turned out for his funeral in a spectacle of wailing and angry tears.

"Even though it may seem like it, box jellies aren't attacking when they sting people. They have complex eyes, with retinas and corneas, just like ours, except there's no brain for them to connect to. But they can see in all directions, tell up from down, navigate, and distinguish light from dark. They'll chase a shrimp to eat it, and avoid *you* if they can, swimming away by squirting water. But during the rainy season, the rivers wash down sediments and the waters get murky."

"Raphael didn't see it?" asked Raymond.

"Probably not."

"He feel it?"

Josie hesitated. "I'm afraid so. A box jelly has, not just one, but three serious poisons. It's got to stun its prey quickly, to avoid damage—from a struggling shrimp, say—so it has one poison to stop the heart, one to paralyze the muscles, and one to kill flesh instantly."

Raphael's mother, Calliope, a large, colorfully dressed woman I knew from the Saturday market stall where she sold seasoning peppers, torch ginger and anthuriums, sat beside Raymond and moaned softly.

"But he would have yelled, Miss. He would have screamed. He was a boy."

"Not necessarily, Raymond. Survivors of a box jelly sting tell of excruciating pain. Victims have been known to die, not from the venom, but from a pain so intense that they go into shock and drown."

A spattering of fat raindrops began to hit the tin roof of the fisheries building and the smell of hot, settling dust wafted into the room.

Josie clicked the slide carousel forward to show an enlarged teardrop shape enclosing a squiggly line. "That's the nematocyst—the stinging cell. And it's full." She clicked again and the same shape became a deflated balloon with a long string. "And this is what it looks like, microscopically, after discharging its stinging cell. Each tentacle may have 5,000 of these."

"Lord, Lord," said Calliope, snapping open her purse to retrieve a handkerchief and dab at her eyes.

Josie flipped to the next slide and a human body flashed on the screen, carefully photographed so as to omit the head. Its skin bore a crosshatch of blackened whip-like scorch marks. The legs looked as if they had been wrapped with burning ropes.

Calliope stifled a scream with her handkerchief and turned to face the back of the room wagging her head, eyes unfocused.

"Witnesses say this unlucky fellow died within three minutes of being stung," said Josie, deep into her scholarly lecture, oblivious to the swelling discomfort of her audience.

Raymond stared at Josie's hand as if willing her to click the forward button. When she did, a translucent jelly, shot from below, haloed by the water's sunlit surface, hung suspended within the slide frame, its long tentacles captured in a floating moment, like a woman's hair drifting behind her in the sea.

Josie wasn't attractive. She carried around forty unnecessary pounds, was heavy thighed, with an extra fold of flesh at the waist. Her skin had a pasty cast, tinged with pink when she'd been in the sun. She didn't tan. Her hair clung to her head, thin and stringy, more reddish than any other color, and her front two teeth were exceptionally large and widely spaced. Her eyes were slightly different colors, too—one blue, one green. She walked with a heavy stride, a self-admitted klutz; her arms and legs bore many scars of miscalculation and fecklessness.

"Gentlemen," she continued, "the most venomous creature on earth is not a snake, or a spider, or even a scorpion. It's this lovely, nearly invisible, prehistoric jelly." She said this with fondness, as if speaking of a beloved pet. The oldest fisherman, seated at the front of the room, sat back in his chair and passed a hand over his closely-cropped white-tinged hair.

"What you need to know—other than to avoid them—is what to do if stung. Box jelly tentacles adhere to the skin. Don't pull them off! It makes them discharge more venom. Pour vinegar over them. You should have several liters in your boat, just in case. It won't help the pain, but it will deactivate the stinging cells and prevent more stings. Then you can carefully pick the tentacles off, using something other than your fingers."

Josie paced the front of the room, striding to the limits of the slide projector cord as she spoke. And Alton James, one of the most handsome fishermen in Dominica, sat forward in his chair, following her with his eyes, attending her every word, nodding in agreement.

From Martin I had learned how Alton gravitated to Josie at their first meeting, following her to the field station, offering nights of pleasure, proposals of marriage, children for her to bear, in the overenthusiastic way of so many local men. I could not imagine the attraction.

When Josie finished her lecture the attendees grudgingly and sparsely clapped, then filed out. Alton walked up as she was placing the slide carousel into its box. Her scholarly demeanor changed immediately. She rolled her neck and leaned back, balancing the box on one hip, pelvis forward. He stood very close, as most island men do, either not understanding or not caring about personal space. He wore long khaki shorts and a loose, short-sleeved shirt in a faded coconut palm print. The bottom three buttons were undone; when he reached for the slides his shorts dropped slightly and a horizontal line of lighter skin shone above the waistband. His stomach was flat, the skin smooth and hairless.

"I will take these to your vehicle," he said, in a sliding voice, like fruit pulled from its husk.

Josie lifted her hair and watched him walk out the door, then turned to me as I stepped forward.

"You must be Tabby," she said. I didn't correct her. We shook hands. Josie's grip was strong. When she smiled her upper lip stretched and vanished, revealing a wide swath of pale pink gums. "Martin's told me so much about you, I feel like I know you," she said.

"And I know almost nothing about you," I lied.

My job, assigned by Martin, was to help Miss Connie, the cook, on weekday mornings. Mondays we rose at dawn and walked down to Mahaut to greet the fishermen and buy directly from their daily catch. Tuesdays we made a trip to town, by bus, to purchase groceries, check mail, and visit the woman who sold bakes, fat wads of deep-fried dough that Connie would stuff with fish or garlicky cheese for lunches the researchers could carry easily into the field. Wednesday was wash day, and anyone could have their clothes cleaned for $5EC a load, which Connie and I bleached and scrubbed on a ribbed concrete sink, then hung out along the fence to dry, wary of sudden rain showers. Thursdays we cleaned the gutters that led away from the dorms, especially the kitchen drain which didn't feed into the small septic tank, but emptied right into the bush and often clogged; squash vines grew spontaneously at this point of egress, twisting and writhing up the trunks of coconut trees.

Fridays we mopped and cleaned the dorms.

When we came to Josie's room, Miss Connie stiffened and hesitated at the door.

"Not here much, is she?" I said.

In response, Miss Connie clicked her tongue and eyed me sideways.

"Where does she go? Does she really work that much?" I asked, knowing the answer, but wanting to hear it from someone else.

"Work," Miss Connie said, rolling her eyes.

"Well, where is she if she's not working?"

"Shaming herself," said Miss Connie, in an angry burst that surprised me.

"Shaming?"

"Chasing down a man. When he got a woman already."

"Alton's married?"

"Woman with a baby."

"Alton?"

"Woman that take care of him. Woman that love him."

"But—"

"Sleeping in a nasty tree house."

When I left Connie, I sought out Martin to speak with him about what I had learned. He told me that Josie had indeed been sleeping on a shoddily built platform in a tree above a bar, next door to the house where Alton lived with his wife and child. Some locals found it amusing that a rich, white American would so degrade herself for the attentions of a poor black fisherman, but most in this conservative, religious, African-style matriarchy found it appalling, and Martin feared that Josie's indiscretions would reflect badly on the field station. He had told Josie as much, and she promised Martin she would put an end to the relationship.

That evening at dinner, a steady rain poured off the roof of the open-air veranda. The gutters rushed with sound, disgorging rainwater and clumps of detritus. Beyond the veranda, the bush shrieked with the incessant trilling of tree frogs. The fading light caused Martin to rise and flip on the bright overhead fluorescents.

Josie joined us then, just as plates were being pushed to the middle of the table and eating began to give way to conversation. It was the first time since my arrival I had seen her at a meal.

She looked disheveled. Not untidy in appearance, so much, but in demeanor, as if she had recently lost her bearings. Distractedly, she over-filled her plate with food, then ate with an alarming aggressive choppiness, repeatedly cutting bite-sized pieces of stewed turkey, holding each morsel up for a pre-bite inspection. This was made all the more disconcerting by the fact that she alone remained eating.

"Practicing dissection techniques?" said Martin, good-naturedly.

"M-m?" Josie looked up and found him at the table. "Oh. Checking for those little sharp bones, actually. Such a nuisance."

"Don't they have strange meat here?" said a female botanist to my left. "I mean, giant turkey legs cut in cross-sectioned slices, bone in the center? Tell me that isn't odd."

"I think they must freeze the legs first, then cut them," I offered. "When Connie buys those at Astaphan's they're smooth and sharply cut. I think that much precision would be impossible if the meat were soft."

"Not with a laser," said Martin, and most at the table laughed, imagining, no doubt, laser-cut turkey legs in a land largely devoid of septic services, ambulances, and dentists.

"Soft meat," said Josie, staring at a bite on the end of her fork.

"Excuse me?" said a wispy-haired, sunburned fellow across from her. I knew him to be engaged in the daily cataloging, weighing, and measuring of *Diadema antillarum*, the spiny sea urchin, abundant on Dominica's reefs.

"Fresh meat," said Josie, still staring at her fork. She looked up, then, and laughed. "Sorry. Thinking out loud. Never mind. What's the weather supposed to be tomorrow?"

"Clear, I think," said Martin. "Should be a good day for field work. The Clemson group arrives in the morning. I scheduled your jellyfish lecture for right after lunch. That work for you?"

As Josie nodded, a small four-legged animal ran across the tiny triangle of centipede grass, our pitiful nod to a lawn, bordered by head-high chicken wire through which the bush encroached, riotous and lush.

"Ooh, look!" cried the botanist, and the diners turned in time to see the animal sprint across the soggy lawn, its large rear legs, tailless body, and short round ears making it look like a very large, long-legged guinea pig. It ran as far as the fence and stopped, dead-ended, then dashed back across our field of vision with its amusing, bouncy gait.

"It's so cute. What is it?" asked the botanist.

"An agouti," said Martin. "A rodent. The island's only land mammal.

It's an herbivore. Harmless. Eats fruit, seeds, roots. Lives in the rainforest."

"Oh, it could be our mascot. For the field station." She smiled expectantly.

"The Fighting Agoutis," said Martin dryly. "Doesn't sound too intimidating, does it?"

When the agouti reached the opening in the fence where it had first entered, it made a quick about-face and splashed away again. Following closely behind the zigzagging animal, a man, wielding a large cutlass above his head, crossed the clearing, cornered the agouti, and with a quick arcing swing of his machete caught the animal in the throat, mid-stride. The small body took a few more steps then crumpled to its side; a rash of red bubbles wheezed up from the severed windpipe. The man bent over, caught the jerking rear legs between his fingers, hoisted the body, and walked off.

"Did I mention that the locals eat them?" asked Martin to a round of nervous laughter.

The botanist's chuckle tapered off and ended in a small sob. Josie made no sound, stared at the place where the animal had been moments before, then abruptly returned to her plate.

"That was awful," said the botanist in a choked-off voice.

"Well, they are supposed to be quite tasty," said Martin. "And the locals have to eat, too."

"Survival of the fittest," said Josie matter-of-factly.

"Well yes, of course," said the botanist, pointing into the yard, "but that was horrible." Her hand shook slightly as she lifted her drink, a lovely, lavender, boiled guava juice that filled the room with its scent.

"Look, it's a simple concept," said Josie. "The strong and clever survive. The rest, the weak, they die. We know this. And we all agree with the theory, right? So why not the practice? I've never understood why it should be harder to accept when it comes down to blood and guts."

"Well, that makes no sense. You're saying humans should feel free to extinguish every species that isn't smart enough to avoid or escape us?" This was said by a herpetologist I knew to be studying the near-extinction of a large local toad, eaten here for years by locals, a delicacy they referred to as *mountain chicken*.

"In Africa they eat bush meat—orangutans, chimpanzees and spider monkeys," I said. "They're our closest kin. It's practically cannibalism."

"Survival of the fittest is a creed. Either you believe it or you don't," said Josie.

Her meal now mostly devoured, Josie set to the task of chasing down the remaining bits of rice with her spoon. Once isolated, she brought each tidbit to her mouth with a quick jerk of her arm and a snap of her lips, grain after grain after grain.

Late the next morning, it being a free Saturday, and the day being hot, I decided to go for a snorkel/swim. I didn't care to be tied to Dominica's capricious weekend bus schedules, so I grabbed my mask, fins and snorkel and walked to Rodney's Rock, a nearby dive site, named for Sir Rodney, the British naval captain who defeated the French at the Battle of the Saintes in 1782. The site surrounded an immense, partially submerged rock situated where the sea floor dropped off steeply within a few feet of shore. Thus I could stay near land but also snorkel in thirty-plus feet of water, allowing me to practice my free diving skills, glimpse large pelagic animals, or drop below the surface and listen for whale songs.

I thought of my mother then, and how much she would have loved to join me. Being my grandmother's sole caretaker, she didn't travel anymore. I knew how much she missed the ocean. I went snorkeling that day as much for my mother as for me.

The road that took me to Rodney's Rock was hot and dusty, the traffic minimal. At the break in foliage that signified the field station's machete-hewn trail, I left the road and pushed through the bush, down the sharp incline toward the water. Scanning the shoreline I noted a fisherman in a dugout canoe floating several hundred yards to the south. Otherwise the surrounding ocean was an empty, welcoming expanse.

The tide was slack and the water smooth so I opted to swim northward along the coast, putting Rodney's Rock behind me, knowing that as the tide turned I could easily drift-snorkel back to my starting point. I spat in my mask, rinsed it clean, and settled it over my eyes and nose, then slid carefully into the water, enjoying the cooling sensation that spread along my skin. I rolled onto my back to don my fins, then bit down on my snorkel, turned, and stretched horizontal, surveying the ocean floor. A school of squid hovered nearby, and for a few moments I held my position while they eyed me warily, flashing neon full-body signals back and forth, side fins undulating like water wings, never breaking their floating V-formation.

Cephalopods—squid, octopuses, and cuttlefish—have always been my mother's favorite invertebrates, after corals. Many times she extolled to me their intelligence and adaptability. Cuttlefish have blue-green blood that uses copper instead of iron and requires three hearts to pump oxygen to all parts of their bodies. The ink of a cuttlefish was the original sepia dye. Their sophisticated eyes function before birth, when they are still inside their clear-shelled eggs. Curvy eyelids make their eyes look like a W. Chromatophores in the skin allow them to change color rapidly and blend into any environment—even when set above a black-and-white checkered background in the laboratory.

A small hawksbill turtle passed at the periphery of my vision and I abandoned the squid to follow her briefly; when she began to head for open water I kicked away and snorkeled far from my original point of entry, hugging the shoreline. After ten minutes, I reversed my direction and relaxed, letting the quickening current carry me back.

As I approached Rodney's Rock, I heard voices above the familiar volcanic click and crackle of Dominica's underwater music. The voices were loud and angry, rising in tenor, incongruous in the space of my languid morning swim. I drifted closer and tilted my head to look above the waterline. The same fisherman and his boat were there, but nearer, and with another passenger.

Reluctant to expose my position, I maneuvered close to the massive rock and held onto a craggy outcropping that barely rose above the water. Still wearing my mask, I peered over the top. The fisherman in the boat I could now discern as Alton, seated in the pointed bow; his passenger, Josie, sat astern. Waves lapped against the faded red boat and the rock to which I held, alternately masking their voices, then delivering whole sentences clearly.

". . . my woman," were the first words I caught, uttered by Alton, in a reasonable voice. He seemed relaxed, sitting in his weathered boat, shirtless, and fresh (I surmised) from checking the status of his fish pots; the contents of a bucket flopped noisily behind him.

"*Your* woman! How is that?" Josie's voice, by contrast, rose and fell erratically. She wore a wetsuit of blue and yellow neoprene and gestured wildly with her arms. A mask and snorkel hung around her neck and her hair was wet. A specimen bag hung heavily over her right wrist.

". . . love. . . heart. My fire." Alton's voice was soft and he held his arms toward her in an attitude of beseechment.

"Ahh," Josie cried, throwing her arms in the air, specimen bag swinging wildly. "Bullshit, Alton . . .shit . . .no good to me."

"Wife keep the home. Woman keep the heart."

"Holy shit!" Josie's voice rose to a shriek then dropped again. She leaned forward and pointed to his chest with the hand that held the bag. ". . .you. Stop."

Alton lifted a short-handled dive knife and pointed to the water. "I going to check . . ." He pointed the knife toward Josie. "You stay."

With an exaggerated motion, Josie transferred the sack to her left hand and slapped Alton with her right, the sound reaching my ears a moment after the act had been completed.

Alton, without expression, dived off the boat, knife in hand. The boat, with Josie in it, rocked wildly and began to drift away. Josie uttered a screeching noise of frustration then scanned the sea and shore. I tucked closer to the rock, grateful for my hiding place.

As I watched, she reached into her specimen bag and withdrew a box jelly, holding it by the non-venomous bell. When Alton surfaced and looked up at her, she threw the specimen against his head. It landed with a slap, tentacles clinging across his face and over one ear; the bell sagging against his shoulder. I rose instinctively from the water as if to help. A muffled noise crept up my throat; I fought the urge to cry out.

For a surprised moment, Alton stared at Josie, then turned his face toward me. Beneath the milky translucent strings, his features contorted in pain. With one hand he pulled at the body of the jellyfish, with the other he reached out in my direction. Josie turned then, too, and I quickly took a breath and dropped below the water.

I pushed against the rock to keep submerged. Alton sank, struggling furiously. The water moved and churned and sand rose up in a cloud around him. I urged my body to move to him, to help, but it would not. I knew from Josie's lecture that it was already too late. He shot to the surface briefly, and attempted to swim toward the boat. His limbs moved in wild circles, then stopped in mid-motion. A high, shrill scream reached my ears—first as a distant above-surface sound, then as a liquid, gurgling shriek that echoed throughout my body as Alton slipped beneath the water, bubbles pouring from his mouth. I couldn't look anymore.

I don't know what Josie did at that point but I turned and fled across the water, kicking furiously, my breath rasping loudly in the snorkel. I reached a shallow spot and exited the water, scrambling up the hill to the road. When I reached the top, my stomach heaved and emptied itself. I don't know if Josie saw me, if she heard, or if she cared.

I suspect she hailed a bus and returned to the field station. I ran—along the road at first—then walked, breathing hard, staring out into the water, tears pouring down my face, imagining Alton's body bobbing on each wave. Then I imagined him climbing over the rocks, exiting the sea, not dead at all. My chest rose and fell and I had trouble catching my breath. I felt the all-too-familiar hyperventilation of crying that I was so susceptible to and tried to breathe slowly, tried not to panic while my frantic heart swooshed blood past my ears. I could barely swallow. My diaphragm began the uncontrollable spasms that my family affectionately called *the snubs*. It was a family joke—not meant unkindly, simply an observation—that their cool, collected, analytical Tabitha cried—*when* she cried—like a blubbering baby.

I walked straight to the police station, snubbing hysterically, to tell them what I had witnessed, forgetting that the Mahaut station was not manned during daylight hours. I stood for a moment, hiccupping for breath, panting and disoriented. Outside the door there was a pad to leave a note. A note! It would be read when they returned for the evening shift. Would they even believe whatever I wrote? How does one describe a murder-by-invertebrate in fifty words or less?

In the end, I left my note, such as it was, and walked back to the station, already beginning to doubt what I had seen, worried about what my confession would bring to Josie, to Martin, to the field station, to me. Should I go back and pull it down? Had I dreamed the whole thing? Had I blacked out and awoken with vague memories of an unconscious time? Would I be implicated for having done nothing? Would I still be able to attend college in the fall? What if Josie hadn't really meant to kill Alton? Perhaps, in her anger, she meant only to hit him with something, anything, and so threw the nearest thing at hand.

My mind bounced between conflicting possibilities. Dread formed a slick pit in the bottom of my stomach. A strange, detached part of me longed to return to my swim. In the water the world had always made sense, it narrowed down to nothing more than breathing and moving, cooling me and rinsing away life's complexities. In the ocean I could float, suspended and weightless, and close my mind to all the clamoring thoughts that plagued me. I could come back to myself. I could drift to the edge of the wall where the island rose straight up through the water. I could look over the shelf, five thousand feet down to the bottomless blue and always get perspective. But not today. Not with what I knew was floating out there, too.

So I walked, instead. And as I walked, I told myself there had been nothing I could do. As soon as the jellyfish hit Alton, he was doomed. If I had tried to pick the tentacles off, I would have been stung. I had no vinegar. I could have died a gruesome death attempting to save a man who was already as good as dead. And what if she had thrown another box jelly? No, there was no way to undo what had already been done. So I walked—hot and sticky and disturbed—keeping near the water's edge for as long as possible, listening to the mellow percussive rocks rolling in and out, over and over with the waves. Listening to the eternity, the inevitability, of the sea.

As I approached the field station compound, a student rang the lunch bell and I followed the sound instinctively, through the gate and down the path, despite my rolling emotions.

Miss Connie had made lunch that day, just like every other day. She served curry soup and fried dasheen with soursop for dessert. I got in line, filled my bowl, and sat at the far end of the longest table. Josie sat at the other end and a group of visiting students filled the intervening seats. They chattered and asked questions that I'm sure I answered, although I don't remember speaking a word.

Mostly I remember watching Josie eat. I found myself fascinated and focused, unable to look away as she slurped her soup, dipping the pieces of dasheen in the broth and sucking them dry after each dip. When the soursop was served, she peeled away the bumpy green skin and slurped the fruit into her mouth, rolling it around until the smooth brown seeds were free, spitting them onto her plate. Soursop juice ran down her wrists and dripped off her elbows to the floor. I thought of Miss Connie, later, on her hands and knees, wiping up the stickiness while shaking her head at the lack of manners displayed by scientists. I imagined Josie eating just this way, but in a cafeteria behind the walls of a prison. With one piece of soursop remaining, she leaned well into the table and pulled it towards her, oblivious to the longing looks of the surrounding students. She licked each fingertip with a loud smacking sound when she was done.

And I wondered where Alton's body was. Had it gone only a short way before coming back to rest on a hump of rounded rocks? Had the hermit crabs found it already? Would it drift and bob its way to another beach? Another island? Or worse, during some future dive or snorkel, would I round a coral head only to find myself face-to-hollowed-out-face with it?

Immediately following lunch, Josie presented her jellyfish lecture to the visiting student group. So as not to arouse her suspicions, I sat in, as I had planned to do. I found it hard, though, to be still and listening, knowing what I knew, knowing what was yet to come, seeing what I had seen. Harder, still, when Josie looked my way and talked about the medusa stage of the jellyfish, her voice dripping with fondness.

"The stage of the jellyfish that we all recognize—the inverted bell-shape with hanging tentacles—is called the medusa stage, the sexually mature phase." Here, she smiled. "Most of you are familiar with the Greek Medusa, a wicked creature, with snakes for hair, so ugly, that to look upon her face turned one to stone. But the original Medusa myth goes farther back, to a time when women were worshipped for their fertility, for their mysterious ability to bleed every month with no sign of a wound. This Medusa got her name from a word that means *sovereign female wisdom*. She was Libyan, with dreadlocks, and a hidden, dangerous face. It was inscribed that no one could possibly lift her veil, and that to look upon her face was to glimpse one's own death, reflected in her eyes."

As Josie talked, I began to think about eyes. About hers, being blue and green, both. And about those strange eyes of the jellyfish. Those eyes, with retinas and corneas, eyes not so unlike our own. Eyes on muscular stalks that turn in all directions, allowing the jellyfish to look away from themselves, out into their watery world, search for prey, and chase it down; eyes that turn to look inside, right through the walls of their own bodies, to see the struggling shrimp and watch themselves devour it.

MADAME TROUSSEAU

They fight all the time. Hushed hisses in a nearby room. Or a hall. Then they talk to me and shout. *Hello, Mother! How are you today!* I never shouted at my father-in-law and he lived to be ninety. Well, maybe once, but he was a Conch and his wife was half Cuban. Or maybe it was him—one of them was half. I have been surrounded all my life by people like that.

My daughter thinks I can't hear the fights. Her first husband Gus was more my kind. The second one—Manny—always brought flowers and smiled and still I did not like him. Quinn did. They joked and called each other military nicknames: *Squid, Tree.*

Did I ever once live with my only daughter in the whole world? No. But her Polish father-in-law did. Cranky old half-blind Bart lived in the apartment attached to their house. He died and they rented it out the next month. Not that I wanted to live in a musty rat hole. But it would have been nice to be asked.

There's a girl here who brings a dog around. A stinky poodle that I am encouraged to pet. I have a poodle puppy at home. We call her *Puddles,* for the obvious reason. A little fluff of white with the grayest eyes that could look right inside you. She died before Leslie started high school. Smart little…little…whisper-snapper.

I do not care for the sassy help around here. They are not at all like our Fanny. They order me around and rape me over the fire coals. I must have Quinn speak to them. I will soon be Mrs. Quinn Baxter and my sister gave me a diary for my trousseau. A diary! Sherry has always been a wolf in cheap clothing. She graduated high school, class of 1959, and thinks she's Queen Bee because she's ahead of me, but Fanny makes a better apple pie.

We bought Puddles when Quinn's pecker didn't make me pregnant. I tell those people what I want for dinner every night. No one listens. But, oh, they sure do shout. *Here are your pills, Mrs. Baxter! Now you know you can't go out there, Mrs. Baxter!* I showed them: I French kissed a dolphin rescuer. He wanted to do more but Quinn had died and I was still a virgin so I said no and went on a cruise instead. My granddaughter Melody moved to the Chesapeake Bay and married a doctor, and me not even out of high school yet! *Pea*, her mother calls her, if you can imagine. What this world is coming to I cannot…cannot…apprehend. How many decades was she lying there?

Nighttime…is a long time. I don't sleep much. It's so quiet you can hear a mouse drop. And white. Hotels benefit from a snazzy color scheme. Ask any decorator. I will have to have a word with the manager. I could give him some recommendations.

Last week, the president was shot in the middle of a bridge game at my house. We all just sat by the radio and cried, Fanny, too. I don't even care for the Catholics, but I brought out the cooking sherry and we had a sip to calm our nerves. The sign says today is Grilled Cheese Wednesday and I will eat it even though I am black toast intolerant. They serve it with tomato soup, which means I should wear red. And then his son, little saluting John-John, in the plane crash. A family curse for sure. How many years ago was she lying there?

Reese has been sneaking out with her boyfriend again but he married her three years ago in a very nice ceremony. Her name is like a candy bar. It was…we ate…well, my wedding cake will be even nicer than hers. Fanny Brown had a chocolate bar and I begged her for a bite. Which reminds me, I need to take Quinn's dress whites to the cleaners. Tabitha never will get married but she brings homemade bread when she visits. Yesterday I cut off part of my finger slicing her bread and it has taken four days to heal. Tomorrow I am going to sneak out like Reese and meet Rudolph behind the air conditioner and neck. I do not know why Mother did what she did. Father was a good man, worth his weight in salt. It was a shame, the whole county looked funny at me.

I need to find a good…musician to cut my hair. Is that too much? Quinn's hair fell out with the chemo and still he thought he had gotten that college student pregnant. I give myself credit; I did not panic. If only the gray roots didn't grow so fast down into the yellow. Two months he thought it over before he came back. *Bluing,* that is how my mother made her hair so pretty white and Leslie cried herself to sleep every night. The day we brought her home I just stared and stared. I couldn't believe we finally had this beautiful little baby all ready to graduate and go off to college. We counted her toes and fingers. She was everybody's baby, but none more than Quinn's, even after he died.

I know Sherry is planning to sneak and read that diary she gave me. After my wedding night I bet she reads every word. Don't be jealous, Sherry, just because Quinn likes me better. She cuddles between us in bed. Quinn didn't want a dog in there at first but Puddles cried, which made me cry, and he relented. He is such a fuzzy dear! Sorry, that's mean to say. I should black out Sherry's name like the censors did on letters from the Pacific. I am a high school graduate marrying a Navy hero who's turning thirty only three weeks after our wedding. My, my.

What dessert goes with a cheese sandwich? Fruit cup? Pudding? Puddles? I need to know because I bought a new navy blue bikini to surprise Quinn. Which is funny, because he was on a ship near Bikini Island when that Atom bomb went off. He saw everything afterward, too, and him younger than me now. Not too late for the G.I. Bill, at least. My husband, the paleontologist. Mrs. Quinn Baxter. *Dr. and Mrs.* Quinn Baxter. I was only four years old when he saw that mushroom cloud. I don't tell him how funny I think that is. He better come and visit today. I have a lot of lovers waiting in the wings.

Seeing something bloody makes a mushroom cloud in your brain. It wipes everything clean. Dark foreign men with box cutters are a mushroom cloud. So is a parent giving up. Ground zero. My mother's bed. Baptism by fire hose.

I need to figure out what to make for dinner if I hope to start a family before my grandchildren are grown. It means so much to Quinn. Fanny called me *L'il Bit* and let me have a bite. Tomorrow I work on my tan so that when he comes home from the Pacific I will be as brown as a native girl. Baby oil and vinegar is my secret. It smells like powder salad but the only dressing here is Thousand Island and my bowels can't handle greens anymore. They are a spring tonic, Mother says. I hope she brings some by today. *Don't bring the spoon, Mother.* How many days ago was she lying there?

The Soviets have put a man in outer space—before us! I don't care so much, except I would like to get a moon rock as a wedding present for Quinn. Roland and Sarah made the down payment; we moved in right after the honeymoon and Melody won a medal swimming Niagara Falls. The pounding water made our jaws drop open and Quinn went to see the fossils. I will unpack my lacy things and surprise him tonight. Next month, I hope to be in a family way. When Mother found out she spanked me with the wooden spoon. I thought it was roses at first, blooming all around her wrists, spreading on the bed.

Was it Anne Frank who called her diary Kitty? We had so many black-and-white barn cats, my father ran out of names for them: *Ice Cream and Chocolate Sauce, Tuxedo, Penguin, Salt and Pepper, Tar and Feather.* Before she spanked me she said I knew better than to eat after a colored. I am going crazy if something doesn't happen soon. Sherry has three children and she married after me! Maybe it is time to think about adoption. It is a baby, I said to Quinn, not rocket surgery. How many hours was she lying there?

I saw the petals everywhere and called for Fanny to come clean them up. She walked in mad but then her hands fell off her hips and her eyes looked like the black parts went on forever. *Oh, my Lord,* she said. *Lord, Lord.* She picked me up and carried me out. She stood in the yard and hugged me hard against her, rocking back and forth. *Oh, L'il Bit.*

Her whole body shook and her apron pressed flat against my face. Her hands on my head were hot, like the sun, and all I smelled was pie crust and salt.

WASTE ISLAND

I

Father had us up again last night.

We have no timekeepers here on Waste Island, but overhead the Pleiades—those seven suicidal sisters in the sky—had reached the apex of their nightly climb when the island finally went dark and Father, instead of talking to us, piped whale songs over the loudspeakers to lull us all to sleep. I must have slept, but by morning my body insisted I had spent more hours awake than asleep. My jaw ached as I watched the sun rise above the water.

My roommate Willow says I make a terrible grinding noise with my teeth in the night. I cannot say—I *am* asleep, after all—but sometimes in the morning the edges of my teeth do feel sharpened, as if I have spent many dark hours whetting them.

Sleep is also complicated by the fact that my chest has become sore. In the time since the last rainy season, I have started to enter my woman-age and it is uncomfortable to sleep on my stomach now.

My birth mother brought us to Waste Island years ago. We came with the first wave of settlers. In the before-time, in a place called Virginia, my mother's name was Melody. She had older sisters. She was beautiful and laughed with a sound like water tumbling over rocks. She wore dresses with colorful patterns and shoes with points under the heels that made her taller, lighter.

Here, she is Sister Moraine and her clothes are the same mud-brown as everyone's. And we are not allowed to talk. *Pass the butter*, this is fine to say to one another, but nothing more intimate. Nothing about the past. Nothing about a love that binds us specially, differently, from the others. We rarely sit near enough at mealtimes to pass food, or anything. And we have no butter. Butter is a distant memory from the time before. As is bread. And the love of my mother.

Mother. This is a word now that is only to be applied to the Great Mother, Mother Earth, the one who sustains us, who makes all life possible. Before-time ties have been discouraged, *forbidden* without using such a word, and my mother—Sister Moraine—is Father's first, most loyal subject.

Moraine. It has some meaning related to glaciers, I know that much, glaciers from the time before the time-before. A tiny difference, this way that Father renames his followers. Take the birth name and shift it slightly, remake it as some feature of the land, the sea, the sky. It is his calling to remake us, to claim us. He bestows it at our rebirthing ceremony. No one on Waste Island is allowed to remain the person that they were before.

And Father has announced that we will accept no more waves of settlers from the mainland. We before-timers are now all there will ever be. For the children that are born on Waste Island, there is no before-time, no need for rebirthing. We are all Brothers and Sisters now: Delta and Crescent, Ria and Quartz, Bay and Valley. No name has been repeated. Further proof, says Father, of the great vastness and variety of nature.

So I remain the only River here. Not old, but old enough to have seen my namesake in the before-time. Rivers, like people, had names then. The old river name I've held in my memory sounds as broad and sweeping as the place in my mind: *Chesapeake.*

Or perhaps that is a word to describe where a river meets an ocean? It has been so long I am no longer sure of names, but I remember a wide expanse of water slowly sliding past, carrying, throbbing, flooding, ebbing. Smelling briny and muddy all at the same time. It was so very long ago, that world in which a little girl, a girl once called Raissa, played in the mudflats and caught crabs on a string.

I remember a big house with marble floors. (We have a Sister Marble here now. I cannot look at her without thinking of the cool, white-and-cinnamon-streaked floors I once walked upon.) I remember a shining pool of blue water with hard sides in a place we called the back yard (*yard*, just one more word no one here will ever use). I jumped from the sides of that water and landed with a splash, into my father's waiting arms. It was not deep—it could not have been, for in my memory my father stands and raises his arms above it. This clear blue spot of water had a sharp smell. I remember it so well, yet have not smelled it since. It sparkled in the sun only feet away from the muddy black edges of the Chesapeake that rose and fell. Even there we had a tide. There was a boat there, too. I remember that. It was ours, I think, tied up to a tree. We used it on days when my father was home and sometimes rode it all the way to the ocean. The ocean. A place where I learned to swim for hours without needing edges or bottoms. Swimming off my father's boat as a child sowed the seeds for the top sister harvester I am today.

Sowed the seeds: another lost phrase. The ocean is our only garden. She sows her own seeds.

I wonder, sometimes, if my father was preparing me. Did he know? Did he sense that in a few years he would be taken by the Plague, with a horrifying gray web grown across the back of his throat and his face gone purple? Did he know the ocean would rise, creeping in to swamp our marble floors?

It was my real father's death that brought Father into our lives. Brinn Ripley, he was called then. I am not supposed to remember his name. Brinn was the only preacher in a hundred miles who would perform funeral rites for Plague victims. He was not afraid. This one fact brought him scores of faithful followers. *He's not afraid* people whispered, as if it were a miracle. His first followers were women, mostly. Widows. Or women who came to worship and brought compliant, tagalong men. Father did not judge his followers by sex or race or creed. He brought his message to everyone.

He adopted so many children orphaned by the Plague that soon the title *Father* stuck, and for those closest to him, *Dad.* I believe he loved my mother. I know she loved him. She walked lighter in his presence, hung on his every word. Perhaps he saw something to admire in my mother. Or something he could use. She was the first of his followers to carry and bear his child, my little sister, chubby baby Rosalie whom we all adored.

Father did not adopt me. I cried and begged my mother, but she said I was not an orphan and I was too old for adopting, anyway, and Father agreed. But I could go with them to the island, he said, smiling, pulling me next to him, stroking my long hair. Yes, I could *definitely come along.* His voice was like the purr of a cat next to my ear. Tiny hairs on my neck shivered under his warm breath. I should understand, he whispered, what an honor it was to be a First Waver. To be an original settler of his new colony, of Waste Island.

He said I would be one of the *chosen.*

The day we left, my mother fluttered around closing the drapes in our house (against what, I don't know), sweeping the floor. Then she laughed and said, "Not that it matters. It's not as if I'll ever come back for any of this." She swept her hand around the room, taking it all in and dismissing it with the same wave of her hand. I don't remember now how we ended up at the dock. Did Father come and pick us up? Did we drive ourselves? Hire a taxi? Of all the things to not remember, that one seems the most odd, but truly it is an empty hole in my memory.

But ask me what the day was like and I can tell you it was warm. I wore a light sweater that I didn't need. My favorite rose-colored one with the soft fur of an animal woven into it and small sparkles that caught the light. I can tell you that the clouds were high, thin wisps that dispersed and reformed in ribbons of white. There was a wide plank that we carried our luggage across, me holding my little sister's hand on one side, pulling my luggage along on the other. Mother was behind us, humming. I hated her at that moment, hated that she could be so happy leaving everything behind.

Now that I am older, I realize I should have been more understanding. People were dying. The world was crumbling. Cities were sinking. It must have been a relief for her to turn her worries over to Father and embrace the new life he offered. To no longer have to cook and clean or keep two children busy, clothed, and fed. I know we made her crazy. She said it many times.

Father had preached of the wonderful new land we would all soon inhabit. As we boarded the big silver ship that day, he stood on deck, on a raised platform. He spoke to us through his megaphone, the breeze off the water lifting his hair and his cheeks pink with excitement or sun. He was so handsome. *Is* so handsome. I understand why mother loved him, why all of us love him. His voice would be enough to make you fall in love. His voice, deep and warm, with a current of love running through it. I have never heard a more consoling speaker, never felt more reassured by voice alone. Not even my birth father could make that soft roll of love come out the way Father does.

There, on our new ship, shiny recycled hull agleam, Father kept up a continuous pre-launch speech of encouragement. Without fail, all those who topped the gangplank smiled in his direction and stopped for a moment to listen and appreciate.

"My dear brothers and sisters, today, with courage and a sense of great adventure and infinite hope, we set forth to our new promised land. We have the magic of the wind and waves to take us—like a horse who knows the way to bring his master back—*to take us home.*"

My mother, still Melody then, lifted my little sister Rosalie (named, Mother told me once, for her aunt and her mother, Rosarita and Leslie, combined into one) onto her hip and beamed at Father. When she finally looked away, she turned to me and said, "This is it, Raissa. This is the first day of our brand new future." Her voice dripped with a certainty as strong as Father's and with the warm sun on my face and the excitement in the air, I let myself believe it.

We would be baptized with new names on the voyage, arriving, as Father said, a whole new group of people, but for now, Mother rested her hand on my head, trapping the warmth from the sun beneath her hand and we stood squinting in the bright reflected sunlight and listened to Father.

"What we do today, my friends, is nothing short of revolutionary. We will be the first floating civilization known to man. And with the help of our new plasma converter, we will grow the island beneath us. We will harvest our food from the bounty of nature. We will be the ocean's first self-sustaining community and we will lead by example and show the world what can be accomplished with faith and love behind us, our fair wind, our following sea."

Even at that age I knew a bit about what we would be doing. I had paid enough attention during the many sermons Father preached to get the basics. We were taking a giant machine that would turn trash into energy and its byproduct was a black slag that floated and would flow like lava and stick to itself so that we could make an island. The boat we were on had supplies enough to hold us for the first month while we built the island. And the ocean had no shortage of trash to provide us raw materials. In fact, we were bound for the Atlantic Gyre, a giant floating trash patch in the heart of the Sargasso Sea. The ocean would provide us with the building blocks for our island and for the power to fuel it and we would remove pollutants that were causing a decline in the ocean's health. A symbiotic civilization, as Father called it.

We were allowed to bring one bag of possessions each. It was a grand celebration, a procession of hopeful followers. Until, that is, a group of angry Plague survivors from town came to the pier to send us off. At first we smiled and waved toward the assembling group. Those still boarding turned and shared triumphant waves at the onlookers. But then they began to chant. We couldn't make out their words at first, and still thought it was some sort of departure song for luck or safe travels.

When the first clunk hit the metal hull of our ship, Father lowered his megaphone and looked around. He didn't understand where the noise had come from any more than the rest of us, so caught up in our euphoria that we could not imagine others might want us gone. By the third or fourth rock, it was clear. We were being pelted with stones—large ones. Large enough to draw blood when one hit me on the forehead. I stood there stunned by the impact of the rock and the impact of the hate that was pulsing our way, pushing us away. Mother hurried us below decks and we found our cabin. Not truly ours, because it was communal and beds for twenty lined the walls in stacked rows of four each. Mother wiped the blood away, looking distractedly around the room as if hoping for some assurance from the others that this wasn't really happening, but we were all equally stunned and some equally injured.

After Mother wrapped a strip of cloth from her nightdress around my forehead, she arranged me on the lowest berth and set my little sister on my lap for safekeeping while she went topside to check on Father and the progress of the others still boarding.

That day, I knew I was twelve years old, holding my little sister in my lap, covering her ears against the curses and the echoing thumps of stones against the hull. Four rainy seasons have passed since that day. Second and third wavers brought news of the Great Melting that submerged the coastal town we had always called home. Do I feel sorry? Not for the rock throwers—I hope they sank when the water rose. But

I do have bad dreams; stoplights shine through the ocean in them, still red, still yellow, still green.

If I add the rainy seasons to my leaving-age, I am sixteen now, or turning so soon. I remember that my birthday was in May, *is* in May, although I am no longer even sure what *May* means. The first season here we used a calendar and the end of May brought the start of the rains. The second season, Father told us June was the beginning of a new year. Now we do not speak of time or of months, not even years, only of seasons: rainy, dry.

At any rate, I am nearly grown. A woman. But saying I am sixteen would anger Father. I am not supposed to think in such before-time ways.

MY CHILDREN, WHAT IS EACH ONE OF US, AFTER ALL, BUT A CASTOFF?
CAST ASIDE BY A SOCIETY THAT NO LONGER WANTS US.
BUT HERE ON WASTE ISLAND, WE FIND LOVING, WELCOMING ARMS.
AND THE WASTES OF THE MODERN WORLD FIND REBIRTH AT OUR HANDS—
RETURNED TO THEIR MOST ELEMENTAL STATES—AS POWER FOR OUR ISLAND,
BRICKS FOR OUR BUILDINGS, THE VERY GROUND BENEATH OUR FEET.
AND I ASK YOU TODAY, DO YOU FEEL UNPROVIDED FOR?
DO YOU FEEL UNLOVED?
DO YOU DOUBT THAT WHAT WE HAVE MADE HERE IS SPECIAL?
THAT *WE* ARE SPECIAL?
DEAR CHILDREN, YOU KNOW HOW VERY MUCH I LOVE YOU. YOU KNOW WE
ARE THE FUTURE OF THIS EARTH. WE ARE THE CHOSEN. CHOSEN BECAUSE
WE HAVE TAUGHT OURSELVES TO MAKE *EVERYTHING* USEFUL.
EVEN AS YOU HEAR MY VOICE TODAY, A NEW EARTH IS BEING BORN.
BORN THROUGH US.
THIS PATH WE HAVE CHOSEN IS NOT EASY.
NO PATH TO SALVATION HAS EVER BEEN EASY. NO PIONEER EVER SAT IN THE
LAP OF LUXURY. BUT SOON WE WILL SEE THE FRUITS OF OUR LABORS. SOON
WE WILL REAP OUR REWARDS.
IT IS THE WORK, MY DEAR ONES, THE WORK THAT WILL SET YOU FREE.

II

I remember being hungry. So very, very hungry. Nights were the worst. Try to ignore the grasping fingers of hunger in the dark, in the quiet. It is impossible. And when you do fall asleep, it is only to dream of food—piles of food, mountains of food, all steaming and delicious.

During the day, we pushed aside hunger as we worked and built and planned—determined to make an island home. I was a primary harvester, working eight hours at a stretch, filling basket after basket with sargassum, also snails, tiny crabs, flying fish eggs, baby eels, and shrimp—whatever we could find, whatever had attached itself to the seaweed—though there was never enough. Our cooks had not yet learned how to process the seaweed, how to dry it and grind it into a flour, how to form it into strips and make a vegetable leather, how to extract juice from it. Sargasso Soup they made at first, which was good, in its way, but here in the horse latitudes rainwater was too precious a commodity to be squandered on soup. Sometimes they simply chopped it and called it salad. Our storehouse of supplies dwindled rapidly. Without Father to keep our spirits up, without his loving hand to guide us, we would all have given up, Mother included, especially after Rosalie took ill.

In the early days of the colony, we were not yet fully separated. We still ate together onboard the ship, but Mother was as busy and exhausted as anyone. Father assigned her night shift on the feedline pushing trash into the plasma converter twelve hours at a stretch. He said she was the only one he could trust with such an important task, the building of our island. It left her no time for us.

Little Rosalie took Mother's withdrawal of affection especially hard. We had slept together every night and suddenly she was sent to the nursery and I to a dormitory room. Father promised Rosalie would receive plenty of love from the caregivers. But at mealtimes she reached out for me or for Mother and let loose a mournful screech of want. Oh, how it hurt to hear! They began to serve her in the nursery, instead. When I inquired, the caregivers said that she had a bad case of prickly heat and refused to eat the strange things harvested from the ocean. I believed this. She had never been an adventurous eater. They told us she was served white rice three times a day. They said it would only disrupt her healing if I visited.

She contracted wet berberi and died within a space of days. They only told us after. There was nothing the caregivers could do. Perhaps her tiny broken heart gave out. I cannot bear to think of it. She was buried at sea.

There is much I would like to ask of Mother, of *Sister Moraine*. I would like to ask her if she misses me. If she misses Rosalie. If she thinks of us as *hers*. I want to ask her what it was like when *she* became a woman, what it felt like to leave her own mother behind. I want to ask her how she let us go so easily. I want to ask her if she sees us in her dreams, the way I see Rosalie and her.

My grandmother believed in Father's vision. She had been a marine biologist when younger and she kept a love of the sea, a fear for its future. I remember sitting on Nana's lap during the funeral for my father. Afterward, she said that Brinn Ripley was a great man. He cared about the ocean and ministered to the lost.

When my mother became pregnant with Rosalie, Nana was less enthusiastic. She cried and hugged my mother close, crooning, "Oh, Pea. Oh, my Sweet Pea," over and over. I remember wishing I had a nickname, too, but it no longer matters now. I am River and River does not lend itself to being shortened. In any case, there is no one who cherishes me enough to try.

But dwelling on the before-time betrays Father's great sacrifice. We are counseled not to allow such thoughts. I must confess and ask forgiveness and hope Father does not think I need time in The Well. My long-ago thoughts are shackles to an old life, a gone life. If I want to move forward, I must shed them. Father instructs us to pluck our old thoughts away like sea lice and put them into an imaginary box, one-by-one. Then we close the lid and set the box of old thoughts adrift on an ocean current. Imagine it carried north, away on the Gulf Stream.

I want more than anything to please Father, so I visualize sending my box of thoughts away. I worry that he knows how badly I fail. But at least I do better than my roommate, Willow, who cries herself to sleep every night.

Willow is a third waver, the last group to arrive—the group that brought us news of the Great Melting—and the last to acclimate. The first week, before her rebirthing ceremony, Father made a sketch on the wall above her bed with a bit of charcoal. It is a drawing of a tree whose arms flow down like a waterfall of leaves. We tried to guess what name it could represent, never dreaming *Willow*. But I understand now why he gave her this name. It is a drooping tree, a sad tree; it suits her temperament.

Above my bed, a charcoal river flows. It curves and washes downward toward my head, toward my dreams. Father said that I am changeable but also constant. Beneath his drawing he wrote, "You never step into the same river twice." And I wonder, sometimes, if I will ever be blessed to see my namesake again.

Willow has been woman-aged for one whole rainy season. She worries that Father has not yet chosen her. She asks me every day how I think she might earn his trust. I am tired of her asking. I tell her it will happen when she is ready, when Father knows she is ready, but privately I wonder. Her face is red with splotches that creep inward from the edges. They rise up her neck when she is anxious. Her cheeks droop and her jaw disappears into her neck, long like a water bird's. Her breasts are large. They are always pulling down at her, making her stoop-shouldered and sad. Her ankles are thick, nothing like a bird.

Do I truly believe Father will call for her, or do I only say it for the satisfied silence the words bring?

Willow works as a caregiver in the nursery, with the babies and young children. She says she cannot wait to have her own baby and help the island grow. I work hard every day. I have no problem waiting. We sister harvesters collect and drag ashore the bounty of nature. At the end of our collective contribution time, we tote everything to the processing center. Each morning I slip into the Sargasso Sea with ten other young women and together we feed the island.

Each afternoon, when Father's loudspeaker calls us from our contribution, we pass a group of brother gleaners carrying pack-baskets filled with trash on their way to the plasma converter.

We sister harvesters, pack-baskets filled with seaweed, travel in the opposite direction, to the processing station. Gleaners collect the floating tons of trash that drift into the gyre and stay—even the tiny pearled bits of photodegraded plastic (Father tells us that they must be gathered piece-by-tiny-piece if we are to truly cleanse the ocean). And the plasma converter turns all this waste into fuel for our machinery and slag that builds and strengthens Waste Island. We grow a little larger every day.

My loyalty is forever and always to Father, as I know it must be, but there is one gleaner whose eyes are a color I have never seen—the golden shade of dried sargassum in the sun, except liquidy, like the ring my mother once wore, before we turned everything over to Father for the collective good. This gleaner's skin and hair—they are nearly the same color as his eyes, so that he looks to be made all of a sunset.

I mustn't think such things, I know. Father would say that I am selfish. That I am not thinking of the collective. But I feel my stomach flip each time I seek out the gleaner in passing only to catch him seeking me, too.

YOUR BEFORE-FAMILY HAS LET YOU DOWN.
YOU HAVE BEEN HURT, ENDURED SUFFERING AND PAIN—I KNOW YOU HAVE—BUT NO MATTER HOW YOU'VE BEEN ABANDONED AND ABUSED, YOU CAN RELY ON ME, MY CHILDREN.
I AM HERE.
I WILL CHERISH YOU AND KEEP YOU SAFE.
WE CAN HAVE A NEW FAMILY, A NEW, LOVING FAMILY THAT I HAVE MADE POSSIBLE.
ALL I NEED YOU TO DO, DEAR CHILDREN, IS LOVE.
OH, HOW I NEED YOU TO LOVE, MY PRECIOUS ONES. TO LOVE WHAT WE ARE, WHAT WE DO, WHAT WE HAVE MADE.
CAN YOU DO THAT FOR ME, CHILDREN?
CAN YOU LOVE?
IT'S A SIMPLE REQUEST. A SIMPLE THING.
LOVE.
DO IT FOR ME, AS I HAVE DONE IT FOR YOU.
WE ARE ONE BODY, HERE, ONE MIND, ONE PURPOSE, ONE HOPE.
WE ARE LOVE, INCARNATE.

III

Today, at the end of our contribution time, as I passed the gleaners going in the opposite direction, I noticed him again, the boy of sunshine and sand.

He broke ranks and approached me saying loudly, "Here, Sister, your strap is twisted," and touched my shoulder in a show of righting what had not been wrong. In my periphery, I saw him slip a note into my pack-basket while he stood close and stared into my eyes for the briefest moment, willing me to understand his intent. I smelled the salt and sea upon his golden skin. His curls were wet from gleaning, still, and dripped upon my shoulder. I was certain I would faint. Later, when I read the note—Branch!

His name is Branch!—it implored me to meet him in private. Oh how I long to! Is it wrong to feel such feelings for a brother? Father would admonish me if he knew. But we came here for love. Ocean love, earth love, love for our ideal of a better life, and, of course, love for Father.

One of Father's anointed brides has given birth this morning—I believe she is younger than me!—and we have all been given the afternoon off. There is a giddy happiness in the air. Our evening meal will be placenta stew in celebration—yes, I know, but truly, it is delicious, and as Father says, an honor to participate so fully in the circle of life. When the others are finishing their stew, when they are celebrating and toasting Father and his newest celestial bride, this is when Branch has asked me to meet him.

If caught, we could be thrown into The Well for *cooling off.* I never want to be so disobedient as to cause Father the pain of disciplining me. It does irk poor Father so, as if he doesn't have enough to do, running the island, caring for us all. It breaks his heart to have to discipline his children. When Brother Geyser was caught stealing food and thrown into The Well, he died while cooling off. Oh, how poor Father mourned that day. He cried, right over the loudspeaker. I could not bear to cause him such an awful pain again. We put so very much on him, it is a wonder he can be as loving as he is.

So I have decided I will meet Branch at the slag pile behind the converter—just this once—to let him know we cannot meet any more, that it is not right. I will not turn him in. But if caught, I can explain my intent, and all will be fine.

WE ARE HERE TO HELP ONE ANOTHER, CHILDREN.
IT IS OUR COMMUNITY RESPONSIBILITY.
OUR LOVE RESPONSIBILITY.
I KNOW BECAUSE I HAVE SEEN MY OWN SO-CALLED PARENTS FILLED WITH HATE. I ESCAPED, AND SO DID YOU. ESCAPED TO THIS PLACE OF LOVE.
IF YOU SEE A BROTHER OR A SISTER STRUGGLING, IF YOU HEAR A MEMBER OF OUR FLOCK EXPRESSING WORRY OR DOUBT, THE BEST THING YOU CAN DO TO SAVE THEM IS TO TELL A COOPERATOR.
WHEN YOU ALERT A COOPERATOR TO YOUR FRIEND OR NEIGHBOR, YOUR BROTHER OR SISTER, EVERYTHING STAYS IN CONFIDENCE. THE STRUGGLING BROTHER OR SISTER IS GIVEN HELP. YOUR CONCERN HELPS OUR FAMILY

MEMBER RECEIVE AN EXTRA DOSE OF LOVE AND CARE.
WE MUST LOOK OUT FOR ONE ANOTHER.
IT IS OUR DUTY AND AN ACT OF LOVE.
PROVE YOUR PRIDE IN ALL THAT WE HAVE BUILT.
PROVE YOUR LOYALTY.
PROVE YOUR LOVE.

IV

Oh, last night! How shall I describe last night? Are there superlatives enough to express the tenderness of Branch's kiss? The longing burn in his golden eyes? His softly whispered avowals of love? He loves me!

We have met the past seven nights and I am quite alive inside. I am unable to concentrate on anything save the sweetness of being held in the strong arms of my love. The days away from him go on forever. I get through them only by remembering the nights.

The passing hours before I see him are an eternity. In my daydreams I long to brush against him again, feel the slide of his muscles beneath my fingers. Feel the warmth of his body beside me, closer, closer. I want to take all of him in, absorb him through my skin and into my bones, make it so I will never have to say good-bye again.

I cannot even name all the things we did, other than to call it love. To shout it—LOVE! We pulled together in the darkness and our bodies led us where they wanted us to go. We felt a pull as if caught on a fishing line and then laughed with surprise when we fit together so well. How good it felt. How we neither one wanted it to stop, ever. This happiness that has overtaken us—the sweetness, the craving, the want.

Oh, how long we kissed! My face is sore. My heart tells me that it could have lasted only moments or an entire lifetime. I finally understand Father's argument against time. It is a pointless measurer of that which cannot be calculated in the heart. Time is perception only. Now I define time this way: that which keeps me from my love.

Last night, Willow caught me sneaking back to our room after hours. The one night she cannot sleep and so she hears me come back in.

"Where were you?" she asked, sitting up awkwardly and smoothing her nightdress.

I thought to lie, but when I hesitated she pleaded so hard, swearing herself to secrecy—and I am full-to-bursting anyway!—and so I told her everything. About the note Branch slipped to me, about our clandestine meetings every night, and our delicious, secret love.

Her eyes shone when I described the joy of love with Branch. This love has expanded my heart until I feel a grand love for everyone. Surely this cannot be a bad thing. I even love poor, sad Willow. Willow, who has no one. Willow who yearns so desperately to be nothing more than one of Father's chosen brides.

SADLY, MY CHILDREN, SOME OF YOU ARE NOT LOYAL IN YOUR HEARTS.
YOU HAVE NOT LOVED OUR DREAM AS FULLY AS YOU SHOULD.
YOU HAVE DOUBTED. YOU HAVE QUESTIONED OUR PURPOSE—AND YES—
EVEN MY VISION. IT HURTS ME TO SAY THIS, BUT SOME OF YOU HAVE STRAYED.
AND YOU HAVE HURT ME DEEPLY.
YOU KNOW WHO YOU ARE.
YOU HAVE BETRAYED THE BROTHERS AND SISTERS WHO COUNTED ON YOU.
AND YOU HAVE BETRAYED ME.

V

Today, after Contribution Time, when the gleaners and harvesters passed one another, I did not see Branch. I tried not to search their ranks for him too desperately, too obviously, but as I walked on I could not find him among the gleaners.

Father's announcement already had me on edge. I felt a trickle of worry-sweat begin under my arms and travel down to my already sweating palms. The day was warm, but this was not a sweat from heat. Branch has a simple, small sickness, I tell myself. I will see him tomorrow. I will look forward to that, but I will worry all night long.

And, what of our planned rendezvous this evening? Should I skip that? Should I risk exposing myself by showing up? What if Branch has turned me in?

But, no, I refuse to believe that. I understand by the way his body pulls toward mine, the way his lips find mine even in the darkness, that my darling Branch would never turn me in.

I HAVE UNFORTUNATE NEWS, DEAR CHILDREN.
WITH A HEAVY HEART, I MUST TELL YOU THAT OUR BEST AND BRIGHTEST GLEANER, BROTHER BRANCH, VENTURED TOO FAR OUT TODAY.

Loyally he swam, out past the edges of the Sargasso Sea, out as far as the mighty Gulf Stream.

He was working hard for us when he was swept away retrieving a ghost net, on my orders.

His fellow gleaners—loyal to a man—were unable to retrieve him.

Several were nearly lost in the trying.

Brother Branch was a fine, hardworking member of our flock.

He will be remembered for his faithfulness, for his tirelessness.

He will be sorely missed.

VI

Sorely missed. Yes.

Father's news tonight—to be heard as an announcement—and not to be able to show my sorrow—and to think of Branch swept away—pulled from the gyre—away from us—away from me, has set me adrift as well. Could he stay afloat? Could he swim enough to reach some place of safety? It is my only consoling thought—that there has been no body. I can dream that he made it away from Waste Island. That he will come back for me. But it is small, this consolation.

And smug Willow is no comfort at all. Father has finally sent for her and tonight she sings and pats her soft, fat cheeks in preparation for a visit to his compound. She asks me to help her with her hair when all I want to do is curl into a ball on my bed and disappear.

She has Father and I have no one. Rosalie is gone. Nana stayed behind. Sister Moraine (not Mother, I cannot call her that) avoids my eyes. Does she know? Does she even care?

I stood at the edge of Waste Island tonight and looked out to sea until the sun fell below the water. Every ripple, every tiny swell gave me hope. Hope that was never answered.

Death is just a portal, my children.

Merely that, and nothing more.

The faithful will not fear death.

The faithful will not grieve for those who have gone before us.

For they are at peace.

They are returned to Mother Earth as nutrients to feed her.

MOTHER NATURE—THE ORIGINAL RECYCLER, ENSURES THAT DEATH FOR ONE IS MERELY REUSE FOR ANOTHER.

THE RIGHTEOUS DO NOT FEAR IT.

THE RIGHTEOUS LOOK FORWARD TO SHEDDING THIS CUMBERSOME MORTAL COIL.

VII

Last night Father sent a Cooperator to fetch *me* to his compound. Me! Not Willow. How does he know when I am so in need? He was kind, as if he knew, or sensed, my burden of sorrow. But how could he know?

He did not speak of Branch, but I felt him in Father's words when he spoke of love, that love can only grow when it is given to the many, that love for only one is narrow—is wrong—that it is an insult to nature's bounty.

He touched me so tenderly that I thought of Branch and let his lips and hands and words press me whole again. I let myself be swept away by waves of sadness and sorrow and love.

I understand now that Mother Ocean took Branch as punishment— punishment for forgetting that love is for all and not for just one.

I will not forget again.

WE MUST REMEMBER, CHILDREN.

EVERY DAY WE MUST REMEMBER THAT OUR BEFORE-FAMILIES HAVE NO HOLD ON US. WE ARE NOT THE PEOPLE WE ONCE WERE.

BIRTH-FAMILIES ARE AN ACCIDENT OF COUPLED GENES.

TRUE FAMILIES ARE MADE BY CHOICE.

WE ARE YOUR FAMILY, YOUR BROTHERS AND SISTERS UNITED IN A DREAM.

A NEW WAY OF LIFE: SUSTAINABLE, LOVING, GIVING, SHARING, UNITED.

OUR NOW-FAMILY WILL SEE US THROUGH TO THE ENDS OF OUR DAYS.

YOU'VE BEEN LET DOWN BY OTHERS—OH, YES—YOU'VE BEEN DISAPPOINTED.

YOUR BEFORE-FAMILIES HAVE FORGOTTEN YOU.

AS YOU MUST FORGET THEM.

BUT I WILL NEVER LEAVE YOU, MY BEAUTIFUL CHILDREN.

I WILL ALWAYS LOVE YOU.

VIII

The moon has filled and emptied many times since Branch's death— his *disappearance*, I want to say. In my dreams, he comes back, touches me and tells me everything will be all right. I believe him. I want more than anything to believe him. Waste Island has changed in all this time, and it has not changed, too. I do not harvest any more. My belly has grown too large. The cooperators have confirmed that I am pregnant. *When* is unclear, but as we have been taught, the "when" of time is not important. Were we even allowed to mark time, I would not be able to say when the seed of this child was first planted.

Last week's storm that cast and spun us about in the gyre delivered a new crop of sargassum and plastic. It also brought a strange ship to the shores of Waste Island. I wondered, briefly, if Branch had sent it. If he had piloted it from afar and come for me. It was not an ancient, reflotsamed ship, but a modern yacht, with a family aboard who looked surprised to find our island and to see us living here. On its prow were the words *La Calma*. I am told it is the ship's name. Their father came ashore to speak with Father.

The wife and children stayed on the boat and stared at us from the deck. Their stares made me feel as if we were longhaired, ragged freaks that might do dreadful, unpredictable things. Father has always told us that the world knows we are here, but the reactions of these people did not support that. I hated how their stares burned my skin.

They *infect* our perfect place.

ANSWER ME THIS:
HAVE I ASKED TOO MUCH OF YOU?
HAVEN'T I GIVEN YOU EVERYTHING YOU NEED?
HAVEN'T I SACRIFICED FOR YOU?
HAVEN'T I BUILT THIS DREAM, THIS UTOPIA ALL FOR YOU?
MY SWEAT AND BLOOD AND TOIL AND TEARS.
ALL FOR YOU.
EVERYTHING I DO IS FOR YOU.
OH, HOW MUCH I'VE LOVED YOU, HOW VERY MUCH I'VE LOVED.
I'VE WORKED TO GIVE YOU A GOOD LIFE, BUT NOW WE HAVE BEEN BETRAYED.
WE HAVE BEEN SO VERY BETRAYED.
THERE ARE PEOPLE AMONG US—FROM THE OUTSIDE—WHO WOULD THREATEN OUR COLLECTIVE BODY—PEOPLE WHO WANT TO STEAL AWAY THOSE WHOSE LOYALTY FALTERS—WHO DO NOT UNDERSTAND WHAT WE HAVE WORKED SO HARD TO CREATE.

OUTSIDERS WHO WOULD DENY US OUR VERY WAY OF LIFE.
WE MUST STAY UNITED.
WE MUST NOT LET THEM DIVIDE OUR HEARTS.

IX

La Calma has been tied to our shore for five sunsets. The family stays inside their ship. I believe they are afraid of us. I do not know what they eat or why they have not left. I have not seen any brothers or sisters go to the ship, but Willow tells me there are traitors among us who board their ship under cover of darkness. They say unfaithful things about Father, they ask to leave. These are the things that Willow knows and I never do.

For my part, I surreptitiously count the days and wonder when the strange people will leave and what they could possibly be waiting for. I try not to think of time. I understand that this obsession with time makes me unworthy of Father's love.

All the other brothers and sisters are so good, so loyal. But I am ungrateful, for I long to cross off days, make tally marks on something. I long to count down the days to my child's birth. And yet all I know for certain is that I am very heavy now and Father blesses me publicly, but does not send for me to be cherished in the night.

Instead, in the dark hours of the morning, when the island sleeps and I am most alone, I lie awake and think of time. This is also when the child in my belly performs a somersaulting dance. This movement is my timekeeper now.

DO YOU NOT WONDER, CHILDREN, WHY THESE OUTSIDERS DO NOT LEAVE?
WHY THEY INSIST ON STAYING AND TEARING US APART?
OFFERING TO TAKE AWAY THOSE WHO WANT TO LEAVE?
THINK ABOUT IT LONG AND HARD, MY CHILDREN.
THINK ABOUT WHAT IT ALL MIGHT MEAN.
AND THEN ANSWER WHETHER YOU WANT YOUR WAY OF LIFE DESTROYED.
WHETHER YOU WANT YOUR LITTLE ONES TO BE FORCED INTO A COLD,
THANKLESS, CONSUMPTIVE SOCIETY THAT DOES NOT CARE FOR THEM, THAT
DOES NOT PROTECT THEIR FUTURE.

X

Late last night, again, the child kicked and kicked inside me and though I tried to stay in bed and sleep, I could not. And so, as Willow snored toward the ceiling, I stepped outside our sleeping quarters to search for the Pleiades in the night sky, hoping for some sense of the closeness of morning. Sadly, sleep is no longer my good friend. Perhaps the child is preparing me to be awake and ready for our nights together after the birth.

Once outside, instead of the starry sisters I found a group of brothers making their way toward the boat *La Calma*, creeping along like lions on the hunt. A wave of dread overtook me at the sight. I did not want to know, but also did not want to leave my witness post. What decided it for me was the knowledge that there was no one I could tell. And so I climbed back in bed and lay there, stomach rippling with life, even as I sensed that life outside my door was ending.

BELIEVE ME, CHILDREN, WHEN I TELL YOU.
THESE DEATHS WERE BEYOND MY CONTROL.
A FEW ANGRY BROTHERS AMONG US ACTED.
THEY DID IT AND NOW IT'S DONE.
THERE WAS NOTHING I COULD DO.
I DID NOT ASK THEM TO DO IT, I DID NOT TELL THEM TO, BUT THEY DID.
AND NOW THE WORLD WILL SEE US AS WE ARE NOT: AS MURDERERS.
THEY WILL COME TO WASTE ISLAND AND STEAL AWAY OUR CHILDREN—
THEY WILL TAKE OUR LITTLE ONES—OH, THEY WILL HURT OUR CHILDREN
AND WE CANNOT LET THIS HAPPEN.
I'M AFRAID OUR EXPERIMENT IS OVER, MY CHILDREN.
DOOMED BY LAST NIGHT'S AVENGERS.
IT IS OVER.
AND I AM GOING TO ASK YOU TO DO SOMETHING THAT I HOPED I WOULD
NOT HAVE TO.

XI

Father called us to the pavilion to prove our loyalty.

Again.

We have had to do this three times in three days and always in the middle of the night.

The siren wailed and we left our bunks and shuffled out with bleary eyes, wanting to reassure Father, willing to do whatever it would take to make him happy again.

.I raised my arms with the others and shouted promises. I vowed my unconditional love and support to the bitter end. Together we cried and swore we would do anything, anything to prove our loyalty. We were dying to reassure him of our love.

Willow rushed forward and threw herself at his feet, weeping and begging to be allowed to go first. Whatever he wanted she would do. She groveled on the ground until a cooperator lifted her and helped her back into the crowd. Others fought their way to the front, making speeches that praised Father's leadership and vowed their unwavering love before us all.

I swore to be loyal, but I was not feeling well, roused from sleep too soon and my belly felt denser, heavier, lower—if that makes sense to say—than usual.

So I vowed my loyalty from a bench in the back.

And I listened.

I KNOW YOUR SUFFERING AND YOUR DOUBTS, MY CHILDREN.

I KNOW YOUR STRUGGLES AND YOUR FEARS.

I KNOW YOUR PAIN.

HAVEN'T I FELT EVERY BIT OF SUFFERING ALONGSIDE YOU?

HAVEN'T I GIVEN UP EVERYTHING FOR YOU?

THE TIME HAS COME TO SHED OUR PAIN AND STEP INTO THE LIGHT.

BE CALM, CHILDREN, BE CALM.

OUR DESTINY IS UPON US.

WE ARE PREPARED, WE HAVE PRACTICED.

YOU KNOW WHAT TO DO, YOU KNOW WHERE YOUR HEART LIES.

WE WILL SHOW THE OUTSIDE WORLD WHAT THEIR DESTRUCTIVE WAYS HAVE WROUGHT.

WE WILL MAKE A STATEMENT THE WORLD WILL NEVER FORGET.

I HOPED IT WOULDN'T COME TO THIS, BUT THEY HAVE LEFT US NO CHOICE.

WHAT WE HAVE TO DO NOW IS SIMPLE, SO VERY SIMPLE.

WE MUST GATHER OUR LOVED ONES, OPEN THE PORTAL, AND STEP THROUGH.

XII

I sat listening in the back, my hands upon my giant stomach as the sun rose in the sky. The bench shifted and the weight of another body dropped beside me. It was Sister Moraine. I stiffened and stared straight ahead. She had not been there in my time of need. She could have cared, but she did not.

I felt her hand on my arm. "Sister," she said, and still I did not look at her.

"We love you, Father. We love you, Father," I chanted with the others.

"Oh, Sweet Pea," she said, and her voice carried so much sorrow. An ocean of sorrow. She put her palms on my belly, and when I finally looked at her, there were tears streaming down her cheeks. "I'm so sorry."

As if in response to her touch, my belly bunched up high and tight beneath her hands. My mother's eyes widened. An extraordinary pain gripped the center of my body and a rush of wetness flooded my thighs.

My first feeling was a wave of embarrassment for having wet myself. But a second pain followed the first and brought another gush of liquid. I knew, then, why I had not been feeling well.

I knew my baby had been counting days when I had not, and it was time.

THINK OF IT AS SIMPLY COCONUT MILK.

JUST A SMALL, SWEET SIP FOR ME.

WITH A LITTLE EXTRA DROP OF LOVE TO MAKE YOU SLEEP.

JUST LOVE. NOTHING MORE. YOU'RE NOT AFRAID OF LOVE, ARE YOU?

THERE WILL BE NO PAIN.

ONLY LIVING CAUSES PAIN.

ONLY THE LIVING SUFFER.

LIARS TELL YOU TO FEAR DEATH—HATERS, COWARDS, NON-BELIEVERS.

I AM ONLY ASKING YOU TO TAKE A JOURNEY YOU'D BE TAKING SOMEDAY ANYWAY. SOONER OR LATER WE ALL TAKE THAT TRAIN.

WE'RE LEAVING A LITTLE EARLY, THAT'S ALL. WE'RE LEAVING TOGETHER.

WE, THE CHOSEN, ARE CHOOSING WHEN TO GO.

WE GO TODAY.

XIII

Willow rushes back to the bench where I sit with Sister Moraine, with *my mother*.

Willow reaches her hand toward us. "Come on, River. Go up with me." When I take her hand, she lifts me to my feet. Her face is pink with excitement and she breathes as if she's been swimming for hours.

I want to show Father my loyalty, I do, but the pain is strong inside me.

"Go ahead, Sister Willow," my mother says. "I'll help River to the stage."

Willow laughs, replete with happiness, and I sit back down. "Thank you," I say after she is gone. Then, "We should not be talking."

"I doubt it matters now." She reaches out and touches my hair with a soft look in her eyes. "There are so many shouting for his attention he will not notice us."

I stare at her, confused. Does she mean *escape*? Together? Before I can ask, another band of pain tightens around my middle. I double over, holding my stomach. Holding it all together.

"Your baby's coming, Raissa."

Raissa. My name, born again, on the lips of my mother.

She looks me in the eye, long and hard. "Do you want to die?"

Do I?

Not so long ago, after Branch's disappearance, I wanted nothing more than death. I would have welcomed it. Every day I imagined swimming until I could no longer see the island, then turning to float on my back, surrendering, beneath a blue-blue sky, surrendering to the pleasant relief of nothingness. I longed to join my love in the dark void, at the bottom of the sea, in the belly of a shark, anywhere that we could be together.

Now, all around me, death has begun. Children cry and cough, parents force their toddlers to drink the bitter liquid. It is not pleasant, not pretty.

This child of mine pushes back. The pain is a white-hot poker. The all-consuming flame of the plasma converter burns inside me.

LISTEN TO YOURSELVES.

DEAR CHILDREN, DO YOU REALLY WANT TO GO THIS WAY?

DO YOU WANT TO BE A WRETCH IN YOUR LAST MINUTES ON EARTH?

Do you want to be a pauper, begging on your hands and knees?
Or do you want to leave this world on your own terms?
I know which one I choose, children.
It is a beautiful thing to be self-reliant, to be one with nature, to turn away from the destruction of our Mother Earth, to make waste into land, into energy.
We have done that.
We have shown the world a better way.
A truer path to righteousness.
We will make the world remember this day.
We will make them remember our courage.

XIV

My mother leans toward me. "You have a child to consider now, Raissa." She kisses my cheek and I remember the familiar softness. I cannot bear it.

"Come with me," I whisper. I desperately want her to. I see how it can be. My mother, back to herself. My mother and me and my child. "We'll hide. Come on."

I stand, and hold my hand out to her. I whisper, "There's still time."

Then Father speaks, with his lips right up against the microphone, slurring slightly. "Sister Moraine."

My mother shakes her head and her lips turn up in a smile. It isn't a smile of happiness. "I can't, my sweet. But you can," she says. "Save yourself for me." She rests a hand on my hard, hot stomach. "Save your baby. Save my grandchild."

She stands then, and shouts along with the others and moves into the crowd. The pain visits me again and there is no chance to stop her. I understand that she does not want to be stopped.

My mind longs to stay, but my body creeps me away from the pavilion amidst the crying, the tears of loyalty, the shouts of admiration, of affirmation.

Across the ground my willful knees crawl me to the room that Willow and I have shared for several seasons now. It is the closest thing I have to a home. In our room, within sight of the pavilion, the smell of salt and sweat is strong.

My renegade wrists pull me, painfully, into the cramped space beneath my bed. From this vantage point, the noise at the pavilion sounds like a celebration party.

Perhaps it is.

YES, MY CHILDREN, YES. YOU ARE SO VERY BRAVE AND BEAUTIFUL.
DO THIS.
DRINK THIS BLOOD OF MY BODY AND OPEN YOUR ARMS TO THE PORTAL.
NO KNOWLEDGE COMES WITHOUT SACRIFICE.
OUR LIVES HAVE BROUGHT US TO THIS POINT OF DECISION.
OUR VOICES WILL RISE ABOVE THE PETTINESS OF LIFE.
WE WILL GO OUT SINGING.
WE WILL START A WAVE.
A TSUNAMI OF LOVE, OF UNDERSTANDING.
TODAY YOU MAKE THE ULTIMATE SACRIFICE FOR THE EXALTATION OF MANKIND.
OUR BODIES—OUR CARBON AND WATER—WILL DISASSEMBLE AND WE WILL RETURN TO THE GREAT POOL OF ELEMENTS. WE WILL FUEL THE UNIVERSE.
OUR MOLECULES WILL BE HEARD.
THEY WILL BEAR WITNESS.

XV

My hiding place under the bed grows painful.

The child tears at my insides and I long to cry out. With a flash of pain that comes from a different place, suddenly I want my mother. Maybe she is already gone. I hold tight to the foot of the bed above me and twist on the floor. I moan in my mind. Colors light the space behind my eyes.

I will surely pass out from the pain, from this twisting, tearing, searing flesh.

But I will not let Father hear me.

YES, CHILDREN.
HOW BEAUTIFUL TO SEE YOU SURRENDER.
BEAUTIFUL THAT YOU LIE DOWN WILLINGLY, RETURN YOURSELF TO EARTH, WITHOUT FEAR, WITHOUT CRYING.
ALL AROUND ME, I FEEL YOU, DEAR CHILDREN.
I FEEL YOUR SOULS SOAR, LEAVING THEIR EARTHLY SORROWS BEHIND.

OH, IT IS A BEAUTIFUL THING TO BE SO LOVED.

BLESSED ARE WE WHO GIVE OUR BODIES TO THE SUSTAINING FLOW OF LIFE.

XVI

The noise at the pavilion dies down. No more children to cry and wail. Father's silky voice rambles on. Unable to stay on the hard floor, I climb onto my bed, hoping he will not come to search for traitors. For that is what I am, I know. A traitor. The only one. I will have to live with that forever. I will have time to count my betrayal for thousands of days.

On the bed, the agony is only slightly easier to bear. Each wave of pain that washes over me crushes the air inside me. Every breath is difficult.

Then, in a sudden rush of feeling, I understand that I cannot *not* push. Every thought in my head says push, push. Every breath in my body comes out in a screaming rush of push. My heartbeat hurts in my ears, beating a rhythm of push, push, push.

And so I do.

BEAUTIFUL, BEAUTIFUL, MY LOVELIES.

ALL IS BEAUTY.

ALL IS YOU.

OUR ISLAND NOW A SEA OF BEAUTIFUL BODIES, COLORFUL, COMFORTING.

YES, YOU ARE LOVE, ALL OF YOU.

...FOR ME, FOR LOVE.

A SEA OF LOVE...ROLLS OUT BEFORE ME.

SO OUR REVOLUTIONARY ACT MAY BE KNOWN, I WILL SET THE TRAITOR SHIP ON FIRE.

IT WILL BURN, MY CHILDREN.

BURN FOR YOU.

BURN FOR ME.

XVII

My child is a son. I will call him Peak. For mountaintop. For Chesapeake. For my short glimpse of love.

Rivers can divide. I learned this recently. When they do, each part is called a branch. I had never known. As my son grows, I will search his face and body for likenesses. I will not be disappointed, whatever I see. He came from me. Father is in him, Branch is in him. When the time comes, I will tell him whatever story he needs to hear.

A long cord attaches us to one another. Thick and purplish, I watch it pulse with blood. When it stops, I bend forward and bite it off, reminded of placenta stew. Were I to cook my own son's afterbirth, there would be no one to share it with tonight.

Father lies in a heap of crumpled limbs, beside the chair on the raised floor of the pavilion. Beyond the dais, beyond the vast sea of bodies, beyond the shores of Waste Island, *La Calma* burns. A long plume of black smoke rises and blooms into the sky above the ship.

I understand that this will be seen for miles. This will bring the curious, the alarmed. Someone will find us.

Us.

I will never be only *me* again.

I look down at the bed, where my small son lies still and blue. I rub his chest and wipe his mouth.

I give him a kiss of breath and he shudders and cries his thin high wail into the stillness.

A Note from the Author

So very many people have read and helped with these stories over the years. It seems an impossible task to thank all the brains that fed them and the hearts that encouraged me, but a few deserve an individual shout-out: Clifford Garstang, Carly Watters, Kevin Watson, Pamela Erens, Maria Robinson, Lu Livingston, Ru Freeman, Jim Tomlinson, Anne Elliott, Katrina Denza, Paula Bolte, Dawn Estrin, Ellen Meister, Ron Currie, Jr., Bonnie ZoBell, Judith Beck, Susan Woodring, Norman Johnson, Tom Lombardo, Sylvia Hoffmire, Jeffery Hess, Suzanne McConnell, Midge Raymond, Christine Norris, Kirsten Menger-Anderson, Laila Lalami, Roy Kesey, T.J. Forrester, Don Capone, Sascha Steiner, Christine Peters, Susie Lawson, Ursula Hegi, Suzanne Kamata, Myfanwy Collins, Kim Chinquee, Claudine Guertin, Andrew Tibbetts and Emily Raboteau.

Thank you to all the wonderful people at Bread Loaf, especially Michael Collier, Noreen Cargill, and Jennifer Grotz. Thank you also to the Virginia Center for the Creative Arts for the generous and timely support.

Thanks to my various family members for love and support: Len Pratt, Sally Johnson, Len Pratt, Cady (tomato!) Guyton, Len Pratt, Charlotte Guyton (mixologist extraordinaire), Len Pratt, Sarah Samarchi, Len Pratt, and Scott Guyton, too, for all those early morning philosophical discussions. Oh, and Len Pratt.

The acknowledgments would grow as long as this book if I listed every person to whom I owe a debt of gratitude for encouragement and support, so I will instead list a few of my favorite *groups* by name and hope the individual members will forgive me: The Second Monday Writing Group, The Red Stiletto Book Club, The Crazy River Think Tank, and Claire's Monday Evening Book Club.

Lastly, I'd like to give a special shout-out to my wonderful friends and supporters at Zoetrope Virtual Studios (too numerous to mention but too important to leave out), where rejection isn't personal, and we all try really hard not to attrish.

About the Author

MARY AKERS is the author of the award-winning short story collection *Women Up On Blocks* (Press 53, 2009). She co-authored a non-fiction book, *Radical Gratitude and Other Life Lessons Learned in Siberia*, that sold in seven countries. She received a Pushcart 2012 Special Mention and has been a Bread Loaf Waiter and work-study Scholar. Mary is Editor-in-chief of the online journal *r.kv.r.y.* and co-founded the Institute for Tropical Marine Ecology, a study abroad marine ecology program originally located in Roseau, Dominica. Although raised in the Blue Ridge Mountains of Virginia, which she will always call home, she currently lives in western New York.

About the Cover Artist

Cover artist **Tim Knifton** lives in South Wales and has been taking photos for many years. He says of his photography, "My main passion at present is urban exploration or the capture of unseen, derelict places and documenting decay that many people would not have the chance to see. I am also a great fan of macro and close-up photography, plus landscape and seascape/beach scenes. Wales is full of rolling landscapes and beaches as far as the eye can see. We are very lucky to have such a rich, long heritage and opportunities on our doorstep. 'Shipwreck' was taken along the coast in the West Country and features the remains of the Norwegian barque SS Nornen, which ran aground during a storm in 1897."

Find more of Tim's photography www.flickr.com/timster1973. He is on Facebook at Tim Knifton Photography, and writes about his work at timster1973.wordpress.com.

CPSIA information can be obtained at www.ICGtesting.com
Printed in the USA
BVOW07s1906210813

329200BV00003B/17/P

APR _ - 2014